I dedicate this book to my friend, Soo— No, wait, what am I saying? My friend? Pah! No, I dedicate this book to the most brilliant mind of the century, to wit – myself: Dirk Lloyd

ORCHARD BOOKS
338 Euston Road, London NW1 3BH
Orchard Books Australia
Level 17/207 Kent Street, Sydney, NSW 2000

First published in the UK in 2012 by Orchard Books

ISBN 978 1 40831 5 125
Text © Jamie Thomson 2012
Illustrated by Freya Hartas
Dirk's Seal by Russ Nicholson

A CIP catalogue record for this book is available from the British Library.

7 9 10 8
Printed and bound by CPI Group (UK) Ltd, Croydon, CR0 4YY

Orchard Books is a division of Hachette Children's Books, an Hachette UK company.
www.hachette.co.uk

JAMIE THOMSON

ORCHARD

MAP OF THE DARKLANDS

Contents

The Story So Far 9

Part One: A New World 11

Prologue 13

Meanwhile, Back on Earth… 15

On That Feteful Day 24

The DarkPhone 37

My Friend's a Huge Monster From
Another World, No Really, He Is… 44

Snot, Pot-bellies and Green Skin 56

An Unexpected Visit 68

Moving House 71

The Moon Queen 91

Part Two: New Friends, New Enemies 99

Home Help 100

The Nanny of Doom 111

The Birthday Party 115

The Paladin, Rufino 130

In the Court of the Moon Queen 146

The Conversation 165

Part Three: Triumph and Despair 179

Under Attack 180

To Battle!   188
Envy and Jealousy   210
Vengeance of the White Witch   219

Part Four: Into the Unknown!   229
The Voyage   230
Foletto the Skirrit King   251
Home is Where the Heart is…
On Your Pink Underpants.   272
The White Tower   282
The Chambers of Correction   302
The Lair of the White Witch   318
The Dark Reliquary   333

Part Five: Metamorphosis   349
A Dark Puberty   350
Return of the Dark Lord   364
In the Court of the Dark Lord   376
Darklands: The Game   384
In for a Penny, In for a Pound   394
Bad Judgement Day   401
The Dungeons of Doom   412
The Fall. Again.   421
Back to School   428

Acknowledgements   438
The Author   440

The Story So Far

Dark Lord: The Teenage Years told the story of how an evil Dark Lord was cast out of his realm and banished to modern day Earth, where he found himself trapped in the body of a teenage schoolboy. Although he tried to tell everyone he was to be called 'Dark Lord', the humans thought he said 'Dirk Lloyd' and that name stuck. Dirk was forced to go to school (School! Noooooo!) where he made some friends: Christopher, Sooz and Sal.

At first, Dirk planned to conquer our world, but soon he realized Orcs and Goblins were no match for tanks, jets and nukes. Instead, he turned his evil genius to the task of getting back home. He tried a kind of magic spell but things went badly wrong, and the school cricket pavilion was burnt down instead. That nearly did for the Dark Lord, but with the aid of Foletto the Skirrit King, he had the pavilion rebuilt.

Then his archenemy, Hasdruban the Wizard, sent the 'White Beast' to kill Dirk, but he managed to outwit it. Dirk needed to get back to the Darklands so he planned another great spell, but instead of sending him back, it sent his friend, Sooz, instead...

Part One:
A New World

Prologue

'AAAaaaaaaaaaarrrrrrrrrrggggggggghhhhhhh!'
Her fall seemed to go on forever through an
endless gulf of space. Then, suddenly—

KER-SPLAT!!!

Sooz lay on her back, exhausted, winded, staring
up at a strange reddish sky... The last thing
she remembered was Dirk's voice, hypnotically
mumbling strange words as the moon's shadow
crept across the face of the sun. And then...then a
burning ruby agony and a feeling of falling, falling,
as if in a dream.

She coughed and turned her head. She was
lying in a kind of dirty water coloured plain that
stretched off into the distance. Her brow furrowed
in puzzlement. The grass was the wrong shade of
green. It was too dark and the sky had a reddish
tinge to it. And...and...there were two moons!

Two! One was a pale white, the other a diseased-looking red. How could that be?

A faint breeze blew up, ruffling her dyed black hair. Her nose wrinkled. The breeze had a strange tang to it, a scent she'd never smelt before. It was like a cross between the sea and cinnamon – a not unpleasant smell in fact, but strange, and because of that, rather disturbing.

This was all Dirk's fault. That strange, funny kid who'd turned up at school claiming to be a Dark Lord exiled from his own lands, lands he called the Darklands. She and her friend Christopher hadn't really believed him, but they had played along – even helping Dirk try to get back to his homeland. The first time, they'd just ended up burning down the school cricket pavilion (and she'd got the blame for it!). Then they'd tried again, with some kind of spell, but this time… What had happened this time?

Sooz sat up. Whatever the smell was, it wasn't the smell of her land. It was the smell of a strange land, a foreign land, a land unknown. It was the smell of the Darklands…

How on earth was she going to get home?

Meanwhile, Back on Earth...

~~October~~ Souls-of-the-Damned 4th
Ten thousand curses on the heads of fluffy little bunny rabbits! I cannot believe what has happened! The Ceremony of the Eclipse of the Gates of the World was supposed to send me back home, but it failed and Sooz has been exiled to the Darklands instead of me! How I fear for the safety of my little Child of the Night. No, wait... What I mean is that I hope my useful servant, Sooz, has not been damaged. That would be inconvenient.

~~October~~ Souls-of-the-Damned 5th
Sooz has been reported missing. Her mum is very upset, as are quite a few people at school, in fact. I never knew Sooz was that popular.

The police interviewed me about it. They asked me all sorts of questions about Sooz such as when I saw her last, what was she wearing (as if I could remember that – Goth stuff, what else?!) and other such petty questions that vex the minds of these puny humans. Anyway, as I am such an honest and upstanding citizen I told them the actual truth – that I had cast a mighty spell, and that it had gone wrong, resulting in Sooz being transported to another plane because she was wearing my Great Ring of Power and she was now in a place called the Darklands, which is very dangerous, full of Orcs and Goblins and ravening Eagle Riders and fanatical Paladins and such like. They didn't believe me of course. Anyway, apparently, now I have to see those feeble-minded child psychos, Wings and Randle again. What a bore!

I have kept a newspaper cutting about Sooz. She would be pleased to see her photo in the paper. Or perhaps 'chuffed'. Yes, that's the word she would use. Chuffed. How I miss her.

Dirk sat in his room, staring glumly out of the window at a cloudy autumn sky, brow furrowed in angry thought. Next to him sat a young boy with bright blue eyes and corn yellow hair, also staring at the darkening sky. The boy seemed to radiate a kind of innocent beauty. Dirk did not. It was as if an angel and a devil were sat next to each other in quiet friendship.

Dirk heaved a sad sigh, full of frustration and despair.

'So, what are we going to do?' said the young boy.

'I don't know, Chris, I don't know,' said Dirk in frustrated tones. He sighed again. 'I can't think of anything. There is no way to get there without the ring, and that's the end of it.'

'But she could be in real danger. I mean really serious stuff. Not like getting an uber-detention for burning down the school pavilion or something, but real stuff, like getting chopped up by Orcs or… Or… It's just so awful I can't bear thinking about it!' said Chris.

'If only I could just talk to her, then I could help, tell her what to do, tell her how to handle things in that dread land,' Dirk said. 'There are

Just Chillin'

great opportunities there, if you know how to take advantage of them.'

Chris lifted up his mobile phone and gazed at it. 'If only we could just call her. I've tried, but it just says, "That person's phone has been turned off or is unavailable".'

'Hah, well, it would, wouldn't it? She's not going to get a signal in the Darklands! Well, not that kind of signal anyway.'

Dirk's eyes narrowed and he began to stare at Chris's phone. A maniacal gleam appeared in his eyes. Always a bad sign, Chris thought to himself, the maniacal gleam. It meant Dirk was coming up with another crazy scheme.

'Not that kind of signal...' Dirk muttered to himself. 'Yes, of course!' Dirk yelled, and he leapt to his feet, snatching Chris's phone.

'All I have to do is modify this device – I'm sure I can get it to transmit the right kind of signal – or more accurately, open a magical doorway between the planes through which sound can travel. We can't travel ourselves, but sound can! Much easier.'

'That's great, but why does it have to be my phone? Why don't you get your own?' said Chris, half-pleased they might be able to help Sooz, half-worried about Dirk's plans for his phone.

'Pah, I'm not getting a mobile phone. Your parents – jailors more like – would use it to track me constantly, as would the High Council of the White Shields, those witless lackeys of my arch-enemy, that old fool, Hasdruban, the White Wizard!'

'I don't think the local council work for the White Wizard really, Dirk. Dark forces, yeah, according to Dad, but not the White Wizard. I mean you're just being paranoid. And my mum certainly doesn't – she's a vicar for goodness sake!' Chris replied.

'All the more reason why she would be working for the White Wizard! Anyway, even if what you say is true, why take the risk? I'm a Dark Lord – I'm supposed to be paranoid. How do you think I've survived for this long?' said Dirk.

'Yeah, well, whatever, Dirk,' said Chris. 'The thing is, will I get my phone back?'

'Well that depends. If my plan works, probably not, no,' said Dirk.

'Why, what are you going to do?' said Chris, worried.

'I'm going to re-engineer it. Magically enhance it.

I'm going to turn it into a DarkPhone.'

'A DarkPhone? What's that?' said Chris, even more worried.

'Well, you know, an evil phone. A kind of undead phone. But first of all I need a little sliver of bone, taken from the skeleton of someone bad, like a murderer or a thief, someone like that. Preferably someone who was hanged for their crimes. Even better, hanged at midnight at a crossroads on All Souls' Eve or Walpurgisnacht or something,' said Dirk, as he removed the SIM card from Chris's phone.

'Riiiight… And where do you think we're going to find that then?' said Chris, shaking his head.

'I'm not sure, but we must at least try,' said Dirk, throwing the SIM card into the bin.

'Oi, what are you doing?!' protested Chris loudly.

'You won't be needing that any more, Christopher,' said Dirk as he pocketed the phone. 'From now on, this phone will run on magic. Necromantic magic. Well, as soon as we can find that bit of bone.'

Christopher stared at Dirk in irritation. Dirk just grinned back at him. Chris gave an involuntary shudder. He'd known Dirk for some time now, but

21

that grin still sent a shiver down his spine.

Christopher didn't really want to encourage any more of Dirk's crazy plans, but on the other hand he was ready to do whatever it took to bring his friend Sooz back. 'Wait a minute…' he said.

Dirk raised an eyebrow. 'Don't imagine for a moment that I shall be returning your phone. It's been requisitioned for the war effort.'

'No, no, I've just had an idea.'

'Really? What?' said Dirk.

'Bog people,' replied Chris.

'Bog…what?' said Dirk, confused. 'Has it come to this, that you now resort to hurling insults at me? It is I that should be handing out the insults, not you!'

'No, no. Bog people. The remains of human sacrifices. Ritually sacrificed and then thrown into peat bogs thousands of years ago. Their bodies are amazingly preserved by the peaty mud. And they were sacrificed by being strangled and then having their throats cut. Really gruesome!' said Chris excitedly.

Dirk's face lit up at the thought of it. 'That is perfect! Absolutely perfect! You are a genius,

Christopher, a genius. Well, obviously not compared to me, but pretty good all the same. For a human child. Anyway, where can we find one of these?'

'There's one in the museum at Fetbury. Fetbury Man they call him,' said Chris.

'Fetbury? Where's that?' asked Dirk. 'And what a stupid name. You humans have such stupid names for places, really you do. Why can't you call it Deadbury or something? You know, where the dead are buried – and rise again to serve their evil necromantic masters – hopefully me. *Mwah, hah, hah!*'

'Deadbury. Right, OK. Well, Deadbury's not far. We could get a bus or a train there, no problem,' said Chris.

'Excellent, we shall go this afternoon,' said Dirk.

'We can't – it's Mum's church fête this arvo, and we have to go to that,' said Chris.

'Nooooooo!' wailed Dirk.

On That Feteful Day

'By the Nine Hells, they're covered in slime and mud like the filth of a thousand years!' said Dirk.

'What, bog people you mean?' said Christopher.

'No, these vile human children! Look at them,' said Dirk, gesturing imperiously with one hand.

Before them, in a large sandpit, several kids played. They were indeed rather dirty, faces smeared with chocolate, hair matted with pink candyfloss, clothes stained with fizzy drinks – and worse.

Dirk and Christopher were standing behind a makeshift stall selling homemade jams, jellies and juices. All made by Chris's mum, the Reverend Purejoie. Several other stalls were scattered around the play area, selling similar goods. It was the church fête.

'*Bah*, I've said it before, and I'll say it again –

they're like an unruly tribe of Goblins, the lot of them!' said Dirk. 'Actually, Goblins would be easier to control – an execution or two, and they'd soon be standing at attention!'

'You can't execute children!' said Chris.

'Why not?'

Chris just looked at him. Dirk raised his eyes and sighed. 'No, I suppose not, more's the pity.'

'Anyway,' said Chris. 'What if they could? You'd be first, probably!'

'Hah! Good point. Now, as the Mouth of Dirk and my closest counsellor, what do you think our plan should be for the assault on the Dead and Buried Museum?'

'Assault? Come on Dirk, we can't attack the place! Anyway, who would do it, you and me? Armed with what? Pencils and exercise books?'

Dirk narrowed his eyes. Sarcasm? Was he being mocked? He was about to admonish Christopher when he noticed something big in the sky. A large balloon, floating serenely by, with a big basket full of humans hanging below it. He gazed up, fascinated, Christopher's disrespectful remark forgotten.

'What makes those float, Christopher?' he said.

'What?' said Chris, following Dirks' gaze upwards. 'Oh, hot air balloons. Helium gas I think.'

'Helium, eh?' said Dirk. 'Interesting. Think of it, a few hundred of those, say, with a crew of Goblins – proper Goblins, not these puny human children. They could drop stuff – you know, like darts and bombs and stones. Make short work of Hasdruban's Paladins, wouldn't they! There are so many things I could do with Earth technology, if I could only get home!'

'They're not easy to make though,' said Chris.

'True, but a lot easier than one of your jet aero planes or a petrol driven tank or whatever,' said Dirk.

Just then, their neighbour, a kindly old lady called Mrs Morris, walked past with a tray.

'Rock cakes, delicious rock cakes, three for a pound!' she said.

'Rock cakes! I love rock cakes, especially hers,' said Chris, all plans to build Goblin-crewed hot air balloons or to raid the archaeological museum in Fetbury forgotten. 'Do you want one, Dirk?'

Dirk frowned. 'Rock cakes? Why would I want to eat rock? Oh, wait, I get it! We use the rock cakes as projectiles to smash a window in the museum and

Let them eat cake!

break in that way. Or better yet, as ammunition for our Goblin battle balloons! You are clever at times Chris, really you are.'

Chris laughed, 'No, no, you numpty, they're not made of rock, they're just called that, they're...'

Dirk suddenly interrupted him. 'Did you just call me a numpty? What is this "numpty"?' he said forcefully, not sure whether to be angry or not.

Chris blinked. The last thing he needed was one of Dirk's tantrums.

'Umm... Err, numpty is like... It's like err...'

Dirk narrowed his eyes once more. Chris was getting really disrespectful these days. If only he could cast one of his spells – that would set him right! Nothing too harsh, mind, but still, something to remind him who was boss. Maybe the Malediction of Unmoving Obesity. If only it worked on this plane...

Chris continued with a rush, an idea popping into his mind, 'It's an old title from history, like Lord High Numpty. A title for foreign ambassadors and that when they visited England in the old days!'

Dirk blinked, almost convinced.

Chris went on. 'Yeah, like a court title. Henry VIII

used it on the French ambassador. No really, he did, I read it in History class. I thought you'd like the title. Lord High Numpty and that, seeing as you're from a foreign land…'

Dirk nodded, buying into it.

'…And deserving of respect,' said Dirk, finishing Christopher's sentence. Christopher nodded enthusiastically. Dirk continued. 'OK. Lord High Numpty. Hmm, sounds good. Well, Christopher, purchase your rock cakes then. Let us see what they taste like! Crunchy I would expect, hah, hah!'

Chris turned away, a look of relief on his face. Moments later, they were both munching on a rock cake.

'Delicious!' said Dirk. 'Now, back to the business of rescuing Sooz, to wit: how to get into the museum.'

'Can't you use the Sinister Hand?' said Chris.

Dirk made a face. 'I could, but it's not a spell that you can use too often. There are risks. And I've already used it more than I should.' Dirk recalled the last time he'd used the spell to detach his hand and send it wondering off on its own – to steal some report cards to give that tyrant, Headmaster Grousammer, a nasty surprise!

'Still, it's the easiest solution. Creep in, creep out, no problem. And we haven't got much time. We have to think of Sooz and her situation.'

Dirk frowned in thought. Then he nodded. 'No, Christopher, you are right; I cannot afford to be safe. We need to take some risks. Sooz is in trouble and we have to do what we have to do. I'll do it, tonight, when you and your parents are asleep.'

'OK, sounds like a plan. Let me know if there's anything I can do,' said Chris.

'Not much, I would think, Christopher. But thanks for the offer anyway,' said Dirk.

'Could I have some of the homemade plum jam?' said a voice. They looked up. A middle-aged man was standing there, pointing at a jar of jam. Beside him, little hand in his was a boy of about seven years of age.

'I love plum jam!' said the little boy.

Chris and Dirk stared at them for a moment, their minds still full of spells and enchantments and how they were going to steal some of the preserved remains of a two-and-a-half-thousand-year-old corpse.

Christopher nudged Dirk. 'Hmm, what?' said

Dirk. 'Oh! Oh, yes, of course, sir, that will be one pound fifty.'

Dirk handed over the jar. 'All proceeds to go to charity,' he said. But then he couldn't help himself and added, 'Pointlessly of course! Why give money away? *Bah*, use it for the greater good – well, my good at any rate. Raise an army! Conquer the world! There'll be no need for charity when I'm in charge, oh no!'

Christopher turned away, trying not to laugh out loud whilst the man stared at Dirk as if he were mad. Then Dirk grinned up at him and he literally flinched back in horror.

Dirk blinked as the man began to hurry away. He realized he may have sounded a little…odd…so he tried to make things right.

'Enjoy the jam, you numpty,' he said at the top of his voice.

Several adults all turned to stare, including Mrs Purejoie. At the sight of Dirk her shoulders slumped, and she put a despairing hand to her forehead. Meanwhile Chris was doubled over with helpless laughter.

'What?' said Dirk. 'What?'

Last night I was woken by a strange tapping on my window. Tap-tap, tap-tap, tap-tap. For a moment I was seized by fear – my feeble body reacting, as would that of any pitiful human child. But then I remembered who I truly was, and resolve filled my heart...

Whatever was doing the tapping, it was they that would be filled with fear, for I am the Great Dirk, Master of the Dark! So I yanked open the curtains.

And there, tapping on the windowpane with its beak was a bird. And not just any kind of bird, but a black crow. Black as blackest night. Its feathers were covered with a kind of oily sheen and its eyes glowed with a baleful red fire. How beautiful it was. At the sight of me, the bird cawed – ah what a sweet sound, that desolate cry! Echoing into the empty night like the cry of a lost soul condemned forever to wander the depths of hell itself.

I opened the window. With another desolate croak, the crow hopped inside.

*And then onto my shoulder... I think
I have found a new friend.*

~~October 10th~~ Souls-of-the-Damned 10th

*I have established what the bird is. It is
a Black Storm Crow, usually found only in
the Darklands. But I believe I know what
has happened. This bird was probably once a
sparrow or a pigeon or some other lowly Earth
bird but it ate of my black, oily Essence
of Evil that I coughed up when I fell to
Earth in that supermarket car park. The
Essence obviously turned the little bird into
a magnificent Storm Crow. And what would
such a bird try and do? Well, find me, of
course! It is drawn to me, drawn to the Dark
Lord, as are all such beasts. What a stroke
of luck! It could prove to be a most useful
pet indeed – they make excellent messengers,
amongst other things.*

*I must be careful though. I cannot let
the Purejoies or any other adults know of
its existence. They might try and take it
from me.*

The White Wizard, Hasdruban, sat at his great desk of living oak, staring at the painting on the wall. It was a painting of the Dark Lord of the Iron Tower of Despair, the Nameless One, the World Burner, the Sorcerer Supreme, etc and Hasdruban's Arch Arch-Enemy. He had to be destroyed once and for all, along with all his works.

A knock at the door interrupted his flow of thought. 'Ah, here she is,' said the Wizard, his voice hoary with age and wisdom. 'Enter!'

A strange apparition walked into his Inner Sanctum. She was dressed from head to foot in long, flowing white lace, an ornate headdress on her head, her face completely hidden behind a veil. Not an inch of her flesh was exposed.

'Ah, the White Witch of Holy Vengeance. Welcome.'

The White Witch merely inclined her shrouded head in acknowledgment.

Hasdruban continued. 'It seems our foe, though he has been trapped in the body of a human child and is weaker and more vulnerable than he has been in a thousand years, was still able to thwart our last attempt to destroy him – he defeated the

White Beast of Retribution. This time, we must try harder.'

He paused, hoping the White Witch would speak, but she didn't. In fact, as far as Hasdruban could recall, she had never spoken. Not a word.

'So, I am sending you this time. You will masquerade as something the humans of that strange plane call a "nanny". I believe their task is to look after other people's children and their families. In this case, the child in question is the Nameless One himself. Though actually, he has a name over there. They call him Dirk. Dirk Lloyd.'

The White Witch stood there, silent.

Hasdruban went on. 'You will beguile the family he lives with, the Purejoie's – they know nothing of the viper they nurture in their midst – or rather they choose not to believe what is obvious. You will...persuade...them that they need a nanny. They will put you in charge of the Dark One. Find out what he is up to, and if you can, destroy him. But be warned! Though he has no sorcerous powers to speak of and inhabits the body of a mere child, he still has his cunning, his endless malice and his evil genius!'

The White Witch inclined her head in acknowledgement. Then she bent low, draping her long veil over her arms and began to do something under her robes.

Hasdruban raised a hairy white eyebrow. After a few seconds, she handed Hasdruban a note written on black paper in white ink. Hasdruban scanned it.

'Ah, how will you get to that plane the inhabitants call Earth? Well, I have some rather special magic for that! Let me show you, my dear…'

The DarkPhone

The Wendle Herald

Local News

GUARD CLAIMS DISEMBODIED 'ZOMBIE' HAND BROKE INTO FETBURY MUSEUM

Alex Marshal, a security guard at the Fetbury Museum, claims that he saw a disembodied hand crawling in through a museum window. He says this 'zombie' hand lifted the lid on the Bog Man's display case, removed a small piece of the body and then dragged itself out of the window. "I was too terrified to do anything, terrified!" The prominent psychiatrist, Professor Wings, said the whole thing was probably a hallucinatory delusion brought on by too many late nights, but another eminent psychiatrist, Dr Randle, said "Poppycock! Wings is an idiot!

Dirk sat at his desk in his room, an open book in front of him. It was a dictionary. This is the entry Dirk was reading:

> **numpty** NOUN, *plural – ties*, *informal –*
> a stupid person
> *Thesaurus* – plonker, numbskull, fool,
> charlie, bonehead, twit, pillock, dufus,
> dweeb, lamebrain, dipstick, dimwit…

And so on.

Dirk narrowed his eyes. That Christopher, he would… What though? Dirk looked at the ceiling, various possible revenge plots and spells going through his head – the Charm of Sudden Baldness, the Cantrip of Uncontrollable Flatulence, the Hex of Hideous Hives or the Malediction of Unmoving Obesity? Oh, if only they worked here on Earth! Perhaps something different then. Hmm… Just then, there was a knock on the door.

'Who dares disturb the Great Dirk?' he said in his best imperial darkness voice.

'It's me – Christopher.'

Dirk snapped the book shut, put it in a drawer

and drew out a small knife.

'Enter,' he said.

Chris opened the door and walked in. 'How's the phone coming on?' he said.

Dirk gestured to the seat beside him, and Chris sat down. Dirk picked up a dirty brown sliver of bone, held it up to the light and began shaping it with the small knife.

'There,' he said. 'A little bit of the Fetbury Bog Man. Deadbury Bog Man, I mean.'

'Did you have trouble getting it?' asked Christopher as he looked at the bony fragment, face wrinkled in disgust. The thing stank.

Dirk stared at Chris for a moment.

'What?' said Chris, brow furrowing in puzzlement.

Dirk made a decision. Payback would be delayed for now – he needed Chris onside until they had resolved the situation with Sooz. Anyway, revenge is a dish best served cold, as the saying goes.

'No, no trouble. Straightforward enough,' said Dirk, as if everything was perfectly fine. 'Well, unless your name's Alex Marshal of course, heh, heh!'

'Who's he?' said Chris.

'A security guard at the museum. He—Oh never

mind, he'll get over it… Probably.'

Chris glanced at Dirk's left arm. There was the telltale greenish scar near the elbow where the Sinister Hand had been detached. He shuddered. He still couldn't really get his mind around that unpleasant spell. Still wasn't sure if it was even real. When he'd first met Dirk, he hadn't believed any of the stuff about being a Dark Lord from another world and all that, he'd thought he was just a mad, deluded kid, and it was all a bit of fun. But after what he'd seen with the White Beast, with Sooz disappearing and all the rest, he knew it must be true. Then he shuddered again – this time because of the cold.

Dirk's window was wide open.

'Can we close that please? It's freezing,' said Chris.

'No, I am expecting someone,' said Dirk as he carefully inserted the sliver of bone into Christopher's mobile phone SIM card slot. It clicked into place perfectly.

Suddenly there was a loud cry and a black flurry of feathers burst into the room. Chris leaped back in shock.

'What the…' he stuttered as a black crow, as black

as blackest night flew in through the window and alighted gracefully on Dirk's shoulder.

Dirk didn't bat an eyelid and continued to work on Chris's phone.

'Hello, Dave,' he said. 'Meet Christopher.' The Black Storm Crow cocked its head and eyed Chris with evil intent, its red eyes glowing. It lifted one claw and extended its talons in his direction.

'Now, now Dave, Christopher is a friend. Do you understand? Friend!' With that the crow gave a disappointed caw, and settled down on Dirk's shoulder.

Chris just stared, gaping. Dirk looked over, a mischievous grin on his face. 'He's a Black Storm Crow. They are drawn to the Dark, to those such as I.'

Chris shook his head in amazement. Yet another freaky Dirk thing! And what had he called it?

'Did you just call it Dave?'

'Yeah! Dave. Dave the Black Storm Crow.'

Chris stared at Dirk, unsure whether this was some kind of joke or not. Dirk carried on working on the phone as if nothing unusual was going on.

'Beautiful, isn't he?' he said, a little smile tugging

at the corner of his mouth.

Chris looked at it. A black crow. Ugly beak. Red eyes. Razor sharp, gnarled claws. Called Dave.

'Beautiful… Riiight…'

Suddenly Dirk cried out in pain, his face a mask of agony. The crow hopped off onto the desk with a caw of alarm.

'What is it?' said Chris. Had the crow turned on him or something, sunk its claws into his shoulder?

Dirk was huddled over, massaging his scarred left arm. 'It's the Sinister Hand spell. I have used it too often and I may have caused some permanent damage – there is always a price to pay when you use dark sorcery. And this puny human child's body is so weak…'

'Do you want Dad to take a look at it? He is a doctor, you know,' said Chris.

'No, no, human medicine won't do any good. Anyway, it doesn't matter – it's worth it. For Sooz. To get her back.'

'Well, if you're sure,' said Chris.

'Yes, I'm sure. It'll get better eventually, though if I use that spell again any time soon, I risk not being able to reattach my arm. Or worse. But the important thing is that the DarkPhone has been created.'

'Can we call Sooz then?' said Chris.

Dirk chuckled. 'Not yet, the DarkPhone will take time to morph into its proper form, to take on its powers. To get charged-up, I suppose you'd say.'

'How long will that take?' asked Chris.

'A few days I would think,' replied Dirk.

'Have we got a few days?' said Chris.

'Possibly not. For all we know, Sooz might already be dead, but this is the best that we can do…'

My Friend's a Huge Monster From Another World, No Really, He Is...

Sooz looked around the grey desolate emptiness of the Darklands. She frowned. She was thinking about what Dirk had told her of this place. When she'd first met Dirk she'd thought he was making it all up for a laugh – all that stuff about Dark Lords, White Wizards and spells and everything. But then she'd started to believe him. And now she knew it was true. And that made her scared. Very scared. According to Dirk, here there were Orcs and Goblins and Dragons and Nightgaunts (whatever they were) and Vampires. Sooz was a Goth girl through and through, it was true. She loved vampires and moons and black stuff and pale skin and that. But real Vampires? Actual real Vampires that lived forever and drank your blood and lived in places called Sunless Keep? No thank you!

And she was on her own. All alone, and lost. Maybe lost forever.

It was all too much for her. She put her face in her hands and sobbed. She wanted her mum.

But then Sooz felt something odd, something that felt hot against her cheek, and it wasn't her tears. It was something on her finger. She glanced down at her hand. Dirk's ring. It was really quite warm. And red runes writhed around it as if alive, coruscating with pent up energy! She stared at it in amazement. It began to glow with an eerie radiance, a kind of dark light. Not exactly darkness, but not exactly light either. The radiance intensified. She was bathed in it, and it made the skin on her hands glow with a perfect gothic paleness. Quickly Sooz reached into her bag and took out her compact mirror. Her eyes, hair and lips seem to shine with a purplish blackness in the bone-pale moon of her face. How beautiful she looked! Like a queen, a beautiful, magnificent Dark Queen of the Night!

'Heh, heh,' she chuckled to herself. Then she caught something moving in the mirror behind her.

She turned – it was her shadow! And what a shadow. It was huge. And it looked like she had some kind of ornate spiked crown on her head, some kind of weapon or staff in her hand, and robes of regal majesty!

Perhaps the magical shadows revealed what the wearer would look like if they were a Dark Lord or a Dark Lady. How cool was that! Sooz jumped up and down in excitement. Her shadow responded with great, majestic leaps.

But then reality came crashing back. She wasn't a Dark Queen, she was just a teenage girl, even if she was a Goth, and the shadow wasn't real, it was just a magic trick.

Still, it wasn't all bad. Dirk's Ring was obviously powerful here in the Darklands. If she could work out how to use it, she wouldn't be totally at the mercy of whatever creatures or people she might find here. Maybe she could even become some kind of Dark Queen. She held it up, examined it against the backdrop of the pale moon in the sky. How beautiful it was, the runes burning with dark energy. As she gazed at the glowing runes, she noticed something out of the corner of her eye, on the skyline. Atop a range of low hills stood some kind of tall tower and…well, was it her imagination or was it pink? Bright pink!

'Hmm, a pink tower. Doesn't sound like it would be dangerous, does it? I mean, if you were an evil Orc Lord or something, you wouldn't paint your castle pink, would you?' she thought to herself. It didn't seem that far away either. Sooz resolved to investigate further. So she set off towards it.

Slowly, oh so slowly, the distant tower grew larger and larger as Sooz slogged across the darkling plain.

Suddenly a large dark shape rose up out of the shadows from behind a nearby pile of tumbled rock. Sooz screamed. Before her stood some kind of hideous demon, at least seven feet tall, covered in scaly skin, with a horned head, talons, and huge fangs. A great leather belt at its waist seemed to have shrunken human heads hanging from it. The thing shrugged – from its shoulders great bat wings extended with a leathery snap. It leant down and hissed at her – plumes of foul-smelling smoke spewing from bony nostrils.

Sooz cowered back, falling to the ground, hand raised in futile defence. She was just a kid! A mere wisp of a girl lost in this terrible land. How could she fight such a monster? Oh, how she wished Dirk was here to help her. But then a thought struck her. The demonic figure looked familiar. She narrowed her eyes and stared. Then she got up, and stared some more, looking the strange thing up and down. This seemed to surprise the huge demon – a look of puzzlement passed across its hellish face.

The creature reminded her of something. Or someone... Oh yes, that concert she went to with Chris and Dirk, where Dirk thought the lead singer was his... What did he call him? Yeah, his dread lieutenant, Gargon, Captain of the Legions of... of... Well, bad stuff. Dirky stuff.

'You look like the lead singer of that band Chris likes so much. What were they called? Morti – that was it,' she said.

The demon blinked.

Sooz stared at it. It looked a bit raggedy around the edges, half starved and filthy. Its feet were scratched and sore. She eyed it suspiciously, not so scared now.

The demon looked back, bemused. Little human girls were supposed to be terrified of him. They

48

Nice to meet you!

weren't supposed to talk back! Then the girl took a step towards him. They certainly weren't supposed to do that!

Sooz frowned up at the demon. Suddenly she extended a hand, and spoke, 'Hello. You must be Gargon. Dirk gave me this ring.' She held up her finger. The ring seemed to respond, as if it knew that it was time to reveal some of its power, and it glowed more intensely with an unearthly light, bathing Sooz's face in a vampiric glow. Mighty runes began to writhe and coruscate around the ring, glowing with crimson fire.

The demon's great fanged jaw dropped and a look of joy crossed its unholy features.

'It is the Great Ring! My lord lives! My lord lives!' said Gargon, in a dark, gravelly demon's voice, for it was indeed him, Dirk's lieutenant, Dread Gargon, the Hewer of Limbs, Captain of the Legions of Dread.

'And he gave you Great Ring! He chose you!' bellowed Gargon. He dropped to one knee. 'Gargon swears fealty to the Dark Mistress, Queen of the Night, and betrothed of my dread lord! I serve you in the name of Dark Lord! I be your faithful servant, my Queen.'

Sooz stood there for a moment. Betrothed? It wasn't an engagement ring; it was Dirk's Great Ring of Power! She wanted to tell him they weren't 'betrothed' – and they weren't going to be either – but maybe that wouldn't be such a good idea. If Gargon believed they were engaged, then maybe it was better left that way.

Anyway, the important thing was Gargon's oath of loyalty. An oath of loyalty from a seven-foot demon who was going to be her faithful servant. How cool was that! A half-smile lifted one side of her mouth. Now she wasn't so vulnerable, so weak, so alone. Now she wasn't a mere wisp of a girl marooned in a foreign land. Oh no, she had protection – and not just any old protection either, but a seven-foot winged and taloned…err…thingy wotsit. Called Gargon.

'So, what are you exactly, Gargon?'

'What do you mean, Dark Mistress?' gravelled Gargon.

'You know, what kind of…well, thing are you?' she asked again.

'Ah… Gargon not know, my Queen. My master, the Dark Lord…'

'Dirk, his name's Dirk,' interrupted Sooz.

'Dirk? His name is Dirk? Really? Are you sure, my Lady of the Dark?'

'Oh yes, that's his real name. Dirk. Dirk Lloyd. Dirk the Dark Lord,' she said.

'D— Dirk. All right, err…my Queen. My master – Dirk – said I was…unique. That there is only one of my kind in all existence,' he replied. He seemed a bit sad at that thought, if a seven foot, winged demon with smoky wisps coming out of his nostrils could look sad.

Sooz looked up at him.

'Hey, I'm loving those bat wings, Gargon,' she said, trying to cheer him up.

'Thank you, my Lady!'

That seemed to perk him up a bit. 'So, what now, O my Dark Mistress?'

'Well, my Dread Lieutenant,' said Sooz, 'I was heading to that pink tower over there,' she said.

Gargon turned. 'The Tower of my master, the Dark Lord, you mean?' he grated.

'The Tower of… The Iron Tower? The Iron Tower of Despair? But it's pink. How can it be pink?' she said confused.

'It was the White Wizard, my Lady. He painted it pink, all over. Pink.' Gargon shook his great craggy head in disgust.

'But why, Gargon. Why would he do that?' she asked.

'I don't know, your Dark Majesty. Gargon not really understand. All Gargon know is that faeries and human children from Gam, the City of Men, visit Tower now. There are slides and rides and things.'

Sooz narrowed her eyes in thought. Propaganda? Was that it? It was a great way to discredit the memory of Dirk by turning his citadel of power into a pink painted amusement park, that's true. But on the other hand, why not destroy it? She shrugged. Anyway.

'So that's the Iron Tower. Then this must be the Plains of Desolation,' said Sooz, almost to herself.

'Yes, my Lady. I have been hiding here, but never in same place for long. Try to avoid Eagle Riders and Paladins of Righteousness.'

Gargon looked up at the sky, fear etched all over his craggy, scaled face. 'They look for Gargon, and if they find me, they kill me!'

'Couldn't you…you know, surrender or something? They're supposed to be the good guys – surely they wouldn't kill you if you surrendered?' said Sooz.

Gargon shook his great bony head. 'No, White Wizard say no prisoners. Darkness to be wiped out from the land once and for all. None can live!'

Sooz frowned. That didn't sound right to her, didn't sound right at all. A look of determination came over her face.

'We must go there, Gargon. I'd like to have a closer look. Maybe we can take the tower back. Take it back for Dirk. Anyway, I need somewhere to hang out, get out of the cold. Can't stay here forever, that's for sure!'

'As you command, my Dark Mistress of Doom!' said Gargon, and a kind of grin split his hideous face. 'It is good to have a Master once more! I mean Mistress. Gargon is happy!'

Sooz smiled up at the vast ugly demon. He was quite sweet really, underneath it all, she thought.

Together they set off towards the Iron Tower of Pinkness…the little thirteen-year-old schoolgirl and the Demon of the Dark. As they walked, she speculated on the Tower. If she'd been one of those 'normie' girls (as she called everyone who wasn't a Goth) she'd love the Tower to be pink and fluffy, maybe with a little pink ribbon around the top. But Sooz was a Goth – pink was hideous. Repainting it black, that would be the answer. Black as night, the colour an Iron Tower of Despair should be! She looked up at Gargon. Would he be any good as a painter and decorator, she wondered?

Snot, Pot-bellies and Green Skin

'YIKES!' yelled Sooz at the top of her voice. A little man-shaped creature had suddenly stepped out from behind the gnarled trunk of a half-dead tree. It looked just like one of those ugly little Goblins she'd seen in films and books back home on Earth, with green warty skin, large, dark eyes, a preposterously long nose, and big ears. He was dressed in tattered leather and had obviously seen better times. If a Goblin could ever be said to have seen better times, that is.

It was about her height and it had some kind of vaguely familiar insignia on its leather chest armour. At its side were a rusty old knife and a big leather pouch. But instead of attacking her, it ignored her. It looked up at the seven-foot demon by her side.

'Gargon, you're alive! That is good news indeed,'

squeaked the Goblin in a surprisingly high-pitched voice.

'Agrash! You made it too, I see,' said Gargon.

'I did. Me and a few mates,' said the Goblin.

The Goblin waved, and from behind rocks and dead trees and bushes and holes in the ground about thirty warty, long-nosed, green-skinned little Goblins emerged. They carried various weapons – rusty old saws, knives, spears, and bill hooks, and were saying things like 'Hey, it's old Gargy!' or 'Gargon lives!' and 'Who's that he's got there then?' or 'Kidnapped some 'ooman girl has he? Good old Gargy', and such like.

Sooz took a fearful step back. She didn't like the look of this, not one bit. She was a schoolgirl from an ordinary school in Surrey and now she was in a place called the Plains of Desolation, with thirty – well, thirty Goblins for heaven's sake! She'd never met any Goblins before! Well, aside from one or two oiks at school, but that didn't count. These were real Goblins. Did they eat people? Or was that Orcs? Orcs eat people in the *Realm of Shadows*, the game she played back home on Earth, but that was a computer game. Real ones could be worse! Maybe they tortured people and then ate them! Or…or… She just didn't know – that was the problem.

Agrash went on. 'We've been hiding out here ever since the Battle. We weren't sure what to do, or where to go, so we…so we didn't do anything or go anywhere… Anyway, you're a big boss right, aren't you Gargon? You had the ear of the Dark Lord himself, you can tell us what to do, can't you?'

'Me? Not me!' said Gargon, pointing at Sooz with a taloned hand.

Agrash's green, warty brow knotted in puzzlement. He turned to look at Sooz as if noticing her for the first time. 'Who's this then? Some girl you kidnapped? Ransom is it? No wait – insurance, I'll bet! Some stinking Paladin's daughter, is that it? Keep her alive and they'll leave you alone, that type of thing? Mind you, she doesn't look like a Paladin's daughter, I have to say!'

'No, no, she is friend,' said Gargon.

Sooz smiled weakly, trying to appear nonchalant and relaxed as if all this were perfectly normal.

'Fr… What did you say?' said Agrash. 'Gargon, Hewer of Limbs, Lieutenant of the Tower of… He's got a…a friend? A human friend? I don't get it!'

Behind him, the Goblin pack formed up into a raggedy band, listening to the conversation with interest. They stared at Sooz avidly, black eyes unblinking, yellow, cat-like pupils fixed on her. Sooz shuddered. She was starting to get really scared.

'She is Dark Mistress now. Our master, the Dark Lord, he send her. Whilst he is in exile,' grated Gargon.

'But… But she's just a girl… A little human girl!' said Agrash.

Sooz began to stare at Agrash. She couldn't help herself; his nose was beginning to fascinate her, even through her growing fear. How could that nose be real? It was so improbably long, sticking right out over the edge of his chin, and it constantly dripped with snot. Green, slimy snot. Agrash noticed she was staring, and put a hand up self-consciously to hide his nose.

'Hey, stop staring like that, it's rude!' he said.

'But…but there's just so much snot,' said Sooz, in fascinated disgust, without thinking.

'Yeah, that's why they call him Agrash Snotripper,' said Gargon. At that, many of the Goblins began to laugh and giggle with curious little goblinish titters.

Agrash broke her chain of thought, wrenching her back to the Darklands, as he turned and shouted at the assembled Goblins, 'Stop that laughing, you idiots! I'm the Captain here! Me! I'm in charge! Why? Because I'm the only one here with a brain, the only one! Remember that, you green-bottomed, pot-bellied morons!'

Chastened, the Goblins hung their heads, the picture of guilty children, shifting from foot to foot to a chorus of 'Yeah, sorry, Agrash', 'Yes, Cap'n', Sorry, sir', and so on.

Sooz began to feel a little more confident about things. They weren't complete savages – they could be controlled. And they were pot-bellied! Each one had a little round pot belly, on top of thin, knobbly-kneed legs.

As Agrash turned back to face her, Sooz realized what the insignia on the armour of the Goblins was. It was Dirk's Seal, the same pattern as on her ring. These were Dirk's Goblins. Of course! That made all the difference. Think! What would Dirk do?

She stepped forward. 'Yes, I am your new Queen. The Dark Lord in Exile has appointed me as your ruler in his absence. You may call me…err…Dark Mistress,' she said.

Agrash looked up at Gargon. 'Wait a minute, this ain't right,' he said. 'Look at her. Granted, she looks like a Nightwalker Vampire and that, but she's obviously not. She's just a kid, I tell you!'

Then Sooz held out her hand. The Great Ring bathed her in its unearthly, dark-bright brilliance, runes twisting and burning across its surface. Behind her the shadow of a Dread Queen of the Night flared up in all its majesty.

Agrash's eyes widened in fear and awe and the company of Goblins took a step back, giving a collective gasp of astonishment.

'The Great Ring! Forgive me, I did not know!' said Agrash.

He dropped to one knee and bowed his head in submission to Sooz. Her heart leapt. First a huge… thingy wotsit…and now a pack of Goblins! Sure, she missed her mum and Dirk and she really, really wanted to go home, but this wasn't so bad. In fact, it was almost fun! She decided to play things up to the hilt.

'Swear fealty to me, your Dark Mistress, your Dread Queen of the Night!' she said, in the most

Just what I've always wanted – minions. Goblin minions.

imperious and commanding tones she could muster. The ring seemed to respond to her need, it began to hum with power, radiating more of its dark light.

Agrash was cowed. 'Yes, your Darkness, I swear allegiance to…umm…' He glanced up at her.

'To Sooz. Sooz, the Dark Queen,' she said, looking down at the kneeling Goblin, one hand on her hip, the other regally holding out her ring hand, the very picture of a haughty queen.

'I, Agrash, swear fealty to Sooz, the Dark Queen, and Mistress of the Night!' said Agrash solemnly. He took Sooz's hand and kissed the ring…dribbling green snot all over her fingers in the process. Sooz tried not to let her disgust show, with limited success, as she looked up at the rest of the Goblins. She couldn't help herself, and gagged a bit, but the Goblins didn't notice. Or maybe they were used to that.

As one, they dropped to their knees and intoned, 'We swear allegiance to Sooz, Dark Queen of the Night and Wielder of the Great Ring!' they said as Sooz tried to shake her hand clean.

She looked over at Gargon triumphantly. He

looked back, and nodded, a wide smile cracking his hideous face in two, revealing huge, sulphurous fangs.

'Good work, my Lady,' he croaked.

'Thank you, my Dread Lieutenant,' she said with a grin of her own.

Then he rose to his feet, trying to change the subject. 'So, Sooz, err, I mean my Dark Mistress, what's the plan?' he said.

'Well, I thought we'd go to the Iron Tower, maybe see if we can take it back. Especially now that there are so many of us,' said Sooz.

Agrash frowned, glancing at Gargon. 'Err… Thirty Goblins are really not that many, my Queen, not compared to Hasdruban's army. It numbers in the thousands. Tens of thousands, in fact.'

'Oh,' said Sooz. But then she brightened and said, 'But on the other hand, we have Gargon and…well, we've got the Great Ring and that, right?'

'That is true,' Agrash said, perking up a bit. 'Yes, that is true, we have the Great Ring and a Dark Lor— Err… Lady. Yes, maybe we can build on that, put another Army of Darkness together.'

'Yeah, absolutely!' said Sooz, though privately

she was kind of worried at that thought. Where was this going to end? Is it possible that she could end up commanding some kind of army of Orcs and Goblins? What would she do with that? She didn't want to fight some kind of fantastical war in a strange land! All she really wanted to do was to go home to her mum, and see Dirk again. But what could she do?

'Well,' continued Agrash, oblivious to her concerns, 'the Tower is currently pretty much unguarded. Just a bunch of pukey fairies and stinky human tourists. It could be fun, we could surprise them and butcher them all! Hack 'em to bits!'

With that, the rest of the Goblins shouted aggressively, waving their weapons in the air. Several said things like, 'Yeah, cut 'em down! Butcher the lot! Blood! Battle! Gore! We loves an unfair fight! Pair of faeiry wings as trophies, yeah! Nothing like a massacre to make your day!' and so on.

Sooz grimaced. 'Oh no, we can't have that!' she said.

'What do you mean, my Dark Lady?' said Agrash confused.

'We can't have any killing!' said Sooz emphatically.

'Can't have any… What are you saying, my Lady? I mean… You know, we're Goblins and that…' spluttered an astonished Agrash.

'There mustn't be any killing! We'll just scare them away. Those are my orders and that's final,' said Sooz.

'But why? I don't understand!' said Agrash.

'Yes,' said Gargon. 'It's not how we usually do things round here, my Lady.'

Sooz thought furiously for a moment, trying to come up with a good reason, other than… Well, other than just doing the right thing. You know, like not murdering people, even if they were naff little pink faeries. She didn't think 'Doing the right thing' would go down well with this lot. She didn't want a rebellion on her hands – that would be a disaster. She frowned, uncertain. But then she had an idea.

'We mustn't antagonize them too much. We are too weak. If we spare their lives and chase them away, we can fortify the Tower. Maybe negotiate a truce or some kind of peace if they don't think we're really dangerous. Otherwise we risk being destroyed. In retaliation. Do you see?'

'Yes… Of course, yes, it makes sense! It'll give us time to build up our forces and then we can strike back with overwhelming force!' said Agrash.

'Dark Mistress is clever!' said Gargon approvingly.

'Right then, on we go, to the Tower,' said Sooz, relieved. 'And remember, if anyone dies, then the... the killer will have to answer to me, the Dread Queen! And...'

She tried to think how Dirk would say it... 'And my wrath shall be terrible. Great will be my anger, and terrible will be the punishment!'

'Yes, Mistress,' said Gargon, Agrash and the Goblins, submissively.

Sooz smiled at that. This was going really well, she thought to herself. She wasn't so scared any more and she was in charge! Dirk would be so proud of her. And hopefully he'd be here soon to tell her. He had to be trying to rescue her, surely? Probably telling Chris what to do as well. At that thought, she laughed – what she thought of as her normal laugh, a kind of girlish giggle. But the ring glowed, and amplified the sound so that it came out as a '*Mwah, hah, hah!*'

An Unexpected Visit

Dr and Reverend Purejoie were Dirk's foster parents. They'd taken him in, convinced he was a poor traumatized boy who'd made up all that stuff about Dark Lords and magic lands and such like to hide the memory of something terrible that had happened to him. Today, their children – the foster boy, Dirk, and their son Christopher – had been packed off to school, and it was now time for them to go to work. As Mrs Purejoie opened the door she was surprised to find someone standing there. A strange figure, examining the doorbell in some detail. It was a woman dressed in a curiously outdated outfit, with a pale face and long white hair. Dr Purejoie regained his composure first and said, 'Yes, can we help you?'

The strange woman looked up at them, as if noticing them for the first time. She stared at them for a moment, saying nothing. Her eyes were such a light grey as to be almost silver.

'Yes?' said Mrs Purejoie.

The strange woman simply handed them each a card. A black card with white writing on it. Mrs Purejoie read it out loud.

'Greetings, Mr and Mrs Purejoie. I am your new nanny, as you requested, sent here by the High Council of the White Shields to look after your troublesome boy, Dirk.'

Mrs Purejoie looked up, a puzzled expression on her face. 'But we didn't ask for a nanny. We don't need one.' She turned to her husband, a quizzical expression on her face.

'No, no, I didn't ask for one either, goodness no! There must be some mistake,' he said.

The strange woman held up a pale hand…and passed it before their faces, weaving a complex pattern in the air. Silvery sparks trailed from her fingers. The Purejoies' faces, amazed at first, suddenly took on expressions of dull acceptance.

'Oh, yes, the nanny,' said Mrs Purejoie in a flat voice. 'Do come in, please, we've been expecting you.'

Dr Purejoie nodded mechanically, and said, 'Yes,

of course, the nanny,' and stepped aside. The strange woman smiled a sinister smile and glided past them into the house…

Moving Home

Sooz craned her neck back and looked up. Up, up, and up at rows of battlements, parapets, pinnacles, gothic arches, buttresses and the rest of the twisted metal and stone that was the Iron Tower of Despair. She was open-mouthed with amazement. It was a work of utter brilliance. Well, except that it was pink.

Sooz was standing in front of the massive vaulted entrance of the Tower, called the Gates of Doom. Great gargoyle skulls of moulded iron adorned the arch of the gates. Pink gargoyle skulls now, of course. Their heads drooped or lay to the side, and their eyes were shut, as if they were asleep. But why would you have sleeping gargoyles over your front door? Very odd, thought Sooz. The gates themselves were carved with the writhing forms of what looked like tormented souls in some kind of crazy hell.

'Cool!' thought Sooz to herself.

Behind her stood Gargon and Agrash. Her Goblin pack – now named Our Lady of the Dark's Royal Goblin Guard – were busy trashing the amusement park that had been set up by the faeries. And having fun doing it. There was nothing a Goblin liked more than mindless vandalism. Though in this case, not so mindless. Sooz was determined to get rid of all the pinks and whites, the strawberry and lime. Time to put some Dirk back into it, as it were, so the twee amusement park had to go. In any case, she wasn't sure whether she could have stopped the Goblins from their looting and smashing and bashing even if she wanted to. It's what Goblins did. Let them have their fun. Well, for now. Maybe she could educate them a bit later. Give them a bit of culture, teach them how to behave properly. She looked back at them, cavorting and leaping and whacking and smacking. But it would take time. Lots of time.

So far though, things had gone well, the previous occupiers having been driven off quite easily. Gargon had gone in first. All he'd had to do was extend his wings, raise his taloned hands, and give one of his great sulphurous roars. The pink-ribboned faeries, the human kids and their parents – they'd all fled almost immediately, screaming in terror. A few 'security guards' looked like they were going to have a go, but when the Goblins came up, they took to their heels too.

And now here she was in front of the Iron Tower of Despair. She turned to Gargon.

'Can you open the gates?' she asked.

'They open only to Dark Lord…or Lady. Just walk up to them, my Queen,' said Gargon.

At that Sooz paused, a worried look on her face. If she walked up to the gates and they didn't open, then Gargon and Agrash would know she wasn't really a Dark Lady or a Dread Queen of the Night at all. And then…what would they do to her? She turned and glanced at Gargon and Agrash. They were talking.

'How did Hasdruban and his lot open the Gates of Doom then?' asked Agrash.

'Doesn't look like they did,' said Gargon. 'Dark Lord…Dirk…say it was indestructible. Gargon not really believe him – he was not known for truth telling, after all – but Gargon think maybe he was telling truth after all.'

Sooz from Surrey at the Gates of Doom

'Ah, that's why they painted it pink, then,' said Agrash. 'That was the best they could do.'

Gargon nodded. Sooz stared at the gates, unsure as to what to do. Agrash went on.

'That means everything inside is still as it was! The Dark Library, the spell books, the Storeroom, the Dungeons of Doom. Everything. That's great, there'll be weapons in there and stuff our Lady can use!'

'Yes, good, very good!' said Gargon excitedly.

'So,' said Agrash, turning to Sooz. 'What are we waiting for, my Lady? Shall we get in there and find out what's what?'

Sooz began to panic. But there was nothing for it. She took a step towards the Gates of Doom.

Suddenly, all the pink gargoyle skulls began to twitch and jerk, as if they were waking up! Several of them yawned with a metallic grating sound. A few shook their heads, and then they were all looking down at her – and doing a kind of pink metal double take. Then one of them turned to another and spoke!

'That's not the Dark Lord,' it said in a rasping, metallic whisper.

Sooz's jaw dropped. Talking pink metal gargoyle heads!

'Is it a vampire? No, wait, it's, it's… No, it's a girl!'

'What do you mean, a girl?' said one of the heads.

'Yes, it's a girl! A human girl! What's going on?' rasped another.

'I don't know, but she has the Ring,' said yet another.

'What, how did she get that?' scraped the first.

'Maybe she slew the Nameless One and took the Ring?' one of them screeched.

'A little girl? No, surely not. Anyway, the Dark Lord must be alive – if he were slain, the Ring would melt away,' said another.

'That's true. Did she steal it then?' said the first.

'No, no, it is not possible for anyone else to wear the Ring, unless it was freely given by the Sorcerer Supreme himself,' said yet another pink skull.

'But then the Dark Lord must have…you know, given the ring to…to a little girl,' said the first.

'Indeed,' grated a pink skull. Then there was a pause as if they were thinking. After a few moments, the first skull said, 'Well, in that case…'

In unison, they spoke, brazen and loud.

'Welcome, Queen of the Night and Dark Lady of the Iron Tower. You may enter your domain, gifted to you by the Dark Lord in Exile!'

With that the great doors began to open, with a sound like a thousand Goblins scraping their nails down a blackboard. Sooz could hardly believe it!

She looked behind. The Goblins had paused in their vandalism, drawn by all the noise, and they were staring at her, any lingering doubts now well and truly dispelled. Then they all knelt. Agrash and Gargon, noticing this, knelt too.

'All hail Sooz, Dark Lady of the Tower,' they chanted.

Sooz had to admit, she really quite liked all the hailing and honouring. It made here feel all puffed up and important. She walked forwards with a swagger, Agrash and Gargon in tow.

Just behind her, she heard one of the skulls mutter, 'Hey, maybe this means we'll get this hideous pink paint removed at last! Back to black, hopefully.'

'Hah, don't be so sure. She may be the Dark Lady but she still looks like a little girl to me – have you any idea what human girls are like? She'll probably put pink ribbons in our hair!' said another.

Sooz turned around angrily, hands on hips, 'FYI pink gargoyle dudes, I'll have you back in black before you can say Rumpledstiltskin!'

'Rumpled what skin?' grated the gargoyle.

'FYI? What… What is she saying? What does that stand for? I don't understand?' said another.

Sooz blinked for a moment. Rumpelstiltskin? Where had that come from?

'Is she telling us to say Rumpel wotsit whenever someone arrives at the Gates? You know, like a watchword or something?' ground out a gargoyle.

Sooz sighed. 'Just forget it, pink gargoyle thingies. The important thing is that you're not going to be pink for much longer, OK?'

'That's good news!' said a gargoyle.

'Great. Thank you, my Lady,' said another.

'Do you think maybe we could get a custom paint job? You know, like maybe green ears, or blue hair. Oooh, oooh! I'd like red eyes! Red eyes would be cool!' one of them rasped.

This was too much – they were driving her round the bend! 'That's enough!' she shouted, stamping her foot. 'Shut up, shut up, shut up!'

Gargon looked up at the chattering gargoyles

distastefully. 'Dark Lord had trouble with them too, my Lady,' he said.

Shaking her head, Sooz turned back to the portal of the Tower. Before her yawned empty blackness. Steeling herself, she crossed the threshold. When she put her foot down, a dull light sprang forth from the floor of the Tower, illuminating her way. She looked at her feet in wonder. As she walked, she left a trail of glowing footprints, enough to see by. Looking back, she saw them slowly fading behind her.

'How cool!' she thought to herself. She jumped up and down. The footsteps glowed even brighter! She looked back. Agrash and Gargon didn't leave a trail, only she did. She ran around in a circle, laughing whilst Gargon and Agrash stood watching indulgently.

She was in a large, circular chamber. The floor and walls were of a glossy ebon blackness, and they gleamed when the light fell on them. It was quite beautiful. Many doors were set into the walls.

'Where do they go?' said Sooz, turning to Gargon and Agrash.

Agrash was staring around in amazement.

'I don't know, my Lady, I was never allowed into the Tower,' he said.

'Yes, he was not worthy,' said Gargon with a grin. Agrash scowled. He pulled out his filthy handkerchief and blew his nose, inevitably spraying snot all over the place. As his snot fell on the ebon floor it hissed and burned away in a moment, leaving it as pristine as before.

'Wow, self-cleaning!' said Sooz.

'Yes, my Lady. "No dust can ever settle in this Tower, no scratch ever mar its perfection", Dark Lord often say. And those doors – they lead to many rooms, many corridors and passageways. No one has mapped them, not even Dark Lord himself,' said Gargon. 'But ahead lies Great Hall, the Great Hall of Gloom, and his…your throne, your Dark Majesty.'

She turned to look in the direction Gargon indicated, but it was wreathed in shadow. So she ran up and down a bit, hopping and jumping. This threw up enough light for her to make out a magnificent staircase of black ebony, sweeping up to a pair of great doors. The banisters of the staircase were made of some kind of precious metal, something similar to silver, but not as bright. In a way, it was more lovely than silver, for it gave off a kind of moon-like radiance when the light struck it.

'Moonsilver,' said Gargon. 'Very hard to get.'

Sooz looked back at him. 'Is it actually from the moon?' she said, awed by the sheer fantastical nature of the place. She'd thought the outside was impressive – well, the inside was even more so! Dirk went up another notch in her estimation.

'Yes, from moon,' said Gargon.

'Which one?' asked an equally awed Agrash.

'Dark Moon of Sorrows, of course,' said Gargon.

Sooz began to walk up the stairs. Each step, a good forty feet wide, glowed with light as she stepped upon it. At the top, she came to a huge door, carved to look like a dragon's maw. Iron bars formed rows of teeth. As she drew near, the doors began to creak open – the lower half of the door falling downwards, like a drawbridge, the top half moving up, the whole effect being that of a great, fanged dragon mouth opening.

Sooz stepped onward.

Into the Great Hall of Gloom.

It was dark, very dark. A light flared up – revealing a tiny statue in a little alcove. It looked like an old bearded man holding a staff in one hand, the end of which gave off a small jet of flame.

The floor was made up of massive slabs of glistening black marble, inlaid with a fine tracery of Moonsilver that glowed in the lamp light so that a soft radiance melted up off the floor to bathe her in its beautiful glow. She paused for a moment. She couldn't help herself, reaching into her AngelBile bag she took out her little mirror to check out how she looked in this silvery light.

'Heh, heh,' she chuckled to herself. She looked really quite beautiful, but not in that magnificent, terrible, Dark Queen kind of way that the ring made her look, but in a gentler kind of way. A melancholy kind of way… 'Hmm, a bit too Emo if you ask me,' she thought, as she snapped the compact shut. Still, it wasn't bad!

She stepped on – another lamp blazed up. And then she caught a movement out of the corner of her eye. It was one of those statues again, in the alcove of another great pillar – and it was moving! As she drew near, the statue reached into its stone robes, pulled out a match and struck it. Then it lighted the end of the staff it held and a flame sprang up. Once lit, the statue became inanimate once more. She looked at it more closely. Every statue was the same, of what looked like an old bearded wizard, holding a staff, carved out of white marble.

'Dark Lord's joke. They are statues of White Wizard,' said Gargon. '"Hasdruban Lamps", he calls them.'

Sooz smiled at that. It did sound like something Dirk would do. Behind her she noticed Agrash get a book out of his leather pouch, and, with a dirty stained goose quill, write something in it.

'You can write! I didn't think Goblins could write,' said Sooz.

Agrash nodded smugly. 'I can write, oh yes. But most Goblins can't. They haven't got the brains for it, not like me.'

Agrash cocked his head, as if struck by a thought. 'I wonder if Gargon can write,' he said mischievously.

Gargon snorted. 'Gargon cannot write it is true but on other hand, Gargon can tear little Goblins in half in a second!'

Agrash gulped, his face turning a lighter shade of green.

After several minutes walking the length of the Great Hall of Gloom, Sooz drew near to the end. There, on a raised dais of inlaid black marble, sat a massive throne. It was made up of hundreds of skulls.

'Throne of Skulls,' said Gargon reverently.

Sooz drew near for a closer look, trying to work out what the skulls had been carved out of. But the more she looked, the more realistic they appeared. And then it dawned on her.

'Ugh, they're real!' she yelped.

'Of course, my Lady,' said Gargon. 'Aren't they magnificent?'

Then the skulls wailed, a terrible wail of awful loneliness, a haunting moan, as of lost souls crying in some benighted wilderness.

Sooz and Agrash leaped back in horror. Gargon chuckled. 'Don't worry, my Lady, they do that from time to time. You get used to it.'

Sooz looked up at him. He nodded at the Throne. 'You must sit on throne, my Lady,' he said.

'Why?' said Sooz. 'It's yucky! I know I'm a Goth, but it's a bit much. I mean, those skulls – they're real! Not only that, they're not quite dead either, for goodness sake!'

'I know what you mean, Dark Queen Sooz, but goodness has nothing to do with it. You've got to stamp your authority on the Tower and on us, your people. That means sitting on your throne,' said Agrash.

Gargon nodded. 'What Agrash say,' he added.

Sooz wrinkled up her face in disgust. 'Well, if I must, but if I'm taking over, then goodness is going to have something to do with it. Things are going to change round here!' she said stamping her foot on the floor.

Agrash raised a snot-drenched eyebrow. 'Goodness, eh? Well, good luck with that, because that's not what we do,' he said.

Gargon rounded on Agrash. 'That sound like maybe Agrash not agree with my Lady! Maybe you not follow orders,' he said leaning down towards Agrash and scowling.

Agrash recoiled in terror. 'No, no, of course not. I'm just saying. You know, I mean… I would never… it's just, it's just not going to be easy, that's all.'

'Huh,' grunted Gargon suspiciously. 'Remember – our Lady is Queen. We swear oath of obedience!'

'Alright, keep your…keep your scales on,' he replied. 'I mean, do we have to do what we're told, even if it means…well, you know, doing good?'

Gargon blinked for a moment, unsure. 'Well… well, yes, I suppose we do,' he said.

'Well, OK then, as long as we're sure,' said Agrash, looking over at Sooz.

She was staring up at the throne. She'd been listening with interest and now she knew she had to sit on that throne. She had to make sure they would obey her. Or else she would end up with blood on her hands, and she didn't want that. She noticed that at each corner of the dais, a large lidded, closed eye had been carved into the marble. It really was a freaky throne! With a sigh, she stepped up onto the dais. The front of the Throne actually came up to her chest. It was obviously built for somebody huge, someone as big as Gargon. Bigger even. She was going to have to climb up.

She put a foot gingerly on one of the skulls. It moaned and she lost her footing. Then she reached for another, and tried to pull herself up. 'Owwww!' it wailed.

She shook her head in disgust. She couldn't do this. It was just too horrible. She turned to Gargon and looked up at him beseechingly.

He looked back. His scaly brow furrowed in puzzlement. Then he got it.

He stepped forward and carefully picked Sooz up. Tenderly (for a hideous monster from another world) he placed her on the throne.

'Thank you, Gargon,' she said as she stood on the throne, patting him on the back of one black taloned hand.

Nobody had ever shown Gargon any affection. Not ever. Gargon blinked at her like a lovesick mooncalf for a moment. The scaly reptilian skin on his face seemed to flush pink. He spluttered in embarrassment and flicked a glance over at Sooz, but luckily she hadn't even noticed. She was staring at the skulls.

Gargon looked over at Agrash. He was standing there, arms folded, looking back at Gargon, a wry smile on his warty little green features. He made a face at Gargon, mocking him for his softness.

Gargon growled at him and drew a taloned finger across his throat, his meaning being clear – if you breathe a word of this, Agrash, I'll rip your throat out!

Agrash grimaced and put his hands up in a placatory gesture, 'Don't worry, Gargon,' he said, I won't say a word, honest. Never, I promise,' he whispered.

'Shut up, fool!' said Gargon loudly.

Sooz looked up. 'What was that?' she said, her reverie broken.

'Nothing, my Lady, nothing,' they both said in unison.

Then Sooz sat down, or rather lay down, drawing her legs up under her, cautiously resting her elbow on an arm of the throne. There was plenty of room for her to stretch out. As she sat, the skulls gave out a sigh, actually like a sigh of welcome relief, as if they were pleased that someone that wasn't too heavy occupied the throne.

From the four corners of the massive dais that the Throne sat upon, the carved eyes suddenly flicked open and out of them came beams of light that bathed her in a silvery glow. The Ring too began to radiate its dark light. The effect was as if she sat on a throne of silvery shadow skulls, her

Our Lady of the Dark

face glowing with dark power, her eyes dark orbs of awful majesty. Gargon and Agrash sank to one knee before her, heads bowed.

'This is going to be fun,' thought Sooz.

The Moon Queen

'That door lead to Dark Library, that one to Dark Lord's – I mean your – Inner Sanctum, and that leads to Storeroom,' said Gargon.

Sooz was standing behind the Throne, looking at three doors set into the back wall of the Great Hall of Gloom, each with Dirk's seal carved on the front where the handle would normally be.

'Just pass Great Ring over the Seal and door will open, my Lady,' said Gargon.

Agrash had gone – Sooz had sent him off to organize Our Lady of the Dark's Royal Guard and get them settled into the reopened Goblin Warrens.

In the meantime, Gargon was showing her around the important places in the Tower.

She walked up to the door of the Inner Sanctum and waved her hand in front of the seal. With a grating shudder, the door swung open. A thrill of anticipation shivered down her spine as she walked into the chamber beyond, into Dirk's Inner Sanctum, his Unholy of Unholies, his private room. What secrets would she uncover here?

Gargon hesitated. 'Are you coming in?' said Sooz. He paused for a moment, and then shook his head. 'No, Gargon not allowed in. No one allowed into Inner Sanctum except Dark Lord or Mistress.'

Sooz nodded. That made sense. She would keep it that way – this would be her place now, her sanctum. Every teenager needed some space for me-time, after all!

'Wait for me, then Gargon. I won't be long,' she said as she entered the room, closing the door behind her.

She stepped into a relatively small room, compared to others in the Tower, this time decked out in shiny ebon black, filigreed with Moonsilver and trimmed with blood red crimson.

The floor glowed as she walked on it and the veins of Moonsilver in the ebon walls reflected this light, bathing the place in a silvery radiance. Taking up the length of one wall was a long workbench cluttered with various flasks, books, instruments, bottles, potions and so on. Underneath it were lots of shelves, piled up with things – tools, scrolls, ingredients, herbs, jars of unsavoury looking pickled creatures or yucky slimy things.

In one corner of the room stood a massive four-poster bed, hung with heavy black drapes and blood-red glyphs of some kind. In another corner, a massive suit of armour rested on a stand, obviously designed for some kind of…well, huge monster really, with cloven hooves and goat legs, though the rest of it looked like it was made for a human. Except maybe the helmet. That didn't look human. Sooz shuddered. Is that what Dirk looked like in Dark Lord mode? It was hard to imagine the mousey haired schoolboy she knew as Dirk looking like that.

Then she noticed a bronze statue in another corner. She walked over to it. Her brow furrowed in irritation at the sight of it. It was of a curvaceous, semi-naked woman, with pale skin, bright red rubies for eyes and long, lustrous black hair. She wore a rather revealing bodice, skintight leather trousers and long black boots. A great cape was flung over one shoulder. Oh Dirk, she thought to herself, this is just tacky. How could you? She turned away, feeling anger and disappointment. Or was it jealousy?

'Gah – boys!' she hissed under her breath, and went over to investigate the bed.

The sheets were of black silk, with Dirk's seal emblazoned on them, picked out in fine red thread. She would at least sleep well!

On a bedside table, carved to resemble a chained, captive elf holding the tabletop over its head, another book rested, as if recently read. As she reached over to pick it up, a little silvery ball, like a miniature moon, popped up to hang in the air over the book. It began to radiate a soft glow, enough to read by. She smiled at that. How cool! She tried to read the cover of the book but it was written in strange glyphs she didn't understand, as were the pages inside. She put the book down.

Along the wall beside the bed was an ebon wardrobe. As she walked up to it, the doors seemed to dissolve away. She stepped back – the doors reformed as if out of thin air. She stepped forwards and the doors disappeared, stepped back – and so on. She got bored of that pretty quick, and moved in for a closer look. It seemed like the wardrobe was hung with row upon row of great black cloaks. She reached for one – a hand popped out, holding the cloak out to her! She stared at it in horror. Gingerly, she took the cloak. The disembodied hand retracted back into the wardrobe with a click. The cloak was large, heavy and covered in strange symbols. She tried to wear it, but it was too big, too bulky. She tried to hang it back up but the hand snapped out again, snatched it out of her hand and hung it up for her.

The rest of the wardrobe was much the same, mostly cloaks, and not much else.

'Well, that's no good. I can't wear any of those. Aren't there any dresses?' said Sooz to herself, as she stood before the wardrobe, arms folded. Suddenly, two disembodied hands flew out of the wardrobe, fistfuls of dresses in each hand. Sooz was chuffed, to say the least, and she spent the next hour or so picking an outfit from the magic wardrobe.

In the end, she chose a dress with several layers of flowing black silk, trimmed with black lace, with strands of Moonsilver woven through the thread. The wardrobe had provided her with a tiara of

Moonsilver too, with a large, glittering black onyx set into it. A black veil covered her face, and she wore tall chunky boots of black leather, inlaid with a thin tracery of Moonsilver as well. They were seriously Goth boots!

When she walked, the Moonsilver in her hair and clothes glowed, so that wherever she went, she radiated moonlight.

The newly attired Sooz put her AngelBile bag on her back, hidden under her cape, and swept out of the Inner Sanctum into the Great Hall of Gloom. Gargon turned to meet her – and his massive jaw dropped in wonder. For a moment, the fanged, horned, be-winged demon-thing was speechless.

Then he said, 'You have become Queen! A great Queen, a Dark Queen – no, wait, Gargon knows, you have become the Moon Queen!' he said, bowing.

'The Moon Queen. Hmm, I like it, Gargon, I like it,' she said.

Later, Sooz, Gargon and Agrash helped themselves to a mighty dinner from the Iron Tower Storeroom, another room that could only be opened with the Ring. Inside was an almost limitless supply of magically preserved food. Afterwards, Sooz began to feel very tired. Exhausted in fact. So much had happened. She retired to bed, an experience she found to be a two-edged sword. Her room was Goth all right, and the silk sheets were great, but it was also pretty scary. Soon, though, her thoughts drifted to other things, to her mum, and what she'd be doing now. Probably she'd be worried sick. If only she could tell her she was OK. More than OK, in fact. Little Sooz from Whiteshields was a queen and everything. How proud her mum would be! She smiled at that.

But then she thought of her own room, and she began to cry. How she missed Mum and all the safe, warm things of home. After all, she wasn't really a queen. She was just a girl who wanted to go home. She promised herself that she'd never be horrible to Mum again, just so long as she could see her one last time.

Her last thought before she fell into a deep, dark slumber was of Dirk. Where was he? Would he come and rescue her?

Part Two:
New Friends,
New Enemies

Home Help

Dirk swept open the door of the Purejoies' home and walked in. Another pointless day at school out of the way he was thinking to himself when he noticed Mrs Purejoie with someone else, someone he didn't recognize, someone…odd. Clearly, they had been waiting for him.

She looked like that character in that sickeningly soppy film Mrs Purejoie forced him and Christopher to watch once. What was it called? Oh yes, *Mary Poppins*. Except that everything she wore was white.

Her hair was completely white, and hung straight down around her shoulders and face like curtains. She had pale, flawlessly pure alabaster skin, no eyebrows, pale lips almost the same shade as her skin, and light grey eyes, so light to be almost white.

'Hello, dear, a visitor has come to see you! She's your new nanny. Her name's Miss Deary. Dumpsy

Deary,' said Mrs Purejoie, in almost hypnotic tones.

'*Bah!* Such an absurd name, it must be false!' said Dirk.

'Now now dear, be nice, there's a good boy. Please don't start with all that business again,' said Mrs Purejoie a look of resigned patience on her face.

'Oh come on, Purejoie! It's obviously not her real name! Look at her! I'll bet she's not even from this plane, by the Nine Hells!' said Dirk in exasperation.

At the sound of the phrase 'the Nine Hells', the strange white woman pointed at Dirk weirdly, and her eyes widened with interest. Dirk frowned. What a strange creature she was! She reminded him of someone…but he couldn't quite think who.

Mrs Purejoie turned to the nanny and said, 'I'm so terribly sorry. He's a good boy really. Just a little…err…eccentric.'

Miss Deary just inclined her head, and smiled. Her teeth were whiter than her pale, albino skin, so white they gleamed. Behind them, a wet tongue flickered red, but no sound or speech came out.

Dirk sighed and raised his eyes. 'Yes, indeed,' he said, 'the geniuses on this plane are always labelled as eccentric.'

'Of course they are, dear,' said Mrs Purejoie, 'I'm sure Miss Deary will be able to help you with that.'

'Wait a minute, I'm thirteen years old, why do I need a nanny?' said Dirk, suspiciously.

'I can't remember why, dear. Perhaps it's something to do with your…eccentric problems and all. She's highly trained and comes well recommended,' said Mrs Purejoie.

'What, don't tell me, by those idiots Wings and Randle, I suppose?' said Dirk.

'No, no, by…umm, actually, I can't remember that either, but highly recommended by someone, I'm sure. Just right for boys like you, in fact,' said Mrs Purejoie vaguely.

Miss Deary just nodded again, saying nothing. She began to stare at Dirk avidly.

Dirk felt like he was being put on the spot, and as a sly, scheming Dark Lord type he really didn't like that! He shifted uncomfortably from foot to foot, and stared back at the strange white lady. Her stare was…predatory! Definitely predatory! He glanced over at Mrs Purejoie. She was looking at them both with an idiot grin on her face. It all seemed fine to her, obviously. But not to Dirk. Something was wrong, very wrong. It was almost as if Mrs Purejoie had been hit by some kind of spell. He narrowed his eyes. For now, he'd better play along until he could find out what was going on.

'Well, what shall I call you then? Dumpsy? Miss Deary? Or maybe Dumpy?'

Miss Deary just smiled at him. Dirk's brow furrowed. 'Or perhaps Old Whiteface? Frumpsy Sneery then?' Dirk added.

But neither Mrs Purejoie nor the nanny said a word. How unutterably strange, thought Dirk to himself. The whole thing just wasn't right.

He hurried away to his room and shut the door, glad to have some time to himself. He sat at his little desk by the window, and opened it. With a loud caw, Dave the Black Storm Crow flew in to rest on the perch Dirk had made by the window, a piece of wood fixed to a bracket on the wall. He'd carved skulls and other necromantic symbols into the wood and then painted it black.

'So, Dave, my pet, what do you make of this Dumpsy Deary character, then?' said Dirk, his chin in his hands.

The crow gave a croak of disdainful contempt.

'Yeah, you're right there, my little Black Pet of Doom! It's as obvious as an Orc at a tea party isn't it! She's no nanny!' said Dirk half to himself, half to the crow.

Just then there was a knock on the door. Dirk's brow furrowed. Could it be her already?

'Who dares enter the dark domain of the Great Dirk?' he said imperiously.

'It's just me, Christopher,' said Christopher as he walked in. 'I wanted to ask how things were going with my phone.'

'Ah, the DarkPhone,' said Dirk. 'Let's see!' With that he yanked open the draw of his desk and pulled out Chris's phone.

'Eurgh,' said Chris, 'it's gone all horrible and vile!'

'Excellent,' said Dirk. 'Look how beautiful it is!'

The phone had indeed mutated. The edges were ridged with what looked like little human leg or arm bones and there was a tiny bone skull at each corner. The rest of it was covered in some kind of yellowed ancient parchment – or more accurately, old and stretched skin… The front, where messages appeared, seemed to be wreathed in black shadow, like a kind of impenetrable darkness.

Yeah, but how many free texts do you get with that?

'So much for my phone then,' said Chris.

'Indeed. It is now truly a DarkPhone,' said Dirk holding it in his hands and stroking it affectionately.

Chris looked on, slightly disgusted. 'Anyway,' he said, 'is it ready yet – you know, to call Sooz?'

'No, not yet, it is still charging. See,' he said, pointing to a tiny glass tube on one side of the phone. It looked like it was slowly filling up with blood. 'We can send and receive here on Earth, but it'll only be able to call the Darklands when it is on full power.'

As if to underline his words, glowing red runic letters appeared in the shadowy darkness of the phone's frontispiece. They formed the words 'Incoming Call'.

And then the little skulls at the four corners began to sound off.

'*Mwah, hah, hah, Mwah, hah, hah,*' they went. Chris stared at it in horror. Dirk stared at it in delight. '*Mwah, hah, hah,*' went the phone, the villainous laughter getting louder and louder.

'Cool ring tone, don't you think?' said Dirk. More words appeared on the dark screen. 'Nutters', it read.

'It's for you,' said Dirk handing the phone to Chris.

Pete Nutley was his real name. Of course, they all called him Nutters. Chris gazed at the phone in Dirk's hand with horror.

Then the ring tone abruptly changed. In a deep, evil Dark Lord's voice, the little skulls said, 'Answer your phone or you will be destroyed! Answer it now, human, or die!'

Chris grabbed the phone. Gingerly, he pressed a little knob of bone and put the phone to his ear. And then gave a howl – little arms came out from below the four skulls and grabbed onto his ear, holding the phone in place.

'Hands-free! See?' said Dirk happily.

Then a voice came out of the phone, thankfully quite a normal voice: 'Hi, Chris, it's Nutters, how's it going?'

'Err… Alright…umm…Pete,' said a disturbed Chris.

'You OK? You never call me Pete,' said Nutters.

'Yeah, yeah, I am – it's just…the phone's grabbed my ear!' stuttered Chris.

'What…?' said Nutters.

'Look, can I call you back? But…not on this phone. In fact, don't ring me on this phone again, OK? Never again. NEVER!!!' howled Chris.

'Yeah, alright, alright, keep yer hair on,' said Nutters.

'I'll get a new phone and call you then. Got to go, sorry, Nutters, sorry,' said Chris.

'OK, OK. Laters, Chris.'

With that, the call ended. The little arms holding the phone up to his ear retracted back and the frontispiece went as black as night once more. Chris handed it back to Dirk who was staring at it with dark delight.

'Now that's a phone,' said Dirk, putting it back into the drawer. 'But for now, we must let it charge up further.'

'Sooner the better – I'm so worried about her!' said Chris.

'As am I, Christopher, as am I. But for now, there is nothing we can do. Anyway, there's something else I wish to discuss with you. Have you met the nanny?'

'Nanny? What nanny?' said Chris.

'You haven't been told about her then? That is

odd,' said Dirk. 'Very odd.'

'No, Mum never mentioned it or anything!' said Chris.

'Yes, well, it's true. We have a new one. Though I think more accurately, I have a new one,' said Dirk. 'You know, because of my...umm...my superior intellect and abilities.'

'Your mental problems, you mean? Oh I see! Perhaps it isn't a nanny so much as a psychiatric nurse, maybe?' said Chris without thinking.

'Mental problems! Typical of you humans that is, typical. You find someone with an intellect way beyond your own feeble capacities and what do you do? Honour them? Give them the respect they deserve? Put them in charge of bio-weapons research or something useful like that? No, they label you insane and put you in a home with some kid called Christopher! Pah!'

Chris raised his eyes. 'Alright, Dirk, sorry, sorry. I don't think you're mad of course. But they do.'

Dirk seemed mollified by that. 'Well, anyway,' he said, 'she's not a nurse or some kind of psychiatrist. I think she is far more dangerous. I think Hasdruban has sent her here to kill me!'

Chris chuckled at that. 'Yeah, sure Dirk, the nanny is from another world and she's trying to murder you. Riiiight.'

'Well, what of her name then?' said Dirk.

'Her name? What is it then – Annabel Lecter? No wait, something more obvious – Dark Lord Slayer? Dirk Killer? Mrs Dirk-Lloyd-Must-Die?'

'No, it's Dumpsy Deary. Miss Dumpsy Deary. What could be a more obvious giveaway than that?'

The Nanny of Doom

Dirk was awoken by a cry of 'Hah!'.

It was Miss Deary. She'd just swept open the curtains bathing the room in bright autumn sunlight that was shining directly onto his face.

Then her pale brow furrowed in confusion. Dirk looked at her.

'You fool, Frumpsy!' he said. 'Did you really think that bright sunlight would burn my flesh?' Dirk shook his head contemptuously.

Miss Deary just glared at him and stormed out of the room.

'What a numpty!' Dirk muttered under his breath. 'Surely she can see I no longer inhabit my old body!'

With that he rose and headed for the door. Time to do the tedious things one had to do when you were stuck in the body of a puny human child –

clean your teeth, go to the toilet, have a shower, clean the blood off your talons – no, wait, he didn't have talons any more.

He opened the door and stepped out – to be met by a deluge of water full in his face! As he stood there spluttering, he began to make out Miss Deary standing in front of him, grinning madly, a look of gleeful anticipation on her features, an empty bottle in one hand. Dirk coughed, puzzled and confused. Why had she thrown water at him? Behind her, Christopher was staring at them both, open-mouthed. It was moments like this that Dirk really missed his old powers and spells, like the Spell of Utter Annihilation or the Claw of Ripping Death. Then he recognized the bottle Miss Deary was holding.

'Ah, I get it,' said Dirk. 'Holy water from Reverend Purejoie's church! Cunning – not!'

Miss Deary's face fell. Dirk began to laugh. 'You fool, Chumpsy! Holy water no longer affects me here on Earth as it would have done in the Darklands!' he said.

Chris interjected, 'What are you doing, Miss Deary? You can't do that! You can't treat him like that!' he said to her in shocked tones.

Miss Deary simply shrugged as if she didn't care. Just then, Mrs Purejoie appeared on the landing.

'Ah, there you are Miss Deary. I wondered where you'd got to!' she said.

'Mum, did you see that? Miss Deary just threw water in Dirk's face!' said Chris.

'Yes, dear, well, I'm sure she didn't throw it. I'm sure she was just washing his face for him, you know, helping to look after him. That's what nannies do,' said Mrs Purejoie. With that, Miss Deary headed off down the stairs. Mrs Purejoie followed her rather more sedately, as if in a dream, leaving Dirk and Chris on the landing together.

'Can't you see your mother has been ensorcelled in some way?' said Dirk.

'What? En… En – what?' said Chris.

'Ensorcelled. You know, enchanted. With a spell. Or hypnosis if you prefer, if that makes it easier for you, though it is obviously sorcery of some kind. Miss Deary has…bamboozled her. And your father.'

Chris's eyes narrowed. Maybe Dirk was right. Mum was behaving oddly and the nanny was definitely weird! And Dirk usually was right when it came to this sort of thing, no matter how outlandish it sounded. But still, there's outlandish and there's outlandish. I mean, Mum and Dad had been enchanted by an assassin nanny from another world? Really?

~~November~~ Rip-out-their-Hearts 4th
It will be Christopher's birthday in a few days. I suppose I should get him some sort of gift. Must make sure he doesn't get the wrong idea and thinks it is some form of tribute though.

The DarkPhone is still charging. I do hope Sooz will be alive to receive my call! It is maddening that she is there and I am here! By the Nine Hells, if only there was some way I could swap places with her.

The Birthday Party

'Happy Spawnday, Christopher, you have been a most excellent servant,' said Dirk, handing Christopher his birthday present. 'I am glad you are finally thirteen, like the rest of us.'

Christopher stared at it in disbelief. It was an A4 sized framed photo of Dirk that hadn't even been wrapped up. The frame was black and covered in little white skulls and other necromantic imagery. The picture itself was like some kind of cheesy publicity photo from a bygone age with Dirk staring off into the distance as if deep in thought. He'd even signed the photo.

There was also a card. The cover was plain black, with the words 'Happy Birthday' on the front written in red letters dripping with blood.

Inside it said:

See, Chris, I have learned some of your human social habits well!

Happy Birth Breeding Vat Day, ~~my friend~~... My lickspittle worm!

Dirk

And he'd marked it off with three little skull and crossbones symbols instead of kisses.

Chris was speechless for a moment. He didn't know whether to laugh or cry. A framed picture of Dirk? Ridiculous! Who gives a photo of themselves as a present except for egotistical, swollen-headed, megalomaniac nutcases that think they're masters of the universe?! Wait a minute…

Dirk was smiling happily, as if he genuinely expected Chris to be pleased with his gift. Chris sighed. Well, Dirk was Dirk after all, what did he expect?

'Thank you, Dirk. What a nice present,' he said. He tried to make it convincing but it didn't quite work. Dirk was not so easily fooled.

'What is it?' he said. 'Don't you like it? No, surely

The worst birthday ever?

you do. I mean, who wouldn't like such a princely gift? Look, it's me. See? Me!'

Chris put his face in his hands. So far it was turning out to be one of his worst birthdays ever!

'What! Surely you cannot be unhappy with my gift!' said Dirk.

'No, no,' said Chris, trying not to hurt Dirk's feelings – such as they were – not to mention avoiding his wrath. 'It's not you, Dirk, I love your present obviously, I'll put it on the table in my room. Thanks, mate.'

'What's the matter then?' said Dirk. 'You are upset about something aren't you? That is a bad sign amongst humans, isn't it – being upset?'

'It's the present from my mum,' said Chris, thinking fast. 'It's a bit…rubbish. Well, not what I wanted anyway.' Which was true, he didn't much like his present from his mum, in fact there hadn't been a really decent present all day and it was very disappointing – Dirk's present was the last straw. Although, to be fair, getting a present at all from Dirk was actually a bit of a surprise in itself…

'Really? What is it then, show me,' said Dirk commandingly.

'Here, look,' said Chris, and he pulled out a gold medallion he had on a gold chain around his neck.

'Ah, some kind of protective talisman or amulet is it?' said Dirk. 'What's wrong with that… No wait, is it some kind of binding talisman, a kind of magical manacle, enchanted by one of her Archbishops or something, is that it? I bet that's it!! Oh, she is cunning, your mother, cunning.'

'No, no,' said Chris, a little smile appearing at the corner of his mouth. 'It's just a St Christopher medallion.'

'A saint!!' said Dirk, recoiling. 'You have the amulet of a saint around your neck? Be careful, my friend, lest it throttle you – or worse, explode, scattering your brains around the playground!'

Christopher was laughing out loud now. 'No, Dirk, that'd be if you wore it, not me!'

'Well, what powers does it have?'

'Powers? Well, none.' said Chris.

'None, what do you mean, none? What is the point of it then?' said a bemused Dirk.

'It's a St Christopher medallion. He's the patron saint of travellers. It's got Christopher on it, carrying Jesus on his back. You know, like his burden. Like one of those parables my mum goes on about,' said Chris.

'Wait, why carry him at all? Simply summon some Skirrits to build a bridge or command Abrakulax, the Dragon King, to fly him over. Or get a boat, for evil's sake!' said Dirk.

'You're not really getting it are you, Dirk? Anyway, it's supposed to bring you luck,' said Chris.

'Ah, so it does have powers, it's a lucky talisman! I see, I see. So, what is wrong with it then? I mean, saints are notoriously hard to defeat, you know. It is a powerful gift.'

'Well, it's not really what I wanted is it? I want a console or a bike or a game or…you know. Not some necklace.'

'Ah, I see. But you have a bike and a console already. And…well, anyway, you have that framed photo of me. That should make up for it, right?' said Dirk.

Chris sighed. 'Yes, Dirk, that makes up for it, really it does. No, really,' he said.

Dirk narrowed his eyes. Was Christopher being sarcastic again? Suddenly Mrs Purejoie's voice wafted up from down the stairs. 'Cake's ready, dear!

Come down and we'll cut it! And bring Dirk with you!'

Chris and Dirk exchanged looks. 'Here we go,' muttered Christopher under his breath.

Dirk grinned. 'I thought you liked cake!' he said.

'I do, it's just all the fuss and attention I don't like,' said Christopher.

'Ah yes, I understand. Mrs Purejoie may decide to hug you!' said Dirk.

'Oh lord no, not that, anything but that!' said Christopher, feigning utter horror, which made Dirk laugh out loud. Together they walked down to the dining room.

Gathered to meet them were Mrs Purejoie, straight from the church, still dressed in her vicar's outfit, her husband, Dr Jack, and the nanny, Dumpsy Deary.

Dirk frowned. 'What in the Nine Hells is she doing here?' he said.

Chris shrugged. 'I dunno – to check up on you, I guess.'

Mrs Purejoie gestured towards the table, smiling happily. In the middle sat a large cake, baked in the shape of a strange looking tower, covered in white icing.

Dirk sucked his breath in at the sight of it. 'The Tower of the White Wizard Hasdruban, may devil worms eat his brains!' he said.

'No, dear,' said Mrs Purejoie. 'It's a nice birthday cake, made just for Christopher by Miss Deary. Isn't that nice of her?' she said, as if on autopilot.

'Yes, very nice,' said Dr Jack.

Miss Deary grinned a sinister grin, white teeth literally sparkling, little red tongue flicking out like a snake tasting the air. She waved her hand towards the cake.

Dirk grinned back at her. Her face fell at the sight of his grin and she took an involuntary step backwards. But then she pulled herself together and gestured emphatically at the cake once more.

Dirk looked at it suspiciously. She'd poisoned it, of course! But the deluded meddler was too stupid to actually poison it with something that would affect humans, because that might kill Christopher too. And that would be against her rules, no doubt. No, she would have tried something that was supposed to work only on him. Something ridiculous!

He stepped up to the table and said, 'What have you done to this cake to poison me, Dumpsy, you absurd do-gooder? Don't tell me, you've added powdered unicorn's horn, known to be deadly to a Dark Lord? Or perhaps along with the vanilla essence, you've added Holy Essence? That would hurt me, wouldn't it? *Bah*, you fool!'

With that he grabbed a great hunk of cake and crammed it into his mouth, smearing it all over his face in the process.

'Oi! My cake!' said Chris. 'You've ruined my cake!'

'Now, now, Dirk, you really should have waited for Christopher you know, it's his birthday after all, not yours!' said Mrs Purcjoic.

The white lady though, she just stood there with a look of glee on her face – that slowly began to fade as it became obvious that Dirk was unaffected by the cake.

'Num, num, num,' mumbled Dirk as he wolfed the cake down. 'See, Grumpsy, you fool!' he said. 'You will not defeat me so easily, oh no, *mwah, hah, hah*!'

Dumpsy Deary glared back at him in frustrated anger. Then she pointed at Dirk's cake-smeared face and smiled, another gleeful smile full of sinister intent. With a sudden movement she whipped out a white flannel and seized Dirk like a falcon swooping on its prey. Before Dirk could even say 'By the Nether Gods, get off me, you absurd do-gooder', she was wiping the cake off his face with the flannel. Mrs Purejoie and Dr Jack looked on approvingly whilst Chris was doing his best not to laugh.

After she'd finished, she stared at Dirk avidly. Dirk coughed and spluttered, and for a moment a look of triumph appeared in Miss Deary's eyes but Dirk began to recover. His nose was twitching. And then he laughed, 'Hah, I know that smell! You soaked the flannel in Aqua Vitae, the Waters of Life, didn't you?' he said contemptuously.

Aqua Vitae was so toxic to creatures of the Dark that it would strip their skin off in seconds. Death would follow in moments. Permanent death.

'Hah, you fool, Lumpsy, you ridiculous fool!' said Dirk. 'I have foiled you once again! *Mwah, hah, hah!*'

Miss Deary grimaced in angry irritation and looked for a moment like she was going to try something else, but then the doorbell rang. It was some of Christopher's friends, coming round for tea and birthday cake. Miss Deary sighed resignedly. She glared at Dirk but then she had to wait whilst Mrs Purejoie poured tea and Dr Jack served cake.

Dirk crossed his arms and settled down into a chair, resigning himself to a birthday tea party. A thirteen-year-old boy, having tea and cake. At his mother's house. And his mother was a vicar. How uncool was that? he thought, the sides of his mouth twitching into a smile. On the other hand, Chris's foster brother was an evil Dark Lord from another dimension. Now that was cool! Dirk laughed out loud, not his trademark evil overlord's laugh, but a simple boyish chuckle.

'What's so funny, Dirk?' said Chris's friend, Nutters, who'd just come in.

'Oh, nothing, Peter Nutley,' said Dirk. 'Nothing at all!'

Later on that evening, just before bedtime, Dirk and Christopher were in Dirk's room with Dave the Storm Crow perched nearby.

'So, how is the phone coming along?' asked Chris.

'Almost ready, my friend,' said Dirk, hunched over the phone, and making tiny adjustments with a little black screwdriver. 'Almost ready.'

'It's been far too long – Sooz could be dead for all we know,' said a worried Chris.

Dirk sighed. 'I know, I know, but there is nothing more we can do but hope for the best. It is a great worry, not knowing what is happening in the Darklands. If only I could get back there and sort things out, take control once more.'

'And rescue Sooz!' said Chris, emphatically.

'Well, yes of course, of course, that's the point, isn't it,' said Dirk. 'Anyway, let's leave the phone problem for now, I want to show you something.'

With that he turned off the light and opened the curtains. Down below, the porch of the Purejoies' house was lit by an outdoor lamp. Miss Deary had just stepped out. Up against the wall was her bicycle, painted all over in white. Even the tyres were white. Miss Deary was changing out of her sensible white plimsolls into a pair of curious Wellington type boots she used for riding. They were bright silver, and covered in strange patterns. She put one foot into a boot.

'Wait for it, wait for it,' whispered Dirk. Chris looked down, intrigued.

Dumpsy put her other boot on – and gave a sudden shriek of horror! Dirk began to chuckle evilly – which set Christopher off too. After removing her foot from the boot rather smartly, the nanny reached in and groped around. Eventually she took out a small metal object.

'Hand buzzer,' spluttered Dirk, barely able to speak through the laughter.

'A what?' said an equally choked up Chris.

'You know, like you get in those old school practical joke kits. When you shake hands, it gives a little buzzing shock – I put one in her ridiculous boots!' said Dirk.

Chris laughed out loud. 'Brilliant!' he said. Dirk was laughing so much, tears appeared in his eyes. If only it could have been a deadly scorpion or snake or something, Dirk thought to himself, but actually, that wouldn't have been nearly so funny, not to mention the unwanted attention from the police and so on.

Just then, the white lady whipped her head round with unnatural swiftness and stared up at the window like a big cat eyeing a gazelle.

Dirk and Chris pulled back out of sight, the

laughter dying on their lips in an instant.

'Creepy! She is well creepy,' said Chris.

'I know, I know,' said Dirk. 'Still, it was fun to get one over on her for once!'

In the distance, they could hear the metallic squeak of the nanny's bike as she cycled off home, wherever that was.

Dirk and Christopher grinned at each other. Then Chris's smile faded.

'I wish Sooz could have been here to see that,' he said.

Dirk frowned. 'So do I, Christopher, so do I. But…what can we do? Our hands are tied.'

Chris sighed resignedly. 'Well, it's been a long day, Dirk, I'm off to bed,' he said.

'Goodnight, Christopher Purejoie, sleep the sleep of the innocent whilst you still can, puny human child!' said Dirk imperiously.

Chris chuckled and shook his head. 'Yes, yes, OK then, night, Dark Lord!'

Just then, a sudden blood-curdling scream came from the phone.

'By the Nether Gods! It's charged up!' said Dirk. 'What's Sooz's number, Chris?'

'It should be there, in the phone's memory. Well, it used to be, before…' said Chris.

'Ah yes, here it is,' said Dirk. 'Quiet now, Christopher.' Dirk put the phone up to his ear – the little hands came out and grabbed it, securing the phone in place.

'It's ringing, it's ringing!'

The Paladin, Rufino

Sooz lounged on the Throne of Skulls, legs drawn up beneath her, one arm draped over the side. Below her stood Agrash and Gargon.

'OK, so there's plenty of black paint in the storeroom and the Goblins can paint the ground level stuff. But how do we paint all those towers up in the air? I mean, we'll need some seriously big ladders and that's before we've even talked about health and safety!' said Sooz.

'Health and… What that mean, Mistress?' said Gargon.

'You know, safety… Err…and health…' Sooz faltered. How do you explain the concept of health and safety to a seven-foot demon monster and a Goblin?

'Actually,' quipped Agrash, 'Gargon can fly up and do it.'

'Hah, easy for you to say, little Goblin,' said Gargon.

'That's what you did the first time round,' said Agrash. 'In fact, you did most of the building work, according to the legends! Isn't that so, Gargon?'

'Yes, yes, Gargon do lots of work on Tower,' said Gargon proudly, puffing his chest out and pointing to himself vigorously with a black taloned thumb.

'So,' said Agrash, 'it should be easy enough for you to fly up there and paint it then!'

'Well, yes, Gargon can paint it,' he said. His brow furrowed in puzzlement for a moment – had he just been tricked into doing something by that snot-nosed little Goblin?

Agrash smiled up at Sooz. She smiled back. 'Well, that's settled then,' she said. 'Agrash and my Royal Guard will paint all the stuff they can get to, Gargon will start on the rest.'

'Yes, my Lady,' said Gargon. 'I start now then.'

Sooz got down off the throne and opened the Storeroom door for Gargon with the Ring. He came out with a big pot of black paint in one hand, and a huge paintbrush in the other, and set off to start work.

'So,' said Sooz, ambling back towards the throne, 'how far have we got with the new design, Agrash?'

'For your personal Seal, my Lady? Let me show you,' Agrash took out a parchment notebook he had in his leather pouch. He opened the first page.

One of the skulls gave off a low moan. Agrash and Sooz glanced at the throne, disturbed by the sheer weirdness of it. For a moment, Sooz's gaze rose up over the throne and around the Great Hall of Gloom. Over her domain. Her domain! How extraordinary it was! 'Hah, what would they say back home if they could see me now? They wouldn't believe it, not for a moment!' she muttered to herself. Then a wave of homesickness washed over her at the thought of home.

A little tear came to her eye.

'Are you all right, Dark Mistress?' said Agrash. 'Don't you want to see the designs I've been working on?'

'No, no, it's not that, Agrash. It's just that…I miss some of my old friends, you know like Dirk and… err…others,' said Sooz, sniffing.

'You miss the Dark Lord?! Why would you miss… Err… Well… I suppose you are his betrothed and that, I just thought…maybe he… Umm… You know…' spluttered Agrash, confused as to why anyone would miss his old master, let alone agree to marry him, come to think of it!

'We're not engaged, for goodness sake,' said Sooz in irritation.

'Not betrothed, my Lady? But then, I mean, how did you get the Ring?' said Agrash.

Sooz realized her mistake. She couldn't let them think she wasn't betrothed to Dirk, she couldn't risk that. It strengthened her position here, even though the idea of it really annoyed her. Well, at first it had annoyed her, but she had to admit, she did like Dirk.

Or not, not when he was rude to her, or ignored her or kept stupid horrible statues in his room. Anyway, for now she had to keep the pretence up.

'No, no, of course we're…betrothed. Yes, of course. He asked me to marry him and gave me his Ring, no, it's true,' said Sooz. 'And I love him so much. I miss him, that's why I'm crying,' she added to give things a bit of weight.

Agrash raised a snot-soaked eyebrow. 'You…love him? Really? But he's so…you know, big and ugly with the horns and the bony bits, and well… He's so mean!'

Sooz stared at him in surprise for a moment. She knew Dirk didn't look like a boy when he was the Dark Lord, but Agrash's description was still a bit worrying. She hadn't thought it was that bad. That armour in his room – could it really be what he looked like?

'He's quite sweet underneath all that,' she said, half to herself.

'Really?' said an unconvinced Agrash.

'No, really. He is. Honestly. Well, to me anyway,' she said.

'Hah, probably needs you for some kind of sacrifice or something, more like!' said Agrash without thinking.

Sooz glared at him. 'No! He really likes me,' she said angrily. The ring on her finger pulsed red for a moment and Agrash paled at the sight of it.

'Umm, no, I didn't mean… Of course he does, my Dread Queen, of course he does, your Majesty!' he said fearfully.

Agrash looked really quite scared which made Sooz feel a little guilty. 'That's all right Agrash, just forget it,' she said, wiping a tear from her eye.

'Would you like a handkerchief, my Lady?' said Agrash solicitously, happy to change the subject.

Sooz pulled herself together in an instant. 'No, no, and definitely no!' she said, almost gagging just at the thought of what Agrash's handkerchief must be like. 'No handkerchief! Just show me the designs.'

'Yes, Mistress,' said Agrash and he opened the book up to a certain page covered in strange symbols. He had been working on a new seal design for Sooz, as she didn't want to use Dirk's glyph as hers. She wanted one of her own.

'I quite like this one,' said Sooz.

'Though really, it's a bit too fussy,' she added.

'What about this, my Lady?' said Agrash.

'Umm, possibly, but again, a bit fussy. Would it work as a seal anyway? What else have you got?' she said.

'Well, there's this,' he said.

'Hmmm…'

Just then there was a frightful scream, a terrible howling noise that filled the entire Tower from top to bottom. Sooz nearly jumped out of her skin. 'What's that?' she said.

'It's the Gates of Doom, your Darkness!' said Agrash, a worried look on his face.

'You mean the gargoyles? They're screaming? Why?' said Sooz with a rising sense of panic.

'It's the alarm, my Lady, the gargoyles are giving the alarm. It means the Tower is under attack!'

'Oh my g… Under attack! What are we going to do?' said Sooz.

'We'll have to…umm… You'll have to get down there, my Lady. See what's what,' said Agrash, stuffing his book back into his leather pouch.

Sooz was seized with terror for a moment, but then she got hold of herself and a determined look appeared on her face.

'Right, we're going to deal with this! Agrash, with me!' she said.

'Yes, Mistress,' said Agrash glumly.

The ring on Sooz's finger began to pulse slowly, its runes beginning to glow as she ran down the stairs, Agrash somewhat reluctantly bringing up the rear.

Sooz ran out of the gate, Agrash in tow.

And pulled up short in horror. The gargoyle heads were still screaming their alarm – and now she could see why.

Striding towards the gates was a tall human, wearing polished steel armour from head to foot, his helmet topped with an ornate unicorn crest. In both hands he held a massive two-handed sword. Behind him marched about fifty or so men-at-arms, in chain mail, holding spears. One of them was casually spearing a Goblin through the throat. The rest of her Goblin guards were cowering against the walls of the tower, holding out their knives and billhooks in wretched defence, hollering to be allowed into the Tower. They were no match for fully armoured humans.

Sooz gasped in horror. This couldn't be happening, it couldn't be happening! Agrash cowered behind her, holding onto her skirts and snivelling in fear.

At the sight of her, the lead figure halted, as did the men behind him. He threw back the visor of his helmet, revealing the face of a middle-aged veteran with a salt and pepper beard and bright blue eyes. 'I am the Paladin Rufino, of the Order of the Sacred Unicorn, and I shall destroy you utterly, vile creature of the night!' he shouted, pointing at Sooz with his sword. Behind him, his band of spearman gave a mighty shout.

It was all a bit too much for Sooz. A huge warrior

with a blood-soaked sword and fifty spear-armed men were about to kill her. She thought of a time when one of the oiky bullyboys back at school had called her some insulting name for being a Goth.

So she just did what she did then, and held the palm of her hand up. 'Whatever, dude, talk to the hand, talk to the hand,' she said uncaringly.

Rufino blinked, confused… That wasn't what he was expecting at all. Without thinking, he stepped forward and addressed her hand, 'Foul daughter of Darkness, you shall suffer and burn for your evil crimes!' He raised his sword as if to strike.

Behind him, some of his men began to mutter, pointing at Sooz. Rufino paused, as if really noticing her for the first time. His brow furrowed in puzzlement.

'But you're…human. And you're…you're a girl!' he said.

Just then a figure swooped down out of the sky – paint pot in one hand, brush in the other, wings outstretched. Gargon crashed to the ground beside Sooz. Rufino and his men took a step back in surprise, and then Rufino's eyes narrowed.

'Ah, a foe I can understand,' he said. 'Great Gargon

Talk to the hand!

himself. A worthy foe indeed!'

Gargon opened his mouth and roared, 'If you harm one hair on my Lady's little head, I'll…'

'What, you'll do what?' said Rufino, glancing down at Gargon's hand. 'Paint us all black?' Behind him his men guffawed.

Gargon blinked, confused for a moment. Then his eyes narrowed. 'No, Gargon will rip your head off, and pour black paint down your neck, human scum!' he bellowed.

Rufino snarled in response, hefting his sword.

Sooz shook her head, as if she were coming to her senses. Suddenly, she was filled with a terrible angry rage. She'd been thrust into this world against her will, and forced to deal with all manner of really weird stuff, like a huge demon, a pack of Goblins, an enchanted Tower and everything and after all that, this fat-brained idiot comes along and just kills some Goblins, for no reason! The Ring on her finger began to pulse strongly with energy and power in response to her mood. All her fear and anxiety drained away. She'd had enough. Sooz walked up to Rufino.

'You monster, you killed them!' shrieked Sooz at the top of her voice, stamping her foot. 'They're just little Goblins, little pot-bellied Goblins, and you murdered them!'

Rufino blinked in confusion once more.

'Monster? Me? No, he's the...' he spluttered, pointing at Gargon. 'And they're...I mean, you know, they're green, by all that's Holy,' he continued, taken aback by Sooz's manner.

Sooz looked up at him, and started to jab him with a finger in his armoured belly. Her dark purple painted nails clicked lightly on his steel breastplate. 'Oh, so you killed them just because they're green, is that it? Look at you! You're a big strong man in full armour, with soldiers and everything, and they're just little Goblins, virtually defenceless! Did you even ask them to surrender or anything?'

'Umm... No, I mean... We just... Umm, surrender? What...' he spluttered.

'I can't believe it!' she shrieked, 'You're no different to a mindless Orc!' The Great Ring responded to her growing anger. It swelled in size, the runes coruscating with dark energy.

Rufino saw it. He gasped in horror and stepped back. 'The Great Ring! She has the Ring! Get back, get back, men!' he shouted.

The dark light of the Ring bathed her in its glow. Sooz's face was a mask of rage; she looked the picture of a vengeful Dread Queen of the Dark. Suddenly a blast of ravening energy burst from the ring to strike the ground in front of Rufino, blowing grass, rocks and earth into the air. Rufino was sent flying backwards, to crash to the ground in a heap. Clods of dirt and pebbles rained back down and clattered off his armour where he lay. The blast left a big, smoking hole where it had struck the ground.

Sooz stared at the Ring in amazement.

'Get in!' she said.

'Nice!' said Agrash, stepping out from behind her skirts. 'That'll teach him!'

'Ah, the Blast of Ravening Flame, good work, my Queen,' said Gargon. Then he bellowed loudly, 'You men, surrender now, or the Dark Lady of the Tower will destroy you all!'

Sooz looked up. Quickly she levelled the Ring at the spearmen, as if ready to blow them all to pieces. Though truth be known, she wasn't sure if she could make it work again. She concentrated, imagining the blast. The Ring began to hum – she could feel it charging up! All she had to do was think...so...

and…so…and then, yes, it would fire! Quickly she reined herself in. She didn't really want to hurt anyone after all.

The spearmen stood there, uncertain. Rufino began to stir. He'd been stunned, but now he was recovering. He got to his feet groggily and removed his helmet.

He glared at Gargon. 'If I had known she wielded the Ring I would have come with greater force,' he said.

Agrash chipped in. 'Well, she does, so there! So you'd better surrender, or she'll blast you back to Gam!'

Rufino frowned. If it were just him, he'd have taken his chances, and if he'd lost it would be a glorious, honourable death. But he had his men to consider. If they fought, many of them would be slaughtered in seconds by the power of the ring. On the other hand, surrender to the Dark usually meant death or slavery. He could expect to be killed and his men enslaved. Except that this time Hasdruban would come. And soon, probably. He'd defeated the Dark Lord, surely he could defeat this Dark Lady. Dark Girl really. And then the White Wizard would free Rufino's men.

Rufino sighed. He'd seen too many battles, too many pointless deaths in his lifetime. Maybe this was it. He'd gambled on a quick surprise attack and it hadn't paid off. Ah well. Time to minimize the damage. He dropped his sword, and signalled his men to do likewise.

'We surrender,' he said. With that, the rest of her Goblins ran forward, full of confidence now, tittering and giggling in Goblin fashion as they began to gather up all the men's weapons.

They piled them up in front of Sooz. She stood there, surveying the field of battle, unsure about what to do next.

'Shall we slay them all, my Lady, or just the Paladin?' growled Gargon.

'No! No. We're not killing anyone. We shall show them mercy, of course,' said Sooz.

'Mercy? Really? Oh well, as you command, my Lady,' said Gargon.

Rufino raised an eyebrow. That was a turn up for the books.

'So, we enslave them then? Put them to work in the Slave Pits of Neverending Toil,' said Agrash.

'No, no, we're not going to enslave them!' said Sooz, shocked. 'We don't do slavery any more around here, all right?'

'No slavery? Oh… Well… Umm, well, as you command, Dread Queen,' said Agrash.

'Gargon, make sure our Goblins give them food and drink whilst I talk with Rufino,' said Sooz. 'Agrash, come with me, and bring your notebook.'

'Yes, my Lady,' said Agrash.

Rufino was staring at her, as if he couldn't believe what he was hearing.

'Now,' said Sooz, walking up to the Paladin. 'We're going to draw up some kind of peace treaty, see if we can live together without all this ridiculous fighting…'

In the Court of the Moon Queen

'So, how is the republication of the Darkland's news-sheet coming along, Agrash?' said Sooz as she lounged on the Throne of Skulls. The throne gave off an inquisitive moan, as if to underlie her question. Sooz smiled at that – she was getting used to the freaky throne at last.

'I have the first issue, my Dark Mistress. The Daily Massacre is back in circulation!' said Agrash enthusiastically, handing her a single sheet of newspaper.

Sooz nodded. 'I like it, Agrash, though isn't there something we can do about the date?'

'Ah, I understand, my Lady, it shall be as you command in the next issue,' said Agrash.

Sooz was holding court, something she had been doing for several days now. It'd been fun, but now it was too much like hard work – she had to make difficult decisions and things. She had to actually rule the kingdom. Or Queendom as she preferred to call it.

The Daily Massacre   15th of the Month of Hellfire
Year of our Dark Lord 2321

BACK IN BLACK

Our glorious and most Dread Queen of the Night, Sooz, sweet Lady of the Dark and most revered ruler has removed the vile pink stain that has desecrated that most ancient seat of Dark Power, the Iron Tower! It is now once more gleaming in purest black!

Our Queen has embellished the Tower in various ways in a new style she calls 'Goth'. How wonderful it looks!

Just below the throne on the left stood Agrash, officially bestowed with the titles Royal Chamberlain and Keeper of the Words of Doom. These were titles she'd allowed him to give himself, though she preferred the one she'd given him – Mr Snotnose Greenbelly. Agrash was dressed in a black tabard with Sooz's new personal Seal inlaid on it, which looked like this:

On her right stood Gargon, the Dread Lieutenant and the Royal Bodyguard or, as Sooz preferred to call him, Me Mate, the Big Horned Demon-thing.

The Great Hall of Gloom was not so gloomy any more. Sooz had stationed Goblin guards beside each great pillar, thus permanently activating the Hasdruban Lamps, so the hall was bathed in a lovely silvery glow whilst still retaining a brooding sense of gothic menace.

What was even more interesting were the group of people – well, some of them were people – who were gathered around her throne.

One was a big, heavy Orc chieftain called Skabber Stormfart and, for an Orc, he was a genius – i.e. about as intelligent as your average human adult. Beside him stood a Nightgaunt, basically an insect-legged, sleek looking bat-like thing about five foot tall with glowing green eyes, black, furry wings and little sharp pointy teeth. Its name was RakRak the

Nest Lord. Nightgaunts were very intelligent, but also kind of weird. Goblins and Orcs were similar to humans, but Nightgaunts weren't, they were very different.

And beside RakRak stood a something that had never been in the Tower before, ever – a Paladin. In this case, Rufino.

Much had happened since she had become the Moon Queen. News of the resurgence of the Dark had drawn many back to the Tower. More Goblins had come to take up residence in the Goblin Warrens. A thousand strong tribe of Plains Orcs had come back and were living in a small city of tents nearby. Nightgaunts had returned to nest in the Eyries of the Night, the topmost battlements and pinnacles of the Iron Tower. Daily they flew out in wide-ranging patrols to report back on goings-on in the vicinity. Both RakRak and Skabber had sworn allegiance to Sooz, accepting her as the rightful Queen of the Dark. Already the Tower was being referred to as the Tower of the Moon, rather than its old title, the Iron Tower of Despair.

And most amazing of all, Sooz had concluded a peace treaty with the local humans and their leader

Rufino. The humans had a small settlement nearby, originally inhabited by amusement park workers and other settlers. They still remained, about a thousand humans, living in peace with the Dark. Some Goblins had even moved into the village and an Orc or two, traders and merchants mostly. And, so far so good, no one had killed anyone. Yet.

But something was up, something to disturb the fragile peace Sooz had managed to put together. Rufino had demanded an audience with the Moon Queen – he had grievances. Sooz had granted his request and here he was.

'Enough of this news-sheet nonsense,' said Rufino angrily, 'I demand to be heard!'

Gargon narrowed his eyes. 'Do not talk like that to my Lady,' he growled.

'*Bah*, you hell-spawned beast, I shall talk to the girl as I like,' said Rufino angrily. 'She has tricked me, tricked us all with her weasel words – I should never have trusted this daughter of darkness!'

'Why? Whassup Rufino?' said Sooz.

Rufino glared at her, though somewhat less angrily. He couldn't help himself, he just couldn't be really angry with her for long – the truth was that Sooz reminded him of his own daughter, who lived with his estranged wife back in Gam, the City of Men.

'Some of my people have been taken,' he said.

'Taken? What – like alien abduction or something?' said Sooz, confused. Then she spotted Agrash shifting uncomfortably from foot to foot and her eyes narrowed in suspicion.

Rufino frowned. 'What? No, not…aliens. No, they have been taken to the Pits. The Slave Pits of Never Ending Toil. Don't pretend you don't know anything about it, my Lady!' said Rufino.

Sooz was staring at Agrash. Snot was beginning to run from his nose, falling to the floor and burning away with a hiss and a wisp of foul smelling vapour as the self-cleaning floor magic kicked in. His nose always started to run more than usual if he was nervous or unsettled.

'Agrash, what have you been up to?' said Sooz silkily, stroking her ring with one hand.

Agrash blinked for a moment, unsure as to what to say. Suddenly he blurted, 'It was Skabber's idea, Skabber! He made me do it!'

Skabber took a step back in shocked horror,

mostly at how quickly Agrash had shopped him.

'You little piece of Goblin snot,' he growled.

Sooz's face scrunched up in anger. She leapt to her feet on the Throne and stamped a foot.

'I told you, I told you!' she shouted, 'I told you we weren't going to open that horrible workhouse pit! And no more slaves, never! But you disobeyed me!'

Rufino stared at her in amazement. Then he smiled, an almost proud, father-like smile. Agrash and Skabber though, they hung their heads like naughty schoolboys.

Sooz crossed her arms. 'Well, why? Why did you do it? Tell me!' she said.

Agrash muttered under his breath.

'What? What was that? Speak up, Snotripper!' she said.

'Well, you know you wanted a proper town built for the Orcs and Goblins to live in with the humans? And you wanted the Warrens refurbished, right, cleaned up, and that? And the river dredged and all the pollution taken out and…' said Agrash.

'Yes, yes, what about it?' said Sooz.

'Well, that's a lot of work. I had to put most of the Goblins on it, lots of Orcs too, working in the Pits.

Skabber thought it only fair we put some humans to work there too, along with the other slave workers. I mean, that's how we get things done around here – slavery in the Pits of Never Ending Toil. It's been like that for a thousand years,' said Agrash.

'That is true, my Lady,' said Gargon. 'All works of the Dark Lord done with slaves in the Pits, just the way of things.'

Sooz shook her head in disgust. Then she sighed. 'Well, I suppose you didn't know any better.'

Sooz sat back down and thought for a moment. Then she stood up once more and spoke.

'Right, this is like a…you know, an official decree type thing. First of all, you will free all the workers in the Pits, especially the humans!'

'Free them all? Are you sure…?' said Agrash.

'Yes, I'm sure, Agrash, just do it,' she said.

'Yes, my Queen,' said the snotty-nosed Goblin.

Rufino spoke. 'Thank you, my Lady. I apologize with all my heart for doubting you.'

Sooz smiled at him. 'That's OK, I understand. Now Agrash, listen to me. We're going to employ people in the Pits from now on. But only if they want to work there! Nobody will be forced to work.

No one is to be forced to do anything, in fact, got that!'

Agrash and Skabber stared at her in amazement.

Sooz continued. 'We've got plenty of gold and that in the Storeroom Treasury so payment won't be a problem. They'll work in five-day shifts, eight hours a day, an hour off for lunch in the middle. Got that?'

Agrash and Skabber's collective jaws dropped. Even Rufino raised an eyebrow.

'Eight hours, is that all?' said Agrash in amazement. 'And an hour for lunch?!'

'Yup. And after five days' work, we give them two days off,' continued Sooz.

'You mean we off them after five days? Seems a bit harsh, even for a Dread Queen of the Night, if you don't mind me saying, my Lady,' said Agrash.

'No, no, we don't off them. We give them two days off,' said Sooz.

'Off? What do you mean – off?' said Agrash, confused.

'You know, off. Days off. They don't have to work, they can rest. Have fun. Do what they like,' she explained.

'Rest? Have fun! DO WHAT THEY LIKE! Have you gone mad, my Lady!' said an astonished Agrash.

'No, I'm serious. Or are you questioning the power of the Dark Queen, Mistress of the Tower of the Moon and Sorceress Supreme?' she said, casually waving her hand, the one with the Great Ring on, the Ring that glowed with a strange darkling light, the Ring with coruscating runes of fiery power that writhed around it like trapped souls in hell.

Agrash's face turned a lighter shade of green. 'Oh no, my Dread Queen, no, not at all! Forgive me, Mistress, it shall be as you command!'

Rufino smiled up at her. 'You are a true queen, my Lady,' he said. 'Dark though you are.' With that he bowed. 'We shall build a great city for your people to live in!'

Agrash raised a snotty eyebrow. 'I just had a thought – what are we going to call your city, Dread One?'

'I don't know,' said Sooz. 'I hadn't thought of that!'

'Soozville!' said Gargon.

'No, City of the Moon!' said Agrash.

Just then, a Goblin messenger ran into the Hall.

'The Black Slayer! The Black Slayer is here!' he said.

Gargon gave a low growl. Rufino reflexively reached for his sword. Skabber looked around as if checking for exits. RakRak the Nest Lord immediately flew straight up into the air, disappearing somewhere into a shadowy corner of the ceiling and Agrash actually cowered in fear.

The sight of them all reacting like that filled Sooz with worry. 'The Black Slayer? Who is that?' she said.

Gargon spoke. 'The Black Slayer, Lieutenant of the Tower of Despair, and Commander of the Legion of Merciless Mayhem. The Dark Lord's most deadly servant…if you could call him a servant. He only obeyed out of fear of the Master and hope of reward.'

Sooz frowned. She vaguely remembered Dirk talking about the Black Slayer and it wasn't good.

'What does he want?' she said.

'An audience,' said the little messenger Goblin, whose name was Larkin-a-boot.

And then, behind Larkin-a-boot, a figure came striding into the Hall. Sooz's jaw dropped. For a moment she thought it was Darth Vader himself, right out of the Star Wars films, but as the figure drew nearer, she could see that the helmet wasn't right, it was black and shiny but more like a crusader helmet from medieval Earth, and the black clothes and cape were cut differently. There was a kind of face mask on the front of his helmet, rather like the face masks of Samurai warriors from back home, but far more terrifying. On his back, a great sword was slung – but openly without a scabbard. The blade was long, wide and leaf shaped and of some kind of black steel, carved with purple runes that glowed evilly in the silvery light of the Hall.

'How did you get in?' said Sooz. 'I thought no one could enter the Tower without my permission!'

'No one save the Lieutenant of the Tower himself, that is,' said the figure. Sooz had half-expected a deep wheezing Darth Vader voice, but instead a thin, ghostly voice came forth, creepy and sinister.

'The Dark Lord, my Master – my true Master, he gave me special dispensation to come and go as I please.'

'I said then it was mistake,' said Gargon.

The Black Slayer waved a dismissive hand in Gargon's direction and strode up to the Throne. Everyone melted away from him in fear – even the

Throne itself gave an involuntary moan of terror. Everyone except Gargon and Rufino that is, who moved between him and Sooz. That made Sooz feel a bit safer, and her heart swelled with affection and gratitude towards them.

The Black Slayer looked them up and down.

'Greetings, Gargon,' he said. 'As loyal as ever, I see, but then again, you are too stupid for anything else. But what is this? A Paladin? That is most unexpected. There hasn't been one of your kind in this Tower for millennia – well, not unless you count those who have sojourned below in the Dungeons of Doom!' With that, the Black Slayer laughed, a sinister, silky laugh of pure malice.

'Do not take another step towards our Lady,' said Rufino, hand on his sword. 'We know you Slayer, we know you of old, of your greed and ambition, your lust for blood and power!'

'What does Slayer want?' said Gargon.

Sooz was staring at the Black Slayer with mounting fear. He looked and sounded really scary. Gargon and Rufino obviously didn't like him, and everyone else was really terrified of him.

'I have heard there is a new power in the land, a

Oh no, it's the Black Slayer!

Queen of the Dark. I have come to see for myself,' hissed the Black Slayer. 'And to offer my services, should she prove worthy.' His face tilted up towards her, and Sooz got the feeling she was being examined closely, examined like a beetle under a microscope.

'But all I can see is a little girl,' he said after a short while. 'A little human girl.'

The blood drained from Sooz's face – this one was going to be trouble, she knew it!

'Queen Sooz is human, and she is young, is true, but…' said Gargon.

'But she wields the Great Ring,' continued Rufino. 'And she knows how to use it, I can vouch for that.'

'Yes, I heard that,' said the Black Slayer, curiosity in his whispery tones. 'That is why I have come.'

Agrash popped his head around the corner of a pillar. 'And she is betrothed to our Dark Master!' he said.

The Black Slayer gave a hiss of astonishment, just as Sooz said, 'No, I'm not…' but then she thought better of it, especially after that reaction. 'I mean yes, yes, we are engaged,' she said. 'And he gave me his Great Ring to wear,' she added, holding it up so the Black Slayer could see the glowing runes.

The Black Slayer laughed. 'Hah, you fools! She is but a child. Somehow a child has taken possession of the Ring, that is all. Look at her, she cannot be the steward, the caretaker of the Dark whilst our Lord is gone!'

'And who should be the guardian of the tower, in your Master's absence, then, eh?' said Rufino. 'I wonder who, eh?'

The Slayer gave a wry, wispy laugh. 'You are astute, I'll give you that, Paladin,' he said. 'But now that you mention it, yes, of course, it should be someone more suitable, someone like me, someone truly of the Dark. Obviously!'

'But Sooz is betrothed,' said Agrash. 'When the Master returns, they shall marry, and she will be Queen!'

The Dark Slayer fell silent for a moment. And then suddenly he reached up for the sword on his back...

'Touch not the Stealer of Souls!' said Rufino as he half drew his own sword and stepped forward. Gargon dropped into a fighting crouch and growled.

The Slayer froze. He seemed to be thinking about things, weighing up his chances.

His hand fell to his side.

'*Bah!* You are all fools and dupes! Can you not see that this little girl has deceived you all?! She has falsely gained the Ring somehow and fed you a lie about this marriage and his friendship! The Dark One would not marry! He does not love! It is I that should wield the Ring in his absence. It is I who should rule!'

Sooz went white with fear – she had been well and truly rumbled, she was for it now, they'd realize everything the Black Slayer had said was true. She was just a little girl, Dirk wasn't her fiancé and she'd only got the ring by accident really. They'd turn on her, these creatures of the dark, they'd turn on her and rip her to shreds. And worst of all – could it be true? That Dirk could not love? Really?

A little tear came to her eye, and she could feel great sobs welling up inside of her. She was just a schoolgirl; it was all too much. Maybe she should start begging for mercy. Maybe they'd let her live if she offered to be a slave in the Pits or maybe the Black Slayer would even let her go or something, especially if she just gave him the Ring! She reached for it, intent on taking it off and handing it over.

But Gargon said, 'Never! NEVER! Gargon swear oath to my Lady, Gargon die first!'

Agrash stepped out from behind the pillar, 'Yes, we Goblins are sworn to her too,' he said fiercely. Then Agrash paled as he realised what he'd just said. 'All right, we might not die first, like Gargon, but we would never serve you, Slayer, never!'

Skabber stepped forward too. 'Orcs are with Agrash. We serve our Lady, Sooz. She's been good to us. Orcs gonna do well under the Moon Queen's rule, I can tell.'

'You cannot win here, Slayer. Even I, Rufino, a Paladin am happy to serve under the Moon Queen, for she is a wise and just ruler, despite her age. Think about it. Orcs, Goblins and humans working together. You cannot defeat that.'

A huge grin split Sooz's face, and she hopped up and down a couple of times on the throne with excited joy. She could hardly believe it! They were all on her side – even prepared to die for her! Well, some of them. Her heart swelled with pride and happiness. In fact, this was probably the happiest moment of her life.

She raised her head and spoke, going into 'decree'

mode. 'I, Sooz, the Moon Queen, Dark Lady of the Tower, do hereby banish you from my domain, Black Slayer!' But she couldn't keep up the queenly stuff for long. 'So, go on, get lost, ya freak!'

The Ring glowed as she said this, lending her power and authority so that she looked and sounded like a Dread Queen, a terrible and powerful Mistress of the Dark.

The Slayer faltered and stepped back. 'So be it,' he hissed. 'Perhaps I have underestimated you, Queen Sooz.'

With that he began to back away. 'Don't think that this is over though!' he said before exiting the Hall.

Everyone sighed in relief.

Just then, a strange noise started coming out of what seemed to be Sooz's back. It was faint, tinny music. Everyone turned to stare. In fact, it was coming from the backpack she was wearing underneath her black and silver cape and it was the first few bars of the Goth band AngelBile's best-selling song, 'I Take My Coffee Black and Bitter, Like My Heart'.

Sooz froze in shocked surprise. It was her phone. Her phone was ringing! How could her phone be ringing?

The Conversation

'Oh…my…g…' she said. Quickly she jumped down off the throne, and rushed off to the Inner Sanctum as quick as she could, checking to see who the phone said was calling. It said the caller was 'Something of the Night'. Weird!

Sooz pressed the answer button on her phone and held it to her ear. 'Hello,' she said tentatively, unsure as to who could be there, hoping against hope.

'Sooz, is that you?' said a voice Sooz had been longing to hear ever since she'd fallen into the Darklands.

'Dirk! Dirk, thank god it's you! It's so good to hear your voice, I can't tell you!' she said, overjoyed.

'Sooz! Are you all right? Are you alive? I'm so sorry, so sorry this had to happen!' said Dirk, equally moved to hear her voice, though he was loathe to admit it.

'Of course I'm alive, fudge boy,' she said, grinning from ear to ear. 'You're talking to me, aren't you?'

'Well, you know, I meant alive alive,' said Dirk, 'as in not turned into the Undead or something.' Of course, he hadn't meant that at all, but he didn't want to sound like a fool in front of Sooz.

'No, I'm not a zombie or anything, Dirk. I'm fine,' said Sooz.

'Thank the Nether Gods for that!' he said. 'I am so relieved. Though this whole thing is really your fault.'

'My fault! What do you mean it's my fault?' said Sooz, annoyed. She'd been through a lot and was in no mood to be blamed for it.

'Well, you and Christopher, in fact. It was the Ring you see, the ceremony shifts the Ring and its wearer back to the Darklands. If you hadn't tried all that skulduggery to keep the Ring I would be there now, not you. So you have only yourself to blame,' said Dirk.

'Only myself to… Ooooh, you stuck up little… little…boy!' said Sooz, so angry she could hardly speak. She stamped her foot and turned off the phone.

She stood there for a moment blinking at the

phone. What had she just done? It can't have been easy for Dirk to get through to her, what if he couldn't ring again? She needed him, she needed his advice, not to mention how good it was just to hear his voice.

She tried the call-back function on her phone, but nothing happened. There was no signal, no connection bars on the display and no way of making calls.

Then it began to ring again with the song 'Black and Bitter'. 'Thank goodness for that!' said Sooz. Then she narrowed her eyes and pressed the answer button.

'You tried to get Chris to steal the Ring for heaven's sake – it was your fault! All you had to do was ask!' she shouted down the phone.

'All right, Sooz, all right, calm down. We can't worry about that now,' said Dirk. 'Chris is here too. He says the first priority is to get you to safety. He is right, of course. I shall assign blame later. Now, tell me, Sooz, where are you?'

Assign blame! Typical Dirk, she thought. But then she smiled as she thought about where she was. 'I'm in the Inner Sanctum,' she said silkily.

There was silence for a moment. 'What, you mean in the Iron Tower?'

'Yes, in the Tower, with the big bed, the armour, and the worktable – well, my dressing table now, and—'

Dirk interrupted. 'By the Nine Hells, my private chambers! Who has imprisoned you there? Hasdruban? Or perhaps Gargon, or the Black Slayer? How did they get in?'

'No, no,' said Sooz. 'It's my private chamber now. I live here.'

There was another stunned silence on the other end.

'Dirk? Are you there Dirk?' said Sooz, grinning to herself.

'What do you mean, you live there? What's going on?' said Dirk.

Sooz couldn't help herself and she giggled triumphantly. 'I've taken over, Dirk. I'm in charge!'

'What... What? How is that possible?' said an astonished Dirk.

'Well, the Orcs and Goblins are on my side now. So is Gargon. We took back the Iron Tower – without killing anyone, I might add – and now I'm the Dark

Mistress of the Tower. The Moon Queen, in fact!'

'By the Nine Hells, Sooz, you have done well! Incredibly well! I am impressed, most impressed!' said Dirk.

Sooz grinned, and jumped up and down excitedly for a second or two.

'I even know how this Ring works. I can blast things with it!' she said excitedly.

There was another silence on the other end. Dirk was beginning to feel rather uncomfortable about how things had turned out. It was great that Sooz was all right, but it was beginning to feel more and more like she'd taken his life over. And not only that, she was doing a really good job of it too. He was beginning to feel a tad jealous.

'So, you've settled in then. In my house, with my ring and my servants…'

Sooz was about to snap back at him, but she got a hold of herself and said, 'Actually, please let's not argue, Dirk. I don't want to be in charge here, or to live here. I want to come home. I want to see Mum. And you and Chris. That's all. When can I come home?'

That made Dirk feel a little better – perhaps she

didn't want to usurp his throne after all. Dirk sighed. 'I know, Sooz, I know. I'm working on it, but I can't think of any way of getting you here, or me there. It's hard enough just getting this phone to work.'

'Oh no, don't say that!' said Sooz.

'I'm sorry, my Child of the Night, but those are the facts. We will have to make the best of things as they are, but I am working on it. If anyone can get you home, it is I, the Great Dirk!'

Sooz smiled at that. 'Well, thanks, Dirk. That's nice, thank you.' After all, he had sorted out the mess with the cricket Pavilion. He'd find a way, she thought to herself.

'Now, put Gargon on, I'd like to talk to him,' he added, rather bossily.

Sooz screwed her face up in annoyance at his tone – though it was typical Dirk once again. Then a little smile crooked up the corner of her mouth, she'd listen in, see how the conversation went. She flicked the speakerphone on. Heh, heh, perhaps some of Dirk's dark cunning was rubbing off on her, she thought to herself.

'All right, hold on Dirk,' she said, as she opened the door and called Gargon over. He loitered in the doorway, unwilling to actually enter the Inner

Sanctum. She held the phone up to him.

Gargon stared at the little device in her hand, a confused expression on his face. Sooz shook it at him. 'Take it, my Dread Lieutenant, take it!'

Gingerly, the Hewer of Limbs stretched forth a taloned hand and took her phone. Dirk's voice crackled, 'Gargon is that you?' The great demon nearly dropped the phone in terror.

Sooz raised her eyes. 'Don't worry, Gargon, it won't harm you. Think of it as a Scrying Crystal, but instead of sight, all you get is sound. Go on, put it up to your ear.'

Gargon sighed a great, sulphurous sigh and lifted the phone to the side of his massive, bony, scaly, fanged head and blinked in worry.

'Gargon? It's me, Dirk. Dirk the Dark Lord!' said Dirk, his voice tinny but quite loud.

Gargon looked puzzled. 'Doesn't sound like you... Master?'

'Yes, yes, it's me, I've been cursed, put into the body of a puny human child by Hasdruban, may a thousand devil-worms gnaw his holy flesh!'

'How do I know it's really you, though, Master?' said Gargon.

'By the Nine Hells, of course it's me! We built the Iron Tower – you remember you had to work fourteen nights in a row and afterwards I rewarded you with a new belt for those shrunken heads!'

Gargon looked away, a look of annoyance on his face. He put his hand over the phone and said, 'It's true, Gargon work like a dog, Dark Master sat on the Throne of Skulls doing nothing and at the end of it Gargon gets a leather belt! Also, Gargon hate shrunken heads! They stink. Pah!'

Gargon spoke into the phone. 'Yes, Master, Gargon remembers. Gargon remembers very well. How are things, my Lord?'

'Could be better, Gargon, could be better, but it's good to hear your gravelly voice after all this time.'

Gargon raised a demonic eyebrow. 'Good to hear my… Are you all right, your Imperial Darkness?'

'Yes, yes, I'm fine. Now listen Gargon, you must look after Sooz. You must protect her. She is very important to me.'

A great beaming smile appeared on Sooz's face when she heard this.

'Ah, you mean she is useful, and must be protected, but when she has outlived her usefulness we can get

It's for you!

rid of her, like the usual standing orders, my Dark Master?' said Gargon.

'Yes, of course, what else, Gargon,' said Dirk without thinking.

The smile on Sooz's face drained away like sand through an hourglass. She scowled. The ring on her finger began to pulsate with angry energy. It began to hum.

'But Gargon doesn't want to get rid of Dark Mistress, Gargon likes my Lady,' Gargon replied, a look of dismay on his scaly face.

'What! You like…Gargon likes…' Dirk went quiet for a moment. It was all so incredible he could hardly believe it. Sooz had really shaken things up!

Dirk continued, 'No, no, you're right, I didn't really mean that, Gargon. We won't get rid of her really. She is my… Umm, she is my friend… I mean a friend! A friend of the dark, you understand? So, do whatever it takes to make sure she never gets hurt, got that Gargon?'

'Yes, Master, I will,' said Gargon.

Sooz was a little mollified at hearing this, but only a little, and she snatched the phone back from Gargon.

'He's sworn an oath of wotsit to me, of course

he's going to look after me,' she said tersely, annoyed that Dirk still didn't have the gumption to really acknowledge her as a friend.

'What, like an oath of fealty and that?' said Dirk, amazed.

'Yeah,' said Sooz, 'so there! And what's this statue of a semi-naked woman in your room all about? She looks pretty dodgy! What's the matter with you, Dirk?'

'Hey, leave it out Sooz, that's my mum, Oksana, the Dark Mistress of the Underworld!' said Dirk. 'All I've got left is that statue of her when she was young.'

'Oh. Oh, sorry Dirk, I just thought… Well, anyway, sorry,' she said. She'd never considered the possibility he had an actual mother. 'I mean, she looks so… Well, like a vampire or something.'

'Well, she was a vampire,' said Dirk. 'The Vampire Queen of Sunless Keep.'

'Riiight,' said Sooz. 'Creepy! And what about that suit of armour, what's that all about?'

Dirk went quiet again. He didn't want to tell her the truth – that his original form was that of a twelve foot horned skeletal Lich Lord with great bony tusks, mighty horns, talons and all the rest. He didn't think that would go down well.

'Umm…well, that's…' spluttered Dirk when Sooz suddenly interrupted him.

'Dirk, the charge on my phone is getting low. Is there anywhere here I can charge it up?'

'What? No, of course not, Sooz, electricity hasn't even been discovered let alone harnessed in the Darklands. We use magic instead.'

'Then it'll run out soon, we can't talk for long,' she said.

'No, you're right, we'd best end this call then, use the phone for emergencies only – you won't be able to call me, but you should be able to text me, which is better anyway as that uses much less power!' said Dirk.

'Right, right, well goodbye then Dirk, goodbye. So good to hear your voice! Say hello to Christopher!' she said.

'Goodbye, Sooz, I shall call again soon – when I have more news. Hopefully of a rescue plan. Goodbye my little Child of the Night,' he said almost affectionately.

The line went dead.

Sooz began to cry. Beside her, a hulking demon

lent down and tenderly put his arm around the little girl's shoulder. She lent into him and sobbed.

'There there, my Lady, there there,' said Gargon.

Sooz suddenly started to cough and splutter.

'Are you all right, my Queen?' he said.

'Wow, those heads on your belt really do hum, don't they, Gargon!'

The Daily Massacre — 17th of the Month of Hellfire, Year of the Moon Queen 1

GOING GOTH IS ALL THE RAGE

A new fashion is sweeping the land, inspired by our Moon Queen Sooz, Dark Mistress of Shadows! Our Queen calls it 'Goth'. Being Goth is easy. Just dress a bit like the vampires of Sunless Keep. Or add a bit of black lace to that black leather battle suit you already have. And don't forget the dark eye liner and make-up! Though your average undead nightwalker looks like that naturally. And your typical orc… Well, you wouldn't notice anyway. But still, Goth is Good!

p.s. Please note new dating system. Everyone is to use this from now on by order of the Moon Queen.

Part Three:
Triumph and Despair

Under Attack

<del>November</del> Rip-out-their-Hearts 13th

*I must say, I was surprised at how well Sooz
has done in the Darklands.*

*She is my friend, it is true, but perhaps she
may also be my rival too? Fortunately she
seems intent on getting back to Earth rather
than ruling in the Darklands, so perhaps I
am getting overly concerned.*

*Still, power corrupts, and absolute power
corrupts absolutely as the saying goes, and I
should know. What if she decides she doesn't
want to give up all that power? I mean, I
wouldn't. In fact, if I were her, I'd get rid of
me!*

*No, no, I am thinking like my old self, not
like Sooz. She is too sweet, too kind. Too weak!
Isn't she?*

It was late, and Dirk was getting into bed. His feet came up against something under the sheets, at the end of his bed. Puzzled, he reached down and felt around. He found something metallic. He pulled it out – a circular medallion, carved with the symbol of the Celestial Court of the Holy Ones.

Obviously that fool Dumpsy Deary had put it there. Normally the Glyph of the Celestial Court of the Holy Ones would sear his feet like a branding iron. It was her revenge for the hand buzzer in the boot episode, no doubt.

Dirk smiled to himself and lay back, resting his head on the pillow. And frowned. The pillow felt strange. He picked it up – and saw a bit of parchment underneath. Some runes had been written on it in blood.

'Aha!' said Dirk to himself. 'The Curse of the Runes of Death. Surely the foolish woman has worked out by now that such spells and magics will not work on this plane!'

He scrunched up the note and threw it at the bin – and missed. 'Pah! Curse this puny human form,' he muttered as he plumped up his pillow. And frowned again – there was something inside the pillow too!

He held it up and shook it – out came a flurry of white feathers. Except that each feather ended in a golden quill, so like real gold to be almost indistinguishable and the feathers were so bright and white they almost hurt his eyes. Imagine what they would have done to his Dark Lord eyes! The feathers had an unusual smell about them too, a surprisingly wholesome smell in fact. How odd! He picked one up – and laughed out loud. Of course! They were feathers of the Royal Griffin, a holy beast of almost pure goodness! Normally the smell would choke him so that he would be unable to say the words of the counter-spell to the Curse of the Runes of Death. He had to admit it was clever, it really was. Unfortunately, it had no chance of working here.

Suddenly, the door swept open and Miss Deary burst into the room. She stared at Dirk, hoping to see him gasping out the last few breaths of his life. But all she saw was a laughing boy. Her face turned into an angry mask of rage.

For a moment, Dirk thought she might physically attack him, which would have been a real problem but instead she took out a piece of black paper, scribbled a note on it in white ink, and handed it to him.

'I shall destroy you in the end, Evil One, for I am the White Witch of Holy Vengeance and Holy Vengeance cannot be stayed!' said the note.

Dirk's jaw dropped. He knew he'd recognized her from somewhere. The White Witch of Holy Vengeance! Normally covered head to foot in white robes and lace and stuff, so he'd never seen her face. Now that he knew who she was, her gait, her smell, her air of sanctimonious righteousness seemed somehow familiar.

This was serious. The White Witch was deadly to servants of the dark, especially those who were unprepared. Though of course, Dirk wasn't a servant of the Dark. He was the Dark, so it wasn't that easy, but still!

Dirk's brow furrowed as he thought it through. Well, it would be serious if he were home in the Darklands. She'd be a serious threat there. But here, most of her powers were useless, just as his were...

Dirk looked up from the note and grinned at her.

'You cannot harm me, Frumpsy, you witch!' he said, and grinned maniacally.

She pursed her lips in frustration. She'd expected Dirk to be terrified by the revelation. Instead, he didn't seem to care. Then her face fell and her shoulders slumped dejectedly. Everything she had done had failed. Completely. She turned and left, the very picture of defeat.

Dirk thrust a boyish fist into the air in triumph and laughed. '*Mwah, hah, hah!*' But his moment of glorious victory was suddenly interrupted by a tinny scream of terror – it was his phone, telling him he'd got a text message.

'By the Nine Hells, it must be Sooz,' said Dirk, and he leapt out of bed and grabbed the phone. A message appeared in dripping red letters.

Hsdrbn & Blk Slayr h8 me! They r allyz.
Big army coming. Hlp! Sooz. xxx.

Dirk's eyes widened in horror. An alliance of the White Wizard and the Black Slayer? By the Nether Gods, taking back the Tower and painting it black was one thing, fighting the White Wizard and the Dark Slayer – that was something else entirely! Even he would have trouble with that one. Poor Sooz!

He could hardly believe it though. The Black Slayer was truly evil, how could the White Wizard ally with him? But then again – the destruction of the Dark, no matter what the cost, that was Hasdruban all over. He'd ally with anyone to achieve that. For the greater good as it were.

Dirk's eyes narrowed. On the other hand, the Black Slayer had his weaknesses… He had to talk to Sooz.

Dirk quickly punched in her number and lifted the phone to the side of his head. The little arms came out and grabbed his ear. Dirk smiled. He really liked the way it did that, it was so creepy and weird!

It began to ring – and was picked up.

'Hello, Dirk, is that you?' said a breathless Sooz.

'Yes, it is I, Nightwalker!' he said.

'Did you get my text?' said Sooz desperately.

'Yes, I did and…' but before he could say anything more Sooz interrupted.

'Dirk, what am I going to do? I'm scared! It's an army and everything – RakRak said it was thousands of that Slayer dude's Orcs and a bunch of humans, with Paladins of the Whiteshields and that, and Hasdruban himself! They're gonna kill us all Dirk. They're gonna kill me!' she wailed.

Dirk blinked. That was serious. But not necessarily fatal.

'Listen, Sooz,' said Dirk. 'There is a way. If you can defeat the Black Slayer, his Orcs will probably desert him – in fact, they may come over to you. If you can swing that, you'll have Hasdruban beat.'

There was silence for a moment.

'Are you still there, Sooz?' said Dirk.

'OK, how do I do that then, Dirk?' said Sooz. Her voice was calmer now that she'd got a hold of herself. She sounded strong, determined. Dirk shook his head in amazement. She was one special girl that Sooz, she really was. For a puny human that is.

'Well, the Black Slayer has one weakness,' said Dirk.

'Oh no! The battery's almost dead. Hurry up Dirk!'

'OK, Sooz, I can't explain on the phone, it will take too long. You have to look it up in the Dark Library.'

'The Library, but it's huge isn't it?'

'You'll find it in the "Employee Records" section, under "Black Slayer's Bane". Shouldn't be hard to find,' said Dirk.

'The… Well, all right, I'll look there. Better go. Goodbye Dirk!' The line went dead.

Dirk sank back into the bed, thinking furiously, but there didn't seem to be anything he could do. There was probably only enough power left in her phone to take one more short call, if that. If only there were a way of recharging Sooz's phone. Or better still, getting back to the Darklands.

There had to be a way, there had to be! He would work on it with all his evil genius, but in the meantime, Sooz was on her own – there was nothing he could do but hope. For now.

To Battle!

'Right, come on, guys, we're off!' said Sooz loudly as she strode out of her room and up to her throne, a box labelled 'Black Slayer's Bane' under her arm. She had found it in the Dark Library, just as Dirk had said. What she'd read had been interesting, very interesting indeed. Turns out Dirk had never trusted the Black Slayer so he'd got some insurance, as it were.

Around the throne, waiting for her, stood her courtiers: Gargon, Agrash Snotripper, Skabber Stormfart, RakRak, and Rufino.

'Off? Is it the heads? Are they humming again, my Lady?' said Gargon.

'Wait a minute, do you mean the gargoyle heads at the gate or on the throne? And they're humming? What are they humming?' said Agrash confused.

'No,' said Gargon, 'the heads on my belt. They

hum. Apparently. She say, they hum,' he added, pointing at Sooz.

Sooz laughed. 'No, no! I mean we're off, off to war!' she said grinning. She was full of a strange, fateful joy, but she knew in her heart of hearts it was false gaiety and bluff. This could be the end of her, the end of them all in fact, but she wasn't going to let that get her down!

'What do you mean, Mistress?' said Agrash, who was looking very worried. 'Don't you mean we're off to make a run for it? We've got to flee, surely!'

'Definitely not, Mr Snotnose! We're going to fight!' she said.

'Are you sure that is wise, my Lady?' said Rufino. 'RakRak reports that the Black Slayer has reformed the Legion of Merciless Mayhem and marches at the head of two thousand Orcs! Hasdruban is with him – he has a thousand stout men-at-arms, including one hundred of the Whiteshields – the best, most fanatic elite Paladins in all the land!'

'I know, Rufino, I know. But still, we're going to march out and meet them head on!' said Sooz, rather enjoying being the warlike queen or so she told herself. Inside, she didn't feel anything at all like a war queen. In fact, she really wanted to go home and watch telly with her mum. But she couldn't and now she had nothing to lose. It was 'victory or death' as they said in her favourite online MMOG, *Realm of Shadows*. And now, here she was in her own real-life version.

'We can't do that – we'll get slaughtered,' stuttered Agrash.

'Hah, you snivelling little blubberer,' said Skabber Stormfart. 'Orcs aren't scared – we'll stand beside her, fight to the last Orc if we have to!'

Sooz smiled at the big Orc. 'Thank you, Skabber,' she said. 'Anyway, I have a plan. Trust me. Now, get the army together, we're setting off right away.'

Skabber gave a kind of rough orcish bow and then turned away to do her bidding. Rufino frowned. Then he shrugged, and nodded. 'Well, if you've got a plan, then I'm with you. I hope it's a good one, that's all.'

'Don't worry, Rufino, I'll fill you in on the way,' said Sooz.

So it was that an hour or two later Sooz found herself riding in a huge chariot of black steel, with wrought iron fittings twisted into all sorts of fantastical shapes and symbols, pulled by two big, black horses called NightMares. These 'horses' had yellow eyes, sleek shiny black coats, snorting sulphurous breath and hooves of what seemed like iron – they gave off sparks whenever they struck stone. Their reins were of shiny black leather, carved with red glyphs and sigils. On the front of the chariot, the Seal of the Dark Lord was picked out in bright, blood red paint. It was called the Midnight Chariot and it looked magnificent but it wasn't exactly comfortable! Sooz was being jostled all over the place. Beside her, in the chariot, stood Agrash. Right behind her, stood Gargon. There was also the driver who was some kind of special Orc known as the Master of the Steeds of Doom and he lived along with his horses in the Dark Stables round the back of the Tower, stables Sooz hadn't even realized existed. In her hand she held a stoppered bottle that she'd found in the Dark Library, a bottle labelled 'Black Slayer's Bane'…

Beside the chariot rode Rufino at the head of a hundred human warriors, the Soozville Militia. On her left strode Skabber Stormfart at the head of five

Outta the way!

hundred Orc warriors, now called the Legion of the Moon Queen. Behind the chariot were a hundred Goblins of her Royal Guard. Above her wheeled thirty or so Nightgaunts, floating effortlessly on the thermals that rose up over the Plains of Desolation. In all, about seven hundred or so soldiers of the Dark, marching out to meet three or four times that number.

A cloud of dust appeared in the distance. The army of Hasdruban and the Black Slayer was marching inexorably towards them.

Agrash gulped nervously. 'Are you sure your plan will work, my Lady?' he said.

'Of course it will, Mr Snotnose!' she said confidently, but secretly she was terrified. She dared not think what would happen if it didn't work, she couldn't bear to even let herself consider it. But she had no choice. There was no other way.

As the two armies drew closer, they began to draw up for battle. Sooz peered over the sides of the chariot at her army – they looked pitifully inadequate compared to those that faced them. Her soldiers were actually quite well equipped, thanks to the Storerooms of the Tower, but they were so few of them and the serried ranks of the enemy looked so much more professional.

A mounted herald came up, a young man on horseback.

'Parley!' he shouted. 'My master, Hasdruban the Pure, and his cohort, the Black Slayer, wish to parley with you under a flag of truce.'

Agrash looked up at Sooz. 'No harm in that, my Lady, we might as well hear what they've got to say,' he said.

'Aye, I second that,' said Rufino.

'OK, then, bring it on,' said Sooz in a querulous voice.

The herald frowned, unsure as to what he'd just heard. 'You mean you will talk under a flag of truce?' he said.

'Yeah, sure!' said Sooz. She was starting to feel really quite out of her depth with all these armies, and heralds and parleys and stuff.

'So be it, your Dark Majesty,' said the herald, and he turned and galloped back to the enemy line.

Sooz had her hands over the lip of the chariot, only her eyes showing. She kept ducking back with fear every now and again whenever she began to think about the sheer size of the enemy forces – row upon row of battle hardened warriors, wielding spears and swords and bows and axes, all ready to rip and tear and kill.

A small group began to approach them from the enemy lines. As they drew near, Sooz could see it was the Black Slayer on a big black horse, and someone else, presumably the White Wizard. He was riding a tall white horse, and wore voluminous white robes. He had white hair, ridiculously hairy white eyebrows and a big bushy white beard. On his head was a crown of white gold, with a bright blue gem at the front that glowed with a strange light and he held a tall, whitewood staff in one hand, topped with what looked like a little human head carved out of white marble.

His eyes though were black, all black with no whites at all. Creepy, thought Sooz. Beside the Black Slayer walked a heavyset Orc in full armour, carrying a big halberd. Beside the White Wizard strode a man in shiny steel armour, with a large white shield in one hand, and a lance in the other – obviously a Captain of the Paladins of the Whiteshields, just like her hometown, Whiteshields in Surrey. Oh, how she longed for home, now more than ever!

As they drew near, Hasdruban said angrily, in a deep voice, 'Rufino! So, it is true. You have joined the Dark. I can hardly believe it, and you a Paladin, too! Traitor!'

'No, no, my Lord, it is not what you think, she is not…' spluttered Rufino.

'Do not speak to me, heretic!' interrupted the Wizard violently. 'You will not corrupt me with your vile weasel words, your traitor's logic! No, death is all you deserve and death is what you will get!'

Sooz was peering over the lip of the chariot in fascination at this exchange. She looked up at the Wizard and the Slayer in fear. These guys were serious! How could she beat them? What was she thinking? She began to shiver and shake in her big, clunky, Goth boots.

Then the Black Slayer spoke, addressing Agrash, Gargon and Skabber in his sibilant, spectral voice. He did not even look at Sooz. 'Hand over the girl to the White Wizard, along with the Ring and you will be spared. I'll take over the Tower and rule the Darklands.'

Just thought we'd drop by for a chat

He glanced over at the White Wizard. 'Rule in Hasdruban's name, that is,' he added. 'Rufino though, the White One wants him, for…err… correction. Everyone else can live, if they swear loyalty to me.'

'Never!' roared Gargon. 'We never give her up to you, or that murderer, the White Wizard! We not give Rufino up either!' he added.

Rufino looked up at Gargon in surprise. He hadn't been expecting that – Gargon had been his mortal enemy for years! Rufino glanced over at Sooz. It was she who had made this happen, this coming together of enemies, he thought to himself.

Hasdruban turned to Gargon, a look of contemptuous loathing in his eyes. '*Bah*, the monster lives! Creature of Hell, you can die along with your evil mistress, if that's what you want!'

'She is not evil…' began Rufino, but the Wizard shouted 'Silence, apostate worm!' and gestured with his hand. The blue gem on his headband glowed brightly for a second, and a white, spectral hand appeared out of nowhere, to clamp itself around Rufino's mouth, silencing him. Rufino glared at the Wizard but he could say nothing. Desperately he wrestled with the white hand, trying to pull it off his face.

Everyone else stepped back in surprise. 'There's a flag of truce, you can't do that!' squealed Agrash.

Hasdruban blinked. 'Well, yes, technically that is true,' he said. '*Bah*, it is but a minor enchantment, it doesn't count. It will soon fade and he will be unharmed!'

'Minor or major, it's still an enchantment! It's still breaking the truce,' said Agrash.

'*Bah*, nonsense! Rufino is one of ours. He has betrayed us. We can do with him as we wish! Now, you have heard our terms. Hand over that hell-spawned daughter of darkness and you live. Do not, we take her anyway and you die!' said Hasdruban.

Sooz stood there frozen in fear, staring and staring, so intimidated by it all that she couldn't even speak. Silence reigned for a few seconds. Then Skabber spoke.

'Belchvile, is that you?' He was addressing the Orc next to the Black Slayer.

'Yeah, Skabs, it's me. How you doing mate?' said the Orc called Belchvile.

'All right, Belchey-boy, all right. Whatchu doing

jobbin' for the Slayer then? He'll drop you in it as soon as look at you!' he said.

'Hah, why you following a girl, then? What's all that about?' replied Belchvile.

'She's the best king… Err, queen…an Orc could have mate, believe me. Plus she's going to marry the big boss himself, the Dark Lord. He'll eat the Slayer for breakfast, when he comes back!' said Skabber.

'Really? I didn't know she was his girl and all! We didn't know that!' said Belchvile.

'SILENCE, you cretins,' yelled the Black Slayer. 'This isn't some orcish veterans reunion, this is serious stuff!' Turning back to Agrash, Gargon and Rufino, he said, 'Now, what do you say to our terms?'

Belchvile shifted from foot to foot. 'You didn't tell us this Queen Sooz was getting married to the Dark Lord. You didn't tell us that. I mean, that puts a totally different complexion on things, don't it!'

'Shut up! SHUT UP, you stupid Orc!' shouted the Black Slayer.

'Oh, it's like that, is it?' said Belchvile. 'Just coz I'm an Orc I must be stupid, eh? That's racist, that is!'

The Black Slayer put his head in his hands and groaned in frustration.

Hasdruban interjected. 'Your concerns are irrelevant Belchvile. The Dark Lord will never return,' said the White Wizard. 'I have exiled him forever to another plane and soon one of my agents will destroy him, if she hasn't already.'

'NO! That's not true!' said Sooz, finding her voice at last. 'He will return, I know he will! I know him, I love him and he loves me. He'll come and rescue me, oh yes he will!' she screamed in a childish rush of words, stamping her foot in anger.

Hasdruban stared at her in astonishment, mouth agape. Sooz went on. 'And I spoke to him on the phone, just yesterday, he was fine. You're not going to destroy him, never, he's too clever!'

Suddenly Sooz lifted up her arm. In her hand, she held the stoppered bottle she'd brought with her from the Dark Library. At the sight of it the Black Slayer gave a gasp of horror. With her other hand, she reached over and pulled the stopper.

'Nooooo!' cried the Black Slayer.

Out of the bottle writhed a shadowy shape, which grew and grew in size until it became a kind of grey

The past returns to haunt him

phantom, perhaps the ghostly form of a young woman.

'At last my love, we can be together!' wailed the phantom in a voice like the howling of the wind on a desolate storm-lashed shore.

It hurtled down through the air towards the Black Slayer. As it struck the Slayer, his armour and clothes burst apart in an explosion of tatters, revealing beneath another shadowy form, this time resembling a young man.

'No, please, no,' wailed the Slayer. The phantoms merged into one mass of shadowy greyness before hurtling up into the sky and away. A final cry of 'Noooooooooooo!' faded on the wind. And that was the end of the Black Slayer.

Everyone stood there in silence for a moment, quite astonished by the sudden turn of events.

Hasdruban shrugged. 'So much for the Black Slayer. You cannot escape your fate, and he reaped what he sowed.'

'Where's he gone, then?' said Belchvile.

'Dragged off to one of the Nine Hells, I would think,' said Hasdruban.

The marble head on the top of Hasdruban's staff

suddenly moved, the red veins pulsing, and then it spoke in a thin, reedy voice.

'Black Slayer's Bane has the Black Slayer Slain!' it said portentously. 'So did the Fates decree!'

'Yes, indeed, Whitehead,' said the Wizard. 'They did indeed.' Then Hasdruban narrowed his eyes. 'Now that *is* a breach of the truce!'

'Not at all,' said Agrash. 'All Queen Sooz did was remove the stopper on a bottle and let fate take its course, a fate the Black Slayer laid down all those years ago when he slew his betrothed on the Altar of the Nether Gods in return for immortality!'

'Yeah,' said Sooz, 'and in any case, you broke the truce first!'

Hasdruban grimaced. '*Bah*, perhaps you have a point,' he said. 'No matter. Come, Belchvile, it is obvious they will not agree to our terms, so we must destroy them instead!'

Belchvile hesitated.

Suddenly Sooz piped up again. 'Belchvile! Join us! I forgive you for serving the Black Slayer, instead you can be my Captain, serve the Dark again, be with your friend Skabber!' she said in a rush, half expecting it not to work.

'Yeah, Belchey-boy,' said Skabber. 'You're not going to fight for 'im are you?' he said, jabbing a black-nailed thumb at the White Wizard. 'I mean, he massacred loads of our pals, didn't he? Loads! Hunted 'em down after they'd surrendered and everything!'

The Orc thought for a moment, but not for long. 'No, course not!' said Belchvile, decision made. 'Now the Black Slayer's gone, we're with Sooz, the Dark Queen! Course we are, and two fingers to that murdering sod, Hasdruban.' And sure enough, he stuck two fingers up at the Wizard.

Hasdruban gave a wry smile at the sight of Belchvile being rude to him, as if he were expecting it. 'How orcish of you, Belchvile,' he said. 'You are perhaps too stupid to realize you have just signed your own death warrant, though it may not be today. So be it then.'

Sooz grinned, and hopped up and down with joy.

'So, White Wiz – who's the Daddy now then!' she said, without thinking.

Hasdruban raised a hairy eyebrow. 'Who's the… What?' he said. Then his eyes narrowed. 'Well, whatever. In any case, it seems we are now the outnumbered ones. But there is no need for further bloodshed is there, Queen Sooz? Will you allow us free passage back to Gam, the City of Men? That way, none of your people or mine need die this day. What say you, dread Queen of the Night?'

Gargon and Agrash shook their heads as one. Even Rufino frowned, as he wrestled with the hand over his mouth. But Sooz ignored them and said, 'Yeah, absolutely, fighting is just stupid anyway, so sure, I agree, let's go home. We've won either way, haven't we?'

Hasdruban nodded, still smiling that wry smile. 'Yes, my Lady, you have won. Until we meet again then!' he said. The Wizard and his unnamed Paladin turned away, riding back to their own lines, leaving Belchvile and the Black Slayer's horse behind. And also his sword. It had fallen to the ground when the Slayer had been carried off to whatever hideous fate awaited him. His sword of black steel, covered in strange purplish runes, the sword known as the Stealer of Souls. Gingerly, Gargon reached down and picked it up.

With the White Wizard gone, Rufino was able to remove the hand over his mouth at last. 'Careful with that blade,' he sputtered. 'It is evil indeed and drinks more than the blood of its victims!'

'Aye,' said Gargon, 'I have seen it do its work. I think best to keep sword in Storeroom, out of way. Especially away from our Queen, yes?'

'Agreed,' said Rufino, looking up at Gargon. Gargon had been one of his most ancient foes, one of the mightiest warriors that the Dark had to offer, second only to the Black Slayer himself. His head was the prize that all foot soldiers of the light sought to gain but strangely now they both had something in common, something that bonded them together. They both wanted to make sure Sooz was safe, no matter the cost.

Soon Hasdruban and his army began marching away, back the way they had come, whilst Belchvile and the Legion of Merciless Mayhem marched forward to join Sooz. Everywhere Orcs and Goblins were celebrating madly. They'd won a great victory, and without shedding any blood – well, except for the Black Slayer but nobody on either side liked him much anyway. And all of this because of their own Dark Lady, Sooz the Moon Queen, and her cunning, bravery and wisdom!

'Queen Sooz! Queen Sooz! Queen Sooz!' chanted her soldiers as they began the march back to the Tower of the Moon.

Sooz waved at them as she rode by – and noticed she was still holding the parchment note Dirk had folded into the box labelled 'Black Slayer's Bane'. This is what it said.

Many years ago, the Black Slayer slew his love on the Altar of the Nether Gods, offering her up in return for immortality. I have summoned her shade from Beyond and imprisoned it in this bottle. It is my insurance policy should the Slayer betray me, all I need do is release the ghost and it will seek him out, to be avenged upon him! She will drink his Soul and he will be destroyed for ever!

Sooz grinned from ear to ear. This was another one of her best moments ever. Thousands of big hulking Orcish warriors, little freaky Goblin things and tall, strong men, all chanting her name. She had her own personal army and everything and they loved her! It was just so cool.

Gargon and Agrash also felt the same but Rufino was frowning to himself and thinking. It'd been too easy. Hasdruban's reaction was too tame when the Black Slayer was disposed of. Had they really won? Or was Hasdruban playing some kind of long game? After all, what had really happened today was that one of the Dark Lord's most powerful lieutenants had just been destroyed. Hmmm… He looked up at Sooz. May the Gods forbid anything happen to her, he thought to himself. It was possible that Sooz could bring them all together, that she could stop thousands of years of conflict and bloodshed, to finally bring peace to the Darklands and the Commonwealth of Good Folk. If anyone could do it, it was this little girl from another world. Rufino vowed to do all in his power to help her achieve it. She was going to need it – after all, it was almost certain that Hasdruban had another plan up his sleeve…

Envy and Jealousy

~~November~~ Rip-out-their-Hearts 15th

I've just seen this in a magazine. Those psycho fools Wings and Randle are up to their old tricks.

THE BOOK VENDOR

Two psychologists have books published about the same case!

Dr Wings and Professor Randle, two eminent child psychologists, have each written a book on a certain case they have been studying, drawing much of their material from the same source – a 13-year-old boy known only as *Child 'A'* – Hannibal or Damien as Wings and Randle call him, respectively.

The books are titled *"The Lecter Boy"* and *"Sauron is Alive and Well and Living in Surrey"* and are a fascinating insight into the origins of psychotic pathology in the young.

Each book comes to a radically different conclusion, however. It is obvious there is no love lost between the psychologists.

'Randle's book is utter rubbish! Don't bother with it!'
Dr Wings.

'Wings' book is total tosh! Just read mine.'
Professor Randle.

Hannibal indeed! Pah, I am above such petty evil! And Damien? As if I were the son of the Devil? I am the Devil!

Dirk sat at his desk, staring emptily up at the ceiling, worrying about Sooz. Around him sat many human children, listening to Grotty Grout the history teacher drone on and on about the Second World War.

Normally Dirk loved History lessons – well, he didn't love them, rather it was one of those classes that he found the least dull, especially when it was about evil dictators and huge battles with tanks and planes and big guns and all the rest. Oh, what he wouldn't give for a few tanks back in the Darklands!

But today he couldn't concentrate. He got the DarkPhone out of his pocket and checked it. No, nothing.

'Dirk Lloyd, no mobiles in class! How many times do I have to tell you!' said Mr Grout.

'Sorry, sir,' said Dirk, putting the phone away, whilst also mouthing the syllables to the Spell of Utter Annihilation and imagining Grotty Grout being smeared all over the whiteboard like strawberry jam.

Grout narrowed his eyes. Something was up with Dirk. Normally he would have come back with a smart comment or corrected him on some historical point to make him look bad in front of the class but today he seemed different somehow. Somehow normal. Almost.

Suddenly, a scream of terror filled the air! Grout and the rest of the class started in shock, except for Dirk, who knew it was the text message alert on his phone. Dirk leapt to his feet, and drew his phone out again.

'I said no mobiles!' said Grout angrily. Dirk just waved him into silence, as if he were an irritating fly.

'How dare you!' said Grout. 'That's a detention right there, boy!'

'Of course, sir,' said Dirk, 'but don't you think you should send me out of the class as well? Only I have an important call to make. If not, I will simply sit here and loudly sing "La Marseillaise", easily the best of all your absurd Earthly national anthems, until you do.'

The rest of the class started to titter and giggle at

this. Grout just stared at him. What was he thinking, comparing him to a normal boy? Then he sighed. What was the point?

'All right then, Dirk. Get out. And stay behind after school for detention,' said Grout, knowing that the best the teachers could ever hope for was that Dirk would at least pay lip service to the rules.

'Thank you, sir,' said Dirk, 'I deserve it, really I do.'

'Hah, I'm sure you do, boy!' said Grout, shaking his head. Only Dirk would thank you for giving him a detention.

Dirk rushed out with unseemly haste. In the corridor, he checked the latest text.

Drk! Cll me!

And that was it. 'By the Nether Gods, I hope she's all right,' he muttered to himself as he put the phone up to the side of his head, waiting for the comforting feel of the little arms as they reached out to grasp his ear. He put his hand down after it had done so. The phone remained in place. See, hands-free!

It rang only once before Sooz took the call.

'Dirk!' she said.

'Yes, it's me. Are you all right? What's happened?' said Dirk.

'Yes, I'm fine, more than fine in fact! It worked perfectly! I got the Black Slayer's Bane from the Library – all that stuff about the ghost of his first love, the woman he sacrificed to evil and that – I mean, wow, what a bad boy that Black Slayer was, wasn't he?'

'Yes, he was a most useful lieutenant, 'tis true,' said Dirk.

'Anyway, we met face to face with Hasdruban and his army and everything. It looked really, really bad, but I did it, I released the ghost, and she got rid of the Slayer! And then Belchvile came over to me with the whole Legion!'

'What, Captain Belchvile and the Legion of Merciless Mayhem?' said Dirk in amazement.

'Yeah, and they all swore that wotsit thing to me as well,' she said.

Dirk's jaw dropped. The Legion of Merciless Mayhem! They were one of his elite legions, one of the best in the whole Darklands horde. He couldn't believe it! They'd sworn an oath of fealty to a thirteen-year-old human girl-child? Incredible!

'So we won, and Hasdruban had to get lost with his tail between his legs, and then everyone started chanting "Queen Sooz! Queen Sooz!". Even my Paladin and my human soldiers!' said Sooz in a rush.

'You have a Paladin? And humans?' said Dirk even more astonished.

'Yeah, Rufino. He and the rest of the humans live with my Orcs and Goblins in Soozville, the new town we're building. They live together in peace and everything!' said Sooz, gushing.

Dirk frowned. He was starting to get annoyed. And jealous! She was taking over, pushing him out! Not only that, she was forging unheard of alliances, and even founding cities. She was doing better than he had!

'Dirk, are you there?' she said.

'Yeah,' he muttered resentfully.

But Sooz didn't notice the tone of his voice, she just gushed on. 'They call me the Queen of the Dark now, the Magnificent Moon Queen, and stuff like that. It's great!'

'I'm so happy for you,' said Dirk sarcastically. 'I hope you're having fun, taking over my life!'

'What? No, it's not like that, Dirk, really. I don't want to take over – I want to come home, I want to see you. I'd much rather you were here, really I would, so that you could do all this ruling stuff.'

'Yeah, right, well for someone who doesn't want to take over, you're doing a great job of doing exactly that – your Magnificence,' he said bitterly.

'Oh please, Dirk, please don't be cross with me… Wait a mo, something's up. Hold on – RakRak's back from patrol.'

Dirk frowned. Things went quiet for a moment or two, and then Sooz came back on, her voice full of fear and panic.

'We've been set up! Whole thing was a trick! An army of elves or something has turned up from the other direction whilst we were doing in the Slayer! And Hasdruban has come back, with the rest of his army, even bigger than before! They were just behind him, hiding behind some hills or something! Help, Dirk, we're surrounded! What do I do?!'

'*Bah*, don't ask me, Sooz, you're the Great Queen of the Dark, you sort it out!' replied Dirk, and with that he hung up, stuffing the phone back in his pocket. Maybe Hasdruban would be doing him a favour, getting rid of this little upstart usurper for him!

He stood there blinking for a moment. He could hardly believe what he'd just done. All right, he'd been angry and jealous – she was doing far too well for her own good, but obviously she was out of her depth now. Hasdruban had managed to get rid of the Slayer, and get most of the army of the Dark in one place. Clever. An army of Elves and Humans in a pincer movement? She was doomed. He'd be doomed if it was him! Well, no, he wouldn't, he'd have found a way – he always found a way. Dirk sighed. He couldn't leave Sooz to her fate like that, he had to help her, put aside his anger and jealousy or he could lose her forever and he couldn't bear that. And none of it was her fault, not really. She didn't ask to go there, any more than he'd asked to come to Earth.

He drew the phone out and called her back. But nothing happened – it didn't ring. After a few seconds, he received an automated message.

'This is the DarkPhone Network. That person's

phone is turned off or is unreachable at the moment. Please try again later.'

Dirk froze. Sooz's phone had run out of power. Desperately, he tried texting, but again it came back with 'Unable to deliver message'. Dirk put his face in his hands. What had he done? Had he just abandoned his friend to almost certain death?

Dirk shook his head in despair. He had to get back to the Darklands. But how to do it? How?

Vengeance of the White Witch

Christopher and Dirk sat in Dirk's room, poring over various maps and notes scattered all over the room. Dirk had drawn a big map from memory of the various planes and dimensions around the Darklands, and had written a list of all the possible spells and ceremonies that could conceivably be used to travel between them. Everywhere lay jottings and scribblings, usually explaining why this or that spell or ritual wouldn't work.

Dirk put his head in his hands. 'It's no good, Christopher, I just can't find a way to get through to the Darklands. The Ceremony of the Eclipse of the Gates of the World is the only one we could even think about getting the ingredients for, but that also needs an eclipse, and there isn't going to be one of those any time soon. What are we going to do?'

'You say that, Dirk, but what about this one, The Sundering of the Walls of the Worlds? It needs the blood of an evil dictator – well, that could be you, right, the feathers of a Black Storm Crow – we've actually got one of those right here!'

Dave the Storm Crow gave a caw of outrage. Chris stared at it for a moment. It was almost as if it understood exactly what he'd just said.

Dirk gave a little knowing smile. 'Go on, Chris, what else?' he said.

'Well, the spell has to be cast in a place that is used for travel or movement and suchlike – we've got loads of those on Earth, like a railway station or a bus station or an airport!'

'True,' said Dirk. 'Go on.'

'And then you need a Reality Knife for cutting the fabric of the Universe itself... Oh...' said Chris.

'No, no, we could actually make one of those, it could be done,' said Dirk, 'so go on.'

'Let me see now... Ah, the still-beating heart of an innocent...recently torn from their breast with the Claw of Ripping Death... Oh...ah...I see.'

'Yes,' said Dirk. 'You see the problem, eh? The

Claw of Ripping Death is a spell that won't work on this plane.'

'Oh, that's the problem is it? Not, you know, killing someone or anything!' said Chris.

'Well, I did consider ripping out your heart, as you're perfect for the sacrifice, but it has to be done with the spell, and that's that,' retorted Dirk.

Chris went pale for a moment, unsure as to whether Dirk was joking or not. Dave the Storm Crow hopped from foot to foot, cawing loudly. Chris stared at it in fascination once more. Was it laughing at him?

Chris frowned in irritation. 'Anyway,' he said, 'I'm not innocent, I'm really bad!'

'Oh please!' said Dirk dismissively. 'Like you're "so baaad". I mean, when was the last time you got a detention even?'

Chris made a face. 'All right, alright – but did you really think about sacrificing me like that?' he said worriedly.

'Of course,' said Dirk. 'You'd make an excellent sacrifice!'

Chris's jaw dropped.

Then Dirk chuckled and clapped him on the

shoulder. 'Don't worry, old friend, I'm joking,' he said. 'I'd never do that to you!'

Chris grinned with relief, that's just what he'd wanted to hear. Of course he wouldn't do that, of course not!

'Well, not to rescue Sooz, at any rate,' said Dirk absent-mindedly as he turned back to his spell lists, his astrological charts, star maps, and inter-planar cartograms.

Chris frowned. He continued to search the spell lists, but every now and then he would glance over at Dirk, that worried look back on his face.

After a while, Dirk looked up. 'What? What is it Christopher?' he said.

'You wouldn't really sacrifice me would you?'

'No, of course not, I told you,' said Dirk.

'Yeah, but…but what if it was… Well, say if it was to save yourself or something?' said Chris.

'Ah, to save myself! Well, now, that's a different matter,' said Dirk, and he gazed up at the ceiling in thought, stroking his chin ruminatively.

Chris's gaped at him. Surely he wouldn't!

Dirk looked back at him. 'I don't think I would.' Then he saw Chris's face, and he laughed.

'No, no, I wouldn't, of course not,' he said reassuringly. Chris smiled back at him weakly.

'That's OK then,' Chris said. And then nodded, having convinced himself thoroughly of the matter. Of course he wouldn't! His thoughts were interrupted by a sudden loud knock on the door.

'Hold on a second,' said Dirk. Quickly he shooed the crow out of the window and hid his strange maps and charts as best he could.

'You may enter the domain of the Great One,' he said imperiously.

The door opened, and in walked Dumpsy Deary. Dirk narrowed his eyes and prepared himself for some kind of magical assault whilst Chris actually flinched back in his chair.

The white lady stood there and then smiled a creepy, red-tongued smile.

'What do you want, Witch?' Dirk said commandingly.

That just made her smile even more. With a sneer of contempt she tossed a sheet of black paper at Dirk. Words were written on it in white ink. Dirk snatched it up and read it. Chris read it over his shoulder.

The White Wizard has your precious little Sooz. She is a prisoner in the White Tower.

'*Bah*, I do not believe you,' said Dirk. 'It's a trick!'

The White Lady smiled again, and tossed a mobile phone at Dirk's feet.

'Sooz's phone!' said Christopher in shocked surprise. This was followed quickly by something else.

'By the Nine Hells, Sooz's AngelBile bag! It cannot be!' said Dirk, leaping to his feet.

Christopher gasped, and Dirk's face fell. 'Noooo!' he cried. 'They have her, they have my Sooz!'

Miss Deary began to cackle insanely, her maniacal laughter getting louder and louder.

'Heh, heh, heh! HEH, HEH, HEH, HEH, HEH!'

She turned and left the room, her laughter echoing down the corridor. Dirk hung his head dejectedly. The Storm Crow flew back in through the window to perch beside them once more. It gave a caw of despair, as if in sympathy.

'What's happened exactly?' said Christopher. 'What's the White Tower?'

'It is the lair of Hasdruban. He has taken her. That

means he has defeated her armies and everything. It also means he has my Ring too. This is a disaster! I have to get back to the Darklands or all is lost! But how, how?'

Chris gazed at the freaky bird, thinking. He cocked his head, struck by a sudden thought.

'Wait a minute,' he said. 'How did Miss Deary get Sooz's phone and her bag? I mean, she must have gone to the Darklands, picked them up and then come back again, right?'

'By the Nether Gods, Chris, you're right!' said Dirk, his face lighting up with a kind of unholy glee. Then his brow furrowed. 'But then again, they could have just sent her stuff over. Though actually, either way, there has to be some way of getting back and forth. We have to find out how! You are a genius, Christopher, a genius – well, as far as a puny human can be a genius, that is!'

'No problem, your Dirkness, happy to help,' said Chris grinning. It wasn't often Dirk called him a genius! Though he did call him a puny human quite often.

'All we have to do is follow her, find out how she does it,' said Dirk.

Chris frowned. 'Won't be so easy to follow her, she'll be on her bike for a start, but also, she's... Well, she's pretty alert and that. She'll spot us!'

'Hmm, you are right, Chris, she can sense us, it is true. Holy Awareness and all that,' said Dirk thoughtfully, stroking his chin like some kind of super-villain – which of course he was.

'Ah,' said Dirk, 'I have it! We'll send Dave the Storm Crow to track her, and we'll follow the bird! That way she'll never spot us!'

'Brilliant!' said Chris. 'But how will you get the crow to follow her?'

'Easy,' said Dirk. 'Dave!' he said addressing the crow. The bird looked up at him, blinking. Dirk leant down and began to whisper something in its ear. After a short while the crow gave a caw of delight, and flew out of the window to perch on the roof guttering overlooking the Purejoies' back porch.

'There,' said Dirk, 'she is waiting for that absurd do-gooder, Humpsy Jeery to leave the house. Then she will track the Witch, and we shall track the crow!'

The Daily Massacre

3rd of the Month of the
Dark Moon of Sorrows
Year of the Moon Queen 1

QUEEN SOOZ HAS FALLEN!

A terrible calamity has befallen the Darklands! Our beloved Moon Queen has been taken in battle by that thrice-cursed, Goblin-killing, Orc-slaying so-called do-gooder, the White Wizard Hasdruban! In a perfidious ambush, the forces of the Dark were scattered and many slain. The Queen was captured and even now languishes in the Dungeons of the White Tower.

Her last act was to get her Court safely into the Tower of the Moon – the heroic Agrash Snotripper, you will be glad to hear, was unhurt, but Gargon, Skabber Stormfart and the Paladin Rufino were all badly wounded. Now they, and the remnants of our army, are besieged in the Tower. RakRak and the Nightgaunts have been driven away once more by the Eagle Riders of the Commonwealth of so-called Good Folk. Without RakRak to forage for food or our Dark Lady to open the Storerooms, we will not last long. When our supplies run out we will be forced to surrender.

This is I fear, my faithful readers, the end.

Agrash Snotripper,
Editor in Chief,
The Daily Massacre

Somewhere deep underground…

The little girl sat on a hard wooden bench in a dirt-floored, stone-walled prison cell and cried. Her hair was a mess and the make-up on her face was streaked with dirt and tears — many tears. Her black, silver-threaded dress was ripped and torn, and her bare feet were scratched and bleeding. One of her hands was bandaged up roughly, the other was cruelly bruised where a ring had been roughly ripped from her finger.

She was alone.

Part Four:
Into the Unknown!

The Voyage

The crow had tracked the White Witch to a remote lock-up in a back alley somewhere in the rougher side of Whiteshields town and now Dirk and Christopher were spying on her through the window. So far, she hadn't noticed they were there because she was so intent on what she was doing. She was standing in the middle of some kind of magic circle drawn on the ground in white chalk. It was made up of a complex pattern of pentacles, triangles, circles, symbols and glyphs. Slowly 'Miss Deary' began to turn on the spot, mumbling to herself. Then she started hopping and stepping on various symbols and glyphs in a complicated dance-like pattern.

Dirk held up his DarkPhone and clicked a button. A slimy looking tendril of pale, pink flesh extended from the back of the phone towards the window.

Which boots are they?

On its end was a little eye.

'Yuk,' cried Chris. 'What's that?'

'Silence, you Goblin-brained half-wit!!' hissed Dirk. 'I'm filming her!'

Chris blinked. Right. The eye was the DarkPhone's camera. Gross!

The White Witch began to chant as she danced, obviously some kind of spell or ritual song. As she began to step on certain shapes, her silver wellington boots began to take on a spectral transparency. Suddenly, she gave a cry, and took several forceful steps and then…disappeared with an audible pop!

Chris's jaw dropped. 'Wow!' he said.

'Of course!' said Dirk, tucking his phone away in his pocket, giving the thing barely enough time to retract its little eye. 'How could I have been so stupid? It's the boots, the silver boots – they're Voyager Boots! Though, err, I am never stupid, of course, being perfect. I must have been fooled in some way – yes, perhaps she cast some kind of spell of concealment or distraction or something, that must be it!'

'Right, there's no way you could ever have actually missed something, is there?' said Chris.

Dirk raised an eyebrow. Was that sarcasm?

'Anyway,' continued Chris. 'What are Voyager Boots?'

'Ah, Voyager Boots. Magical boots used for voyaging or journeying between the many planes of existence. She is using them to literally walk to the Darklands!'

'Really? Well, if that's true, then we've got to get those boots, so you can use them to fetch Sooz,' said Christopher.

'Indeed,' replied Dirk, 'but there is a problem.'

'What's that then?' asked Christopher.

'Well, umm. I'll tell you later,' said Dirk.

Chris narrowed his eyes, suspiciously. Dirk was holding something back, and that usually meant bad things would happen. And not to Dirk.

'Anyway, I got it all on my phone, every move,' said Dirk, changing the subject.

'So?' said Chris. 'Don't tell me you're going to post it up on the net, or email it to people? I mean it's freaky, and weird, but the disappearing bit at the end – people will think you faked it somehow.'

'No, no, I've filmed it so we can learn how to do it. We have to get the dance exactly right, or else we could end up somewhere else completely different!' said Dirk.

'What do you mean?' said Chris.

'Well, if we get it wrong, we could end up walking into the wrong dimension. Could be really bad if we ended up somewhere like the Realm of Eternal Flame or the Plains of Instant Death!' said Dirk.

'Plains of Instant... You're kidding right?' said Chris.

'No, I'm not. It's a real place! It's only safe to go there if you're already dead,' said Dirk, as he turned and set off for home.

'Riiight,' said Chris. 'Safe if you're already dead. Of course!'

'Indeed,' said Dirk. 'You can't be killed twice after all, can you? Well, actually you can, but I mean... Well, anyway, it's safe for the Undead. Many of them choose to make it their home. Can't get disturbed by meddling do-gooders out to destroy them and that.'

Chris shook his head. 'Anyway, what's next, Dirk?' he said.

'We go home, and wait until morning. Stumpsy Queery will turn up for work. You know what your mum is like, she'll insist she doesn't wear her boots inside the house, so she'll leave her bike and her boots outside as she always does. We shall take the boots, come here and depart immediately,' said Dirk.

'But won't that mean we'll have to bunk off school? Mum will kill me!' said Chris.

Dirk stopped and stared at him. 'By the Nine Hells, Chris, we're not bunking off to go and hang out at the bike sheds or to mindlessly tag bus shelters, we're going to go travelling across the Universe, to a different dimension! Not to mention rescuing Sooz.'

'Yeah, well, when you put it like that… But it's still truanting though, isn't it?' said Chris sullenly.

Dirk shook his head. 'Well, think of it this way then – every now and then you get to go on school trips and that, don't you, because sometimes there are better ways of learning things than sitting in class.'

'Yeah but…' said Chris.

'Well, you'll learn far more than you ever could voyaging to some distant dimension than you will sitting in some dusty old classroom!' said Dirk.

'Hold on a second, what's all this "we" stuff? I mean, I'll help you and everything, but I'm not actually going to another world myself, am I? What do you need me for?' asked Chris.

'Yes, you have to come with me, Chris,' said Dirk. 'There is no other way.'

'What! Why?' said an astonished Chris.

'Well, I told you there was a problem.'

'Yeah…' said Chris.

Dirk stopped and turned to Chris. He looked at him for a few seconds, scratching his chin and thinking. Then he said, 'Only those of pure heart can wear the boots.'

Chris blinked.

'But… But… But I can't go into the Darklands on my own and rescue Sooz – I'm just a kid. How would I survive?'

'I know,' said Dirk. 'But have you considered the saint?'

'Saint? What saint?' said Christopher.

'Your namesake, the absurd St Christopher.'

'Wha— St Christopher? What about him?' said a confused Chris.

'Think about it!' said Dirk. 'What did you tell me

about the absurd do-gooder?'

'What … Wait, no! Don't tell me you want me to carry you on my back?' said Chris.

'Got a better idea?' said Dirk.

Chris stared at him. 'So, what you're saying is that I have to have you on my back, whilst doing some freaky spell dance thing and then carry you off to another dimension?' said Chris.

'Exactly so, Christopher! It'll be the ultimate truancy, the ultimate bunking off of school! It'll be so much fun!' said Dirk as enthusiastically as he could.

'Right…' said Chris, thoroughly unconvinced.

'Also, you're going to have to practise all night long,' said Dirk.

'What?' said Chris. 'Practise what?'

'You have to learn the ritual by heart – all the words and especially the dance. You have to get it exactly right, and you have to do it with me on your back!'

Chris narrowed his eyes in anger. 'I could kill you Dirk,' he said. 'I really could!'

'Hah, join the queue!' retorted Dirk. 'Just remember though, it's the only way to rescue

Sooz – bear that in mind!'

Chris raised his eyes and sighed resignedly. 'Well, in that case, I suppose so…' But then he had a sudden thought. 'Hold on a minute – I'm not pure! That White Beast thingy, in that car park, it turned on me because I betrayed you, right, do you remember? Because I wasn't pure any more. That means I can't go either. Hooray!'

Dirk smiled at him and shook his head. 'I'm afraid not, little human. You saved me, remember? You jumped on the Beast's back, distracted it while I cast a spell. You took far more of a risk doing that than you did just blocking its way. It could have killed you. So, I'm afraid you were redeemed, even purer than you were before. "Bad luck, old chum" as the saying goes! You'll have to come with me after all. *Mwah, hah, hah!*'

The next morning, Chris and Dirk set off as usual for school, though both of them were really quite tired. They'd been up most of the night practising the Ritual of the Dancer on the Sea of Infinity, as Dirk called it.

They had it pretty much down pat but it wasn't perfect. Still, there was no more time, and they had to go with what they had. It was the best that they could do. Every hour wasted could be the difference between life and death for Sooz.

Dirk had Sooz's bag on his back, with all her stuff in it, but they'd had to leave the crow behind. He couldn't come with them so Dirk had left plenty of food out in the garden and said his farewells, hopefully only for a day or two.

The boys left the house for school like they usually did, but then grabbed the Voyager Boots and rushed off as quickly as they could to Miss Deary's lock-up before the witch could notice.

It wasn't long before Christopher was stomping around the magic circle in her lock-up, panting out the words of the spell, with Dirk on his back.

Chris was nearing the end of the ritual. He gave a shout and took three forceful steps – just as Dirk slid off his back, shouting at the top of his voice, but he couldn't hear what he was saying. Chris turned. All he could see was fire, fire everywhere! His hair was on fire, his clothes were on fire! Then he felt a hand on his collar and he was yanked back out of the flames.

He collapsed in the middle of the magic pentacle,

smoking. Dirk was desperately putting out the fire in his hair. 'Are you alright, Chris?' he was saying.

'Yeah, yeah,' said Chris, checking the exposed parts of his body. After a few seconds, he got to his feet. 'Yeah, nothing serious,' he said, though a bit of his hair was gone and his eyebrows were badly singed.

'That was the Realm of Eternal Flame. You got the ritual wrong! A few more seconds and you'd have been incinerated!' said Dirk.

'Wow,' said Chris. 'I never thought this was going to be that dangerous! Do you think we should leave it for a while, get some more practice in?'

'No, we cannot, for Sooz's sake. There's no time,' said Dirk.

Chris frowned. 'But…'

'Again,' said Dirk forcefully. 'We must try again, and this time, make sure you get it right!'

Chris nodded resignedly. 'Well, I guess we have to, but I'm really scared Dirk – what if we end up in the Plains of Instant Death or something?'

'Don't worry, I won't let anything happen to you. Now, let's go again, from the top,' said Dirk.

Dirk climbed up on Chris's back. Chris began

the dance once more. This time, when it reached its climax, he strode forcefully forward, in what he thought was the right place – and suddenly they found themselves in total darkness. They couldn't see a thing. Everything was as black as the deepest night and as silent as the deepest grave.

Dirk slid off Chris's back slowly. They stood quietly for a moment, scared of disturbing the silent emptiness.

Eventually Chris whispered, 'So, is this why they call it the Darklands, then? I didn't realize it was literally a dark land, as it were.'

'No,' whispered Dirk. 'No. This isn't the Darklands. This is somewhere else. You've got it wrong again.'

'What?' hissed Chris. 'Well, why don't you take us back then?'

'I can't,' he whispered. 'It's too late. I thought for a moment we'd just arrived at night, but it's much too dark even for that. I'm sorry, there's no going back, only forwards.'

'Where are we?' muttered Chris.

'I think it is the place they call the Valley of Unending Night,' whispered Dirk.

'Unending Night? That doesn't sound good. And

why are we whispering?' whispered Chris.

'So they don't hear us,' whispered Dirk.

'Who? So who doesn't hear us?' said Chris a bit too loudly.

'Shhh! Them! The Denizens of the Unending Night,' hissed Dirk.

'What... The denizens? What are they then?' whispered Chris fearfully.

'You don't want to know. Luckily, it's quite easy to travel out of this plane,' whispered Dirk.

'Really? How?' said Chris. Suddenly there was a sound nearby. Both of them froze. Something was... slithering. After a few heart-stopping moments, the noise began to fade away. Whatever it was, it was heading away from them.

Dirk breathed a sigh of relief. 'Well, any light in the Unending Night will tear a hole in the fabric of this dimension, like a portal or doorway to somewhere else.'

'That's great! But where to?' whispered Chris.

'The Abyssal Gulfs,' whispered Dirk.

'Abyssal... That doesn't sound much better!' whispered Chris.

'It is a kind of gulf between all the worlds. Not

entirely safe but not nearly as dangerous as here. Anyway, we have no choice,' whispered Dirk.

'OK, anywhere's got to be better than here – so, well… Ah…. Have you got a torch, Dirk?'

'Umm no… You?' whispered Chris.

'No. What about my phone?' whispered Chris.

'My phone you mean. Hmm, yes, that might work. Good thinking,' whispered Dirk.

Dirk reached into his pocket and drew out his phone. He flipped the lid – the face remained dark. Dirk felt around and pressed a button – but he hit the wrong one! It began to play the video of Dumpsy Deary doing the Ritual of the Dancer on the Sea of Infinity. The sound of her chanting seemed to echo around the Unending Night like a car alarm going off in a broom cupboard! Dirk shut it off as quick as he could, but at least the phone was now on, releasing a beam of soft reddish light.

'That noise will bring them down upon us for sure! Quick,' shouted Dirk, directing the light onto the ground.

Suddenly, into the light a vast shape loomed. Chris and Dirk cowered back in horror.

'Arrgh!' howled Dirk. 'An Abominable Swallower!'

Christopher simply whimpered in paralyzed terror.

Above them rose the pale form of what could only be described as a gigantic fish-like maggot, its body mottled and lumpy. If that was bad enough, it was nothing compared to its truly terrifying head! It looked a bit like this, according to a picture Dirk drew later.

Fortunately for Dirk and Christopher, it flinched back from the red glow of the phone, dull though it was, just for a second or two. At their feet, where Dirk shone his phone, a circle of light was burning a hole in the ground.

'Quick,' said Dirk. 'Jump in!' As quick as they could, they jumped into the hole, just as that hideous head whipped down, the snapping jaws of the Abominable Swallower closing over where they'd been standing just seconds before.

They fell for a short distance – to appear suddenly in the air over a small platform of rock that seemed to be floating aimlessly in a vast gulf of space. They hit the ground bone-shakingly hard but apart from a few bruises, they were all right. Certainly they were better off than they had been a few seconds before!

And then they began to look around. In the distance was a never-ending star-filled black sky, a 360-degree backdrop of diamond-studded night. Nearby, islands of rock floated in an abyss of space, some covered in vegetation and trees, some bare and dusty, others with rocky outcrops and hills, still others burning with baleful fire. Shooting stars shot past in the distance, flaming comets hurtled across the near sky, planets and moons hung like Christmas tree baubles in the vast emptiness of space – all sorts of planets, gas giants, ice balls, blue Earth-like worlds, red dusty barren Mars-like worlds, and many more. And everywhere they could hear a roaring, rushing sound, the sound of suns burning and planets spinning in space. Chris stared at it all in astonished wonder.

'Welcome to the Abyssal Gulf,' said Dirk wryly.

Chris could hardly believe his eyes. 'But… I mean… Aren't we in space? How come we can breathe? And we're not freezing! Shouldn't we be freezing, you know like, instantly?' he said.

'Well, we're in a kind of space. Sort of. Technically we are in the interstices, the in-between places that exist betwixt the many worlds and planes of the Multi-verse,' said Dirk. 'It's not real space, it's not really your universe even. It's… It's somewhere else, with different laws. That's why it's warm and we can breathe. In fact, here everything can breathe whatever their natural atmosphere. Even fish would be fine – in fact, there are some over there!'

A shoal of fish was indeed floating by – swimming by in fact, just as if they were in some sea somewhere, in this case the Abyssal Gulf rather than the Gulf of Mexico or wherever.

'Wait a minute,' said Chris. 'Those are – whatchamacallits – Sailfish! From Earth! How'd they get here?'

'Ah, well,' said Dirk. 'Sometimes accidents happen and holes appear in the fabric of reality, allowing travel between the planes. In this case, they probably came from the Bermuda Triangle. It's

Worlds and stuff

a kind of hotspot on Earth for inter-planar events. Every place has at least one.'

Chris gazed at them in wonder as they swam sedately past, as if space was just one vast ocean. 'Wow,' he said. 'This place is fantastic!'

'It is, but still…' said Dirk.

'What? What do mean "But still"?' said Chris, folding his arms.

'Well, it's a sightseer's wonder, that's true, but… Well, we're kind of marooned here,' said Dirk.

'Marooned! You mean there's no way to get out of here? Why we'd come here then?' said Chris angrily.

'We couldn't exactly stay where we were, could we? And anyway, it's not my fault is it? You got the dance wrong, didn't you, you stupid human!'

'What! MY fault! Hah, but I had some fat idiot on my back didn't I?' said Chris waspishly. 'That didn't make it any easier did it?!'

Dirk narrowed his eyes. 'How dare you address me like that!' said Dirk. 'Fat idiot? Me? How dare you, I have punished people severely for far less than that!'

'Oh, so you're going to punish me now are you? How, eh? What could be worse than this?' shouted

Chris, pointing around. 'To be stuck here forever? And it's your fault, not mine! I'm just a kid from Surrey. It's not my fault you can't wear the Voyager Boots coz you're such a bad boy, is it? It's not my fault Sooz is stuck in some dungeon somewhere! If you hadn't come along, everything would've been all right wouldn't it? None of this would have happened! Me and Sooz would have been fine, she'd have picked me, not you, you…you…'

His voice tailed off and he started to cry. It was all too much for him.

Dirk folded his arms and pursed his lips. He had to admit, Chris had a point. Dirk sighed. He put his arm around Chris's shoulder. 'I'm sorry, Christopher, you're right. I got you into this. Both of you. But I'll get you out, I promise.'

Chris looked up at him. 'How? I thought you said we were marooned?' he snivelled.

'Well, that's true. But there are people who live in the Abyssal Gulf. Well, I say people – they're not humans or anything, they're Skirrits.'

'Skirrits? Like the creatures that built the Pavilion?' said Chris.

'Yes, indeed. This is where they live, in between

the worlds. That is why it is so easy to summon them. They'll find us, I'm sure of it. They know pretty much what goes on anywhere on this plane.'

'How?' said Christopher, who had finally stopped crying.

'They can detect movements between the planes, openings and that. Usually they come looking for what's turned up, like scavengers or salvagers.'

'OK, cool,' said Chris. 'At least we've got some hope, then!'

'Oh yes, there is hope.'

Foletto the Skirrit King

Not long after, a strange golden barge appeared in the distance – the Skirrits called them Sky Boats. The Skirrits had taken Christopher and Dirk to their city, home to thousands and thousands of Skirrits. It was called Wispwillow and it was built on a large floating island not far from where Chris and Dirk had landed. Skirrits were short, thin little creatures with spindly limbs and spiky hair, a bit like the gnomes and fairies of Earth legend but more…well, more real for a start. Wispwillow was quite a wondrous sight. It was made up of one huge artificially constructed crystal tree from which depended multicoloured houses and buildings like Christmas tree decorations. Travelling around the city was done with little cable cars that were slung below every crystal branch.

So it was that Christopher and Dirk found

themselves stood before the Skirrit throne, upon which sat a little sprite-like fellow, with arms and legs that were really long and thin, with a crest of spiky white hair, peppered with black. Hanging off his head was a gold cap, lined with red velvet, the Royal Cap of the Skirrits. He wore a loose fitting robe, also of gold, covered with little shiny gems of many colours.

'Greetings, Foletto, King of the Skirrits!' said Dirk as imperiously as he could.

'Greetings, your Imperial Darkness,' said Foletto in a squeaky high-pitched tone. 'I see that little has changed since I spoke with you last – you are still trapped in the body of a human child. How disgusting!'

Dirk remembered the last time only too well. Foletto had found him back on Earth, and they'd done a deal. Foletto had performed various useful tasks for him – but he'd had to give the Skirrit King the deal of a lifetime. A deal he didn't really want to bring to Foletto's attention.

'Indeed, but soon I shall return to the Darklands, there to wrest back my Iron Tower, restore myself to my original form and take my vengeance on that thrice-cursed meddler, Hasdruban the Pure!' replied Dirk, trying to sound as confident as he could.

Foletto put a hand to his long, warty chin and raised a spiky eyebrow.

'Yet it seems you are lost between the worlds and have ended up here, in our realm, all alone and trapped in the body of a weak, defenceless human child,' he said silkily.

'I, the Dark Lord, Master of the Shadow Magics and Sorcerer Supreme – lost and weak? Never! We have deliberately travelled here, on our way home,' blustered Dirk.

Foletto frowned, not quite sure what to believe. To him, they just looked like two typical Earth children, lost in the abyss between the worlds. On the other hand, he may be trapped in the body of a human child, but he was still the Dark Lord; Foletto could sense that, just like last time. And Dark Lords were powerful and cunning, oh yes, oh so cunning! He had to be careful, just in case. But still, maybe there was some advantage to be gained here.

Foletto said, 'And who is this with you? Have you taken to frequenting the company of other human children?'

'Ah…well…this is Christopher,' said Dirk. 'He too is a great mage – thought not in my league of course – who has been similarly cursed!'

Chris looked over at Dirk quizzically. Dirk nodded at him encouragingly, as if to say, 'Come on Chris, play along now!'

'Christopher? Doesn't sound like the name of a great mage,' said Foletto.

'Umm… Christopher is my alias whilst I am trapped in this…err, this foul form! *Bah*, humans! Revolting!' said Chris, making a face and spitting in disgust, doing his best to play along.

Foletto frowned. Boy spit, yuk! He signalled with one hand – two Skirrits capered forth and began to clear up Chris's spit with little white cloths.

'Ah…umm… Sorry about that,' said Chris.

Dirk glared at Chris. 'Numpty!' he said without thinking, using the word Chris had called him back on Earth at the church fête. It seemed like years ago now!

'Numpty? What is Numpty? Or is that his real name?' said Foletto

Dirk blinked for a moment, non-plussed. But then he had an idea… Revenge! 'Oh yes. It is a term of high status, isn't it? Numpty,' said Dirk sarcastically, glaring at Christopher. 'Or so it says in my dictionary.'

Christopher's face fell as he realized what Dirk was saying. He had no choice but to play along. 'Yes, your Majesty, yes. Umm… I am Numpty. Err… Numpty the Wizard!' he said.

Dirk put a hand to his mouth, stifling the uncontrollable giggling that threatened to consume him at any moment.

'And where do you hail from, Numpty?' asked Foletto.

'Whiteshields, your Majesty,' he said without a thought.

'Whiteshields? No! You are one of the Whiteshields? The elite Paladins of Hasdruban the Pure? But you are sworn to destroy the Dark Lord – you cannot have betrayed your oath, it is not possible, surely!' said an astonished Foletto.

'Ah well…' said Dirk, trying to cover things up with another lie but Foletto interrupted him, pointing at Christopher with a thin, spiky finger.

'Ah, wait, I've got it! That is why you were exiled and regressed into the body of a boy, just like the

Dark One! Hah, you are a traitor and you have been punished for it!' he said. 'Who would have thought it? A Paladin of the Order of the Whiteshields betraying everything like that!'

'Indeed, indeed,' said Dirk, going along with the flow. 'You have divined the truth with admirable insight, Foletto!'

It was rather improbable, thought Dirk to himself, but it was better than the real truth – that he did indeed 'frequent the company of human children' and that basically, yes, they were lost, and worst of all, neither of them had any magical powers to speak of and were completely vulnerable to whatever Foletto wanted to do with them. It was vital Foletto didn't realize that.

Foletto nodded, pleased with himself.

Dirk began to address him, 'Now, my friend, we have need of—' but Foletto put up his hand to silence him.

Dirk's jaw dropped. 'How dare you, Foletto,' he said. 'How dare you!'

Foletto gazed at him for a moment, as if considering ignoring him or having him arrested or something but at the last minute he relented, afraid to take the risk.

'Forgive me, your Imperial Darkness, forgive me!' he said. 'Please, give me a moment, I beg you.'

Dirk, playing the mighty Dark Lord to the hilt, nodded regally and said, 'I shall be magnanimous! I accept your apology. As you wish, Foletto, take your moment.'

The Skirrit King stared at Dirk for a second or two, thinking about what he was going to say, and what the Dark Lord's reaction might be. He adjusted his cap nervously, and then said, 'Didn't you give me a promise last time we met, Dark One?'

Dirk shifted from foot to foot uncomfortably. 'Yes, yes, I did. How could I forget?' he said.

'What was it now? Oh yes, my heart's desire! In return for…umm, let me think, some trivial thing. Oh yes, the rebuilding of that ugly wooden earthling pavilion. Hah! So easy!' said Foletto.

'Yes, that is true, a rather uneven agreement, as you yourself have recognized,' said Dirk.

'Nevertheless, 'twas agreed,' said Foletto.

'Yes, it was agreed,' nodded Dirk, resignedly.

'Well, I think I know what I want now,' said Foletto.

'Oh yes, and what will it be?' said Dirk jauntily, although inside he could feel his stomach lurching. Why had he agreed to such a stupid deal? He'd been desperate, really desperate, but even so, he should have thought it through, taken his time.

Foletto smiled. 'One of our Gods… Well, I say a God. Others say he is some kind of super powerful being that inhabits the Gulfs, just like us. Anyway, either way, we are forced to treat him like a God. In any case, what else is a deity but a super powerful being who…'

'Yes, yes, enough of your meandering philosophy. What's your point?' said Dirk impatiently.

'Well… the God in question is called Nephthos, the Eater of Sins, and he is an angry vengeful God. Often do we have to appease him with sacrifices and suchlike. The sacrifices must be those who are full of sin and evil. And there is nothing he likes more than the taste of a traitor, and the worse the betrayal the better the taste!'

Dirk gasped in horror. Christopher frowned – he hadn't quite got it yet.

'So, what I want is Numpty the Paladin. Or ex-Paladin I should say. What a perfect sacrifice he would make to Nephthos! A Paladin who has turned to the Dark? Oh, how perfect!'

Christopher's face fell. He was getting it now!

'*Bah*,' said Dirk. 'Never!' Christopher looked over at Dirk gratefully. Dirk did not look back.

'What, you would refuse me? You cannot!' said Foletto.

Dirk stared for a moment, thinking furiously. 'Well, if I agree, will you give me safe passage to the Darklands?' he said.

'What?' said Christopher. 'You said you wouldn't do this, that you wouldn't sacrifice me, even if it was to save yourself, and here you are, literally sacrificing me! I can't believe it!'

'I lied,' said Dirk, staring at the Skirrit King. He wouldn't even look at Christopher.

'Hah,' said Foletto, slapping a thin, bony thigh with pleasure. 'This is delicious. Delicious! Yes, your Darkness, I guarantee your safety, even though technically that's an extra clause in the contract I don't have to agree to, but yes, done!'

'All right, so be it,' said Dirk. 'I agree!'

'No!' wailed Christopher. 'You can't do this to me, Dirk, you can't!'

'Take him away, and prepare him for the ritual,' said the Skirrit King, grinning madly from ear to ear like a deranged sock puppet.

A rush of little Skirrit guards swept towards Christopher, capering and dancing, giggling and sniggering. 'No,' said Chris, as the Skirrits swarmed all over him. 'Wait, you can't do this! Help, Dirk, help me! Nooooo, help meeee!' wailed Chris as he was dragged out of the throne room to whatever fate awaited him.

'Goodbye, Numpty, it was nice knowing you,' said Foletto. He was staring at Dirk all the while. Dirk looked up at him. 'So, what does the preparation for sacrifice consist of?' he said airily.

'The Chosen One is…' began Foletto before Dirk interrupted him.

'The victim, you mean,' he said.

Foletto grinned. 'Yes, the victim. The victim is stripped naked, except for a pink loincloth covered in little crimson hearts…'

'Pink underpants!' interrupted Dirk, a little smile appearing at the corner of his mouth.

'Indeed, pink underpants. Pink is sacred to Nephthos apparently and the hearts represent the love we have for him and that, though actually we're just terrified of him, but that's all part of the game. Anyway, then the Chosen…the victim I mean, is covered from head to foot in Goonut butter, and…' continued Foletto, only to be interrupted once more.

'Goonut butter! What is that?' said Dirk.

'The Goonut grows on certain trees on certain floating islands in the Abyssal Gulfs. It is said to be the favourite delicacy of Nephthos the Sin Eater, though to us it smells faintly of dung so we don't touch it,' said Foletto.

Dirk smiled broadly – he couldn't help himself, and he chuckled. Foletto frowned. That wasn't the reaction he'd been hoping for.

Foletto leaned forward, annoyed at Dirk's cavalier attitude and said, 'And then the victim is strapped down on the Altar of Nephthos and his throat is cut by the High Priestess with the Sinblade, a jagged, obsidian dagger that really, really hurts!'

'Nice,' said Dirk. 'Can I watch?'

Foletto's jaw dropped. 'You want to… Hah!' He slapped his thigh again, and grinned. 'You are truly the Evil One, are you not?'

Dirk took a bow. 'Indeed, so I am. What did you expect?' said Dirk

Foletto's face fell at that. Here was proof positive of the boy's true nature. He may be trapped in the body of a human child, but it was the Dark Lord himself, here in his throne room, face to face with him… As evil and as cunning as he'd ever been. Foletto shifted uncomfortably.

'And afterwards, you will take me to the Darklands, yes?' said Dirk.

'Oh yes, absolutely. Straight away!' said Foletto, stepping down from his throne. 'Shall we go to the Temple of Nephthos then? They'll be doing the sacrifice quite soon,' he added, rather eager to get this Dread Lord out of his hair.

Dirk nodded, and followed the Skirrit King through the corridors of the palace to take one of the cable cars that ran up and down the branches of the great crystal tree of Wispwillow.

The view from the cable car was magnificent but all too brief. Soon they arrived at the Temple of Nephthos, a pyramidal building that hung from the tip of a long crystal branch. Foletto, Dirk and several Skirrit priests and worshippers made their way to the Great Hall of Sacrifice, a chamber in the Temple that was almost completely bare save for a bloodstained black rock altar in the middle of the room. Leering over the altar was a statue of Nephthos the Sin Eater. He looked like a huge, tall, spindly Skirrit, but with the head of some kind of vulture, with a taloned beak, and bright, beady eyes of ruby.

Christopher was strapped to the altar. He was wearing pink underpants and was covered in a dirty brown paste. He was gagged so he couldn't speak, but he was glaring at Dirk, sometimes angrily, sometimes imploringly.

A Skirrit Priestess, dressed in long, pink robes, walked slowly up to the altar, a crystal ball in one hand, and a nasty looking obsidian dagger in the other.

She leaned over the altar. Christopher was staring at her in fascinated horror. She placed the crystal ball on his chest, passed her hand over it in an arcane gesture, and said, 'Numpty! You have been chosen. Now you shall be tested,' and she began to mumble some kind of prayer or spell over him.

Dirk leaned forward, frowning intently. Foletto

What are friends for, after all?

glanced over at him. Slowly the crystal ball began to fill up with a pinkish, whitish light. Dirk sat back with a sigh of relief. Foletto looked over at him once more. It was his turn to frown.

Suddenly, the High Priestess snatched the ball away.

'This one won't do!' she said in a reedy voice. 'This one won't do at all!'

'What do you mean it won't do?' said Foletto, confused.

'I'm sorry, your Majesty,' said the High Priestess, 'but there is hardly any sin in this one at all. In fact, it's almost totally innocent!'

'What?!' said Foletto. 'But he's Numpty the Wizard, an ex-Paladin of the Whiteshields who has forsworn his oath! He's turned to the dark side and everything! I can't think of anyone who'd be more full of sin – well, except… But he's…' Foletto glanced nervously over at Dirk as he finished his sentence.

'No, Foletto, this one is not,' said the High Priestess. 'He's just a boy, a simple human child. More innocent than most, in fact.'

'But…but…' spluttered Foletto. He turned to

Dirk, who was standing there, looking up at the temple roof and whistling to himself, as if nothing was amiss.

Foletto's eyes narrowed. 'Well, can't you sacrifice him anyway?' he said. 'Got to be worth something, even if he is blameless!'

'No! Definitely not! Such an offering would enrage Nephthos. It'd be like feeding him dirt or worse. He'd likely go on the rampage, start trashing our city, like the last time!'

'Oh dear,' said Foletto. 'We can't have that!'

'No, we can't!' said the Priestess. 'We'll have to release him.' With that, she leant forward and used the obsidian dagger to cut Chris's bonds. Christopher sat up, rubbing his wrists, staring around wildly as if he couldn't quite believe what had just happened.

Foletto glared at Dirk. Dirk smiled back at him, hands behind his back, rocking back and forth on his heels, whistling.

'Wait,' said Foletto, still staring at Dirk angrily. 'What if we just killed the boy, you know, just for fun, no rituals or anything. Or threw him into space or marooned him on one of the Floating Islands!'

'No, no, you can't do that,' said the High Priestess. 'He's been consecrated now, anointed for sacrifice. If we kill him, it'll still count as a sacrifice. No, the best thing we can do is get him off this plane as soon as possible – if he dies here in the Abyssal Gulfs, Nephthos will take him, and we'll get the blame!'

Foletto blinked as he digested this. Christopher, listening avidly, stood up and removed the gag on his mouth.

Foletto put his hands on his hips. Then he raised them to his head. And then folded them. Then put them back on his hips. And then back to his head. 'Arrrgh!' he cried.

Dirk chuckled.

'Arrrgh!' he said again. 'I can't believe it! You have outwitted me!'

'Indeed,' said Dirk. 'I am the Dark Lord after all, the Master of Cunning.'

'But wait, don't think that I shall be taking you to the Darklands!' said Foletto.

'Yes, you will! You must, as agreed!' said Dirk, grinning.

'But the boy!' said Foletto.

'I gave him up to you, as agreed. It is hardly my

fault that you now must release him, is it?' said Dirk, smilingly.

Foletto spat. '*Bah*,' was all that he could say. Two little Skirrits ran forward to clear up the spit. Foletto kicked one spitefully.

Then he sighed. 'Ah well, I suppose so. I guess we have not lost much really, it's no big deal to transport you to the Darklands, and you might as well take the boy with you. We can't keep him here anyway!'

Foletto signalled, 'Take these two…guests…to the Portal to the Darklands. Take them wherever they want to go there,' he said.

'What about my clothes and stuff?' said Christopher.

'Hah, don't push your luck, Numpty! Don't push your luck!'

'My name's not Numpty, it's Christopher, and I want my stuff, especially my boots!' said Christopher angrily.

'Forget it, Numpty. I've had enough. Any more trouble from you, and I'll send the Dark One to the Darklands, and you to the Holothurian Deeps! Remember, I have no agreement with you!

Now, get out of my sight.'

'Holothurian Deeps, what are they?' said Christopher, turning to Dirk.

'Not good, Christopher, you won't die, but you'll get turned into… Anyway, best we just take what we've got, believe me. Come on, we'd best go whilst we still can,' said Dirk under his breath so that Foletto couldn't hear him.

'But what about the boots?' said Christopher.

'We have to give them up,' hissed Dirk, grabbing Christopher by the arm.

'What? How will we get home without the boots? And take your hands off me, you…you betrayer! How could you do that to me, I was nearly killed! It was terrifying!' shouted Chris angrily, as a little Skirrit guard pointed the way down a corridor.

'But you didn't get killed did you? And we got what we wanted in the end – safe passage to the Darklands for both of us,' said Dirk, following the little guard.

'Got what you wanted, you mean! Look at me, I'm wearing pink underpants, and I smell of poo! It's horrible!'

'I know, I know,' said Dirk laughing and wrinkling

his nose up in disgust at the same time, 'but it was worth it, believe me. Not to mention the fact that I managed to get out of a bad deal I'd made with Foletto back on Earth! Clean slate and everything, and it cost me virtually nothing!'

'Oh, worth it for you, I'm sure! And how did you know about that freaked out Neph wotsit and the innocent sacrifice thing?' said Chris angrily.

'Well, I met him once, a long time ago. He's actually the ruler of one of the Nine Hells. Mind you, I wasn't entirely sure, but the whole sin/purity thing seemed quite likely,' said Dirk.

'What? You weren't even sure I'd survive? How could you, you... You total... You total numpty!' said Chris so angry he could hardly speak.

'What, numpty as in Lord High Numpty to the court of Henry VIII?' said Dirk waspishly.

Chris just blinked for a moment. 'No, not that kind of numpty. Umm... Anyway, the proper numpty, you know what I mean!'

'Indeed I do,' said Dirk happily. 'Did you really think you could fool me so easily?'

Behind them, Foletto the Skirrit King stood despondently, listening to their banter, a puzzled look on his face. The last thing he heard was Dirk's loud '*Mwah, hah, hah!*' echoing down the corridor. Foletto sighed. He wasn't entirely sure what had just happened, but what he did know was that he was glad to see the back of them.

Home is Where the Heart is...On Your Pink Underpants

It was dawn. A light breeze murmured through the trees that overlooked the garden of the abandoned farmhouse, abandoned quite recently, by the look of it. The wind brought with it a mild odour of spice – a whiff of cinnamon mixed with the briny tang of the sea, the unmistakable scent of a foreign land, a land that was not Earth.

Suddenly, a circle of light appeared in the air, hanging a couple of feet off the ground. It flashed with ruby light for a moment, and then it went black, coal black. An arm emerged from the empty blackness, followed by a leg, and then a head and a body, and a human child fell forward to the ground. Another, dressed only in pink underpants,

Home at last!

came after the first, to land on top of him with a wet, slapping sound. Behind them, the black, inter-dimensional portal (for that is what it was) flicked out in an instant, gone forever.

'*Eurgh!*' shouted Dirk. 'You've got Goonut paste on me, you Orc-brained lackwit!'

'Sorry, sorry,' said Chris, 'but it's your fault I'm covered in it at all, so there! Eat it!'

'What? I am not Nephthos! I refuse to eat it! Peanut butter, yes; Goonut butter, never – it smells of dung, and so do you!' said Dirk, pushing Christopher off him.

'No, no, "eat it" – like take it, you deserve it, you know, like suck it up!' said Chris getting to his feet and looking around.

'Suck it up? What are you saying?' said Dirk.

'You know, like… Oh, never mind,' said Chris with a smile. But then his face fell and a tear came to his eye. 'My mum used to say it to Dad, when, when she beat him at chess. I miss home!'

'Well, I am home, Christopher. This is my world,' said Dirk. He was running his hands up and down his arms, inspecting his legs and body as he said this.

'What are you doing?' said Chris.

'Just checking. I had hoped I would revert to my original, powerful form,' replied Dirk, 'but it appears I am still in the form of a human child. Hasdruban's enchantment was strong indeed.'

'Your original form? What's that like then? Like a grown man or something?' said Chris innocently.

Dirk just stared at him for a moment. 'On second thoughts, perhaps it is just as well I have not,' said Dirk.

'That bad, eh?' said Chris with a grin.

'You have no idea!' Dirk said. 'I suspect the only way that I could regain that form is to drink of the Essence of Evil once more.'

'You mean that revolting black oily stuff the White Thingy of Wotsit lapped up back in that car park?' said Chris.

'You mean the White Beast of Retribution? Yes, that's the one,' said Dirk. Then he took a few deep breaths, savouring the exotic smell. He heaved a great sigh. 'I have striven for so long to get back, and here I am at last! It is good to be home, it is good indeed!'

Dirk began to gesture oddly with his hands,

making patterns in the air. Then he muttered something odd, staring at Christopher avidly the whole time.

Chris stared back.

'What was that all about?' he said.

'I was trying a spell. But it hasn't worked,' he said, gazing at the top of Chris's head.

'What spell?' said Chris nervously.

'The Charm of Sudden Baldness,' said a distracted Dirk, deep in thought.

Chris felt for his hair, his face paling with outrage.

'You tried it on me! How could you?'

Dirk shook his head. 'Don't worry, I didn't think it would work, it doesn't feel right. I was hoping that all my spells and power would come back to me here in the Darklands, but it hasn't.'

'Well, I'm sorry and all that, but you can't just practise on me, you know, I'm not some kind of guinea pig!'

'Actually, you are an excellent guinea pig, Christopher, but that's not the point. I can only assume that my magic is somehow tied to my form. This body is just not suited to the casting of certain magics, I guess.'

But Chris wasn't really listening any more. His jaw had dropped open in amazement – he was staring up into the sky over Dirk's shoulder. Dirk followed his gaze.

'What is it, Chris, is something wrong?' said Dirk. 'Eagle Riders, is that it?'

'No, no… It's…umm. There are two moons, Dirk, two moons!' said Chris.

'Well, yes, there've always been two moons. We call that pale one the Dark Moon of Sorrows and that red sickly looking one the Blood Moon. Though the Commonwealth of so-called Good Folk call them the Eye of Tranquillity and the Sky Rose. Typical lacklustre goody-goody names if you ask me.'

'It's the weirdness of it all,' he said. 'You know, the smells, the colours – the moons! Everywhere so different to Earth – it's kind of scary! I've got no idea what to expect next. I'm scared. Scared of the unknown and that.'

'I know, I know,' said Dirk, resting a hand on Chris's shoulder. 'But don't worry, I am here. I know this world inside out, it's mine! I'll protect you, fear not. And this isn't like the other places we've visited, it's not so dangerous, it's a bit more like Earth. Well relatively speaking that is.'

Chris started to feel a bit better after hearing that. Until Dirk added without thinking, 'I mean, having said that, it is still far more dangerous than Earth of course.'

Chris raised his eyes. Dirk was so astonishingly insensitive sometimes.

'So, how did you cope when you fell to Earth for the first time?' said Chris.

'Well, I didn't actually panic or anything, of course, not like you. Although I was pretty confused. Instead, I decided I'd conquer the place.'

Chris chuckled at that which made him feel a lot better. 'Conquer the Earth? Typical!'

Dirk lifted his hand from Chris's shoulder. His hand was covered in Goonut butter. He couldn't help himself and he sniffed it without thinking.

'Eurrgh,' he said, wrinkling up his nose in disgust.

Christopher burst out laughing. 'The Great Conqueror returns, eh!' said Christopher. 'I shall destroy you all, just as soon as I've cleared this stinky stuff off my fingers,' he said in a passable imitation of Dirk's best imperial voice.

Dirk smiled sarcastically. 'Right, now that

you've recovered,' he said, 'let's see what we can do about getting cleaned up. We'll start with that old farmhouse.'

As they walked over to the farmhouse door, Chris asked, 'So, where are we exactly? Near your part of the world?'

'No,' said Dirk. 'We are in the Commonwealth of the Good Folk, not far from the White Tower. That's where they've got Sooz.'

'But isn't that where Hasdruban lives too?'

'Indeed it is, but we must take that risk. Though in fact, in many ways, we are in the perfect disguise – two innocent little human children, so actually it is doubly better that I did not revert to my original form.'

As they walked up to the entrance of the abandoned farmhouse, they saw a piece of paper nailed to the door, which read:

By order of HASDRUBAN THE PURE and the Blessed Tribunal of Incriminators:

The inhabitants of this house have been incriminated in heresy and arrested. All their goods and chattels have been confiscated.

'*Hah!* Heresy indeed. Ridiculous. Why doesn't he just lock people up, steal their stuff, and be done with it, instead of dressing it up with all this legal mummery,' said Dirk, shaking his head as he pushed the door open.

The farmhouse had been pretty much stripped of almost everything, but they did find a still functioning water pump, which they used to wash the stinky Goonut butter off. They also found some stale bread and cheese, which was a welcome relief as they hadn't eaten for a while, and some clothes for Christopher to wear – a simple brown linen shirt and trousers, and a pair of old wooden clogs.

'*Ugh!* I look like some kind of mutant Pinocchio!' said Chris.

'Who is Pinocchio?' said Dirk.

'A kind of wooden puppet who could talk and… Oh never mind, the point is that I look ridiculous!'

'Actually, you don't. You look normal for this part of the world. It's me that looks out of place, with my jeans, T-shirt and trainers.'

'*Humph,*' said Chris. 'Why am I always the normal one?'

'I guess because you are, my boy,' said Dirk with

a laugh. 'Anyway, it is time to go, the White Tower is not far, perhaps an hour's walk at most.'

They set off together following a path that led out of the farm. 'Interesting idea though, that talking puppet of yours,' said Dirk. 'What if we made an army of such creatures? What damage could they wreak?'

Christopher looked over at Dirk and shook his head in amused despair.

'What? What's wrong with an army of puppet monsters? Come on, it's a great idea!' said Dirk.

'You haven't seen the film, have you?' said Chris.

'No, no. What's that got to do with it?' said Dirk.

And so the conversation went…

The White Tower

Dirk and Christopher had left the old farmhouse behind them some time ago. They were making their way down the main road of a bustling market town called Magus Falls. Either side of them were shops and stalls, taverns, inns, houses and so on. It wasn't a big town, like the sprawling metropolis that was Gam, the City of Men, but it was sizeable enough, its primary purpose being to serve the various needs of the White Tower. Most of the taverns and inns had names like 'The Wizard's Retreat' or 'The Beard and the Staff' or 'Inn of the White Eyebrows' and suchlike. They served beer like 'Purewhite Wheat Beer' or 'Hasdruban's Hoppy Harvest Ale'.

Dirk was glaring about him in disgust. 'Toadying lickspittles,' he hissed. 'Look how they suck up to that meddling fanatic! *Bah!*'

But Chris was looking around in awed wonder – it was almost as if he'd stepped into one of those computer role-playing games he was so fond of, like *Battlecraft* or *The Dungeons of Death*. Except here there were no save games, no reloads, no healing potions or spells and death was real and permanent. Also, he was like a first-level school kid, with no powers or special abilities whatsoever and with maybe five hit points, possibly less! Chris gulped nervously.

Fortunately, nobody took much notice of them – they were just two more kids walking down the high street, going about their own business.

'Hah, if only they knew who I really was! That they had the Dark Lord himself in their very midst, then they'd tremble in their boots, the fawning knee benders!' muttered Dirk.

After a short while, they left the town on a wide paved road that led up into some low hills. On top of one of the hills rose the White Tower, gleaming so brightly in the sunlight it actually hurt their eyes. Around its base various buildings were scattered – barracks, courthouses, a drill square and other administrative or military structures. As they drew nearer, they could see that the Tower was quite thin and tall, and almost featureless. The walls were of smooth polished white stone and there appeared to be no windows at all. On top of the tower was a multifaceted polygonal structure made entirely of glass, held together with white-painted steel girders. A great sky telescope poked out of the top, pointing upwards to the heavens.

A regular stream of traffic was travelling to and from the Tower. Supply wagons, soldiers, messengers, tourists, merchants, petitioners, litigants, monks, priests, mages, and so on. One group of what looked like pilgrims or monks were whipping themselves with ropes, and wailing 'We are not worthy! We are not worthy!' and 'All praise the White Wizard! We suffer for him as he suffers for us' and stuff like that.

'*Bah!* Fools!' said Dirk. 'If they want to be whipped, they should come and see me. I'd put 'em to work in the Slave Pits, where they'd get whipped for free!'

Christopher frowned. 'You have slave pits?' he said. 'With actual slaves? And you whip them?'

Dirk glanced over at him. 'Goblins and Orcs need

to be whipped,' he said automatically, but then he thought better of it and said, 'Umm… Used to, I mean! We used to have slaves. In the old days – umm, you know, like you used to on Earth. Before health and safety and workers' rights and that. It's all modernized now of course.' Dirk rubbed his jaw, thinking to himself. He'd have to hide the Slave Pits of Never Ending Toil from Chris, obviously, should they ever return to the Iron Tower. In fact, he'd have to hide a lot of things.

'So, no more slaves then?' said Chris.

'No, no, no more slaves!' said Dirk breezily. 'Ah, look, we're nearly there,' he said, changing the subject.

As they approached the White Tower, they saw that the entrance was flanked by two vast jackal-headed statues.

'What are they?' said Chris in awed tones.

'The Watchers at the Gate, ever vigilant guardians of the Portal of the White Tower.'

'What do you mean "ever vigilant"? Are they like alive or something?' said Chris.

'Well, sort of. Enchanted certainly,' said Dirk. 'They are ever alert, ever on guard against evil.'

'Won't they know who you are though, Dirk? I mean, it was probably built because of you, right?'

'Well, the Watchers at the Gate can sense evil, it's true, but you have no evil in you to speak of, Chris, and my Essence of Evil was taken by the White Beast. So, to the Watchers, we will be two ordinary human children, nothing of note at all. Hopefully.'

'Wait a minute, you can walk through the Watchers at the Gate but you can't wear the Voyager Boots? What's that all about then?'

'Ah well, the Watchers can't be as sensitive as the Boots, can they? I mean, if they were, half of these people couldn't enter the Tower, could they?' said Dirk, waving a hand at the long queue waiting to get in. 'And certainly not those little fascists, the Holy Incriminators! They say they're holy, but let me tell you, what they do is evil, really evil! You see, Chris, most people just aren't as nice as you are, it's as simple as that. Though give it time, give it time. I'm working on it!'

'What, you mean like trying to make everyone as nice as me?' said Chris.

'What? No, don't be ridiculous, the other way round, of course!' said Dirk.

Chris smiled weakly at him. Dirk went on. 'And also, from the Watchers' point of view, we're just kids. After all, what could two boys do to the White Wizard in his White Tower, eh?'

'Well, he's about to find out, isn't he?' muttered Christopher under his breath.

'Yes, indeed he is my stalwart friend, indeed he is!' said Dirk, impressed with Chris's spirit.

Christopher spotted a group of schoolchildren, much the same as schoolchildren back home (i.e. noisy, troublesome and vaguely goblinish) dressed in tunics, little round caps and woollen trousers of blue and white. They were carrying parchments and quills instead of pens and notebooks. The similarities with modern Earth school kids were striking, though none of them had any dyed hair, earrings, nose rings, mobile phones, iPads, laptops, big chunky Goth boots, bags with band names on or designer labels or handheld gaming consoles. They were led by a big fat fusty old teacher, with a silly hat and a thin, white cane, which he used to hit the kids with when they were naughty. Another big difference, Christopher thought!

Dirk and Chris waited for them to come by and

then sort of attached themselves to the rear of the group. No one really noticed, so they followed the school party into the Tower. As they passed beneath the statues of the Watchers, Dirk's skin began to crawl. He half expected that the alarm would be given and swarms of Paladins, Holy Incriminators and Tower guards would appear to take him away to the Chambers of Correction underneath the Tower. But nothing happened.

Lining the entrance way stood guards wearing shiny steel armour with great white shields held in front of them. Dirk eyed them suspiciously. Paladins of the Order of the White Shields. They stood there, legs apart, hands on the top of their shields, unmoving, except for their heads, which turned back and forth constantly as they scanned the crowds for signs of wrongdoing, heresy or evil.

Dirk froze for a moment as one of them glanced at him, but the Paladin's attention moved on, dismissing Dirk as just another sightseeing kid, come to gawp at the Tower of the great White Wizard, the wise and benevolent ruler of the Commonwealth of Good Folk. Or so they believed. The abandoned farmhouse with its poor owners

The school trip

carried away for some fabricated crime put the lie to that, Dirk thought to himself.

They stepped into the main entrance hall of the Tower. It was wide and round and spacious. The walls were like smooth alabaster with great white oak doors spaced evenly around them, leading to various rooms and chambers. The floor was of white marble, veined with blue. High up near the ceiling, a ball of flaming gas hung in the air, filling the place with bright, white light. It was basically a little artificial sun. Dirk raised an eyebrow at that. Impressive, he thought to himself.

Most of the entrance chamber was taken up with several large desks, behind which sat clerks, sheriffs, clerics, bureaucrats, and scribes dealing with issues of governance, law and justice, such as it was. Long queues of people waited in line to see them.

'Well,' said Christopher, 'we can hardly queue up and ask to see Sooz, can we!'

'No, indeed,' said Dirk, who was looking around, fascinated. 'I've never been here, you know. Sure, I've dreamed of it, dreamed of coming here with a battalion of great ogres, to rip it down, brick by brick. Who could have possibly imagined that one day I would just walk in, free as a bird!'

Nearby the fat teacher was lecturing his class, pointing to the paintings that were hung around the walls – huge, tall paintings of various men and women, all dressed in white robes, wearing silver circlets with blue stones set into them and carrying various kinds of magic-looking staves.

'These are all the Enchantresses and White Wizards that have ever been, from the First Wizard to our present Wizard, the greatest and best of them all, may he live for a thousand years – Hasdruban the Pure.'

Dirk folded his arms, and settled in to listen, a wry smile on his face. Christopher was equally interested.

'The First Wizard was appointed thousands of years ago, in response to the rise of the Vampire Lords of Sunless Keep. Not long after the destruction of that fell place came the Dark Lord – a far greater peril! He sent forth his Orc legions to terrorize us all. It was after the burning of the city of Old Mylorn by that dread foe that the Commonwealth of Good Folk was formed as a bulwark against evil, and we haven't looked back since!'

Christopher looked over at Dirk. 'Thousands of years ago?' he said. 'How many Dark Lords have their been?' he asked.

'Just one,' said Dirk absently.

'But that means...you're... I mean, are you really that old?' said Chris.

'Indeed. But I can't remember it all. Some of that was spent in enchanted sleep, enchained in the World's Heart, deep in the dark, empty places below the earth,' he said distractedly, all his attention on the 'Fat Teacher' as he now thought of him.

Christopher stared at him in amazement.

'And the Wizard before this one died in battle with the Dark Lord,' continued the Fat Teacher.

'No he didn't,' said Dirk from the back. 'He was poisoned, and it wasn't me... I mean, and it wasn't the Dark Lord!'

'What! How dare you! That's heresy, that is,' said the teacher. 'Everyone knows he was slain in the Borderlands by the Dark Lord's treacherous magic!'

Dirk glared. 'No, that's not...' he began, but Christopher tugged on his sleeve, nodding in the direction of the entrance. One of the Paladins was looking over, drawn by the mention of heresy.

'We're attracting too much attention,' hissed Chris. 'Remember why we're here!'

'By the Nine Hells, you're right,' Dirk whispered back, before continuing on loudly. 'Yes, sir, of course! I thought it was poison. My mistake, forgive me. I was getting confused with the thirteenth wizard, Gatulac the Impure. He took poison, didn't he, out of shame?'

'Yes! That is right. And there is his portrait! Gatulac the Impure – he tried to come to terms with the Dark. Imagine that! He betrayed us all and in the end, took his own life when he realized the enormity of his crime,' the teacher said enthusiastically, Dirk's interruption forgotten. 'Remember that children! There can never be peace with the Dark Lord, never! He must be destroyed, along with all his works and all his vile folk – the Orcs, the Goblins, the Nightgaunts and the like. All of them must be eradicated utterly! Destroyed once and for all, their vile stain expunged forever from the face of the world!'

His voice rose at the end, spittle flying from his lips as he declaimed his fanatical creed. Dirk shook his head in despair. 'See what I'm up against,

Christopher? They're mad, all of them!' he said.

'Anyway, enough of that, children,' said the Fat Teacher. 'We shall now begin our tour of the White Tower, starting with the levels down below. Come along, follow me, we have a special treat for you today, oh yes indeed!'

Dirk nudged Chris. 'We should tag along, this is an excellent opportunity to get below!' he said.

They followed the school party down some stairs. At the bottom, two guards checked the teacher's paperwork, and then waved them through, not even batting an eyelid when Dirk and Christopher came too.

Down below, they were shown around various displays of Hasdruban's great achievements – models of his building works, copies of his new laws and rules (in general, a tightening up of his power and control but sold to the people as enlightened, wise rulership in the face of the terrible threat of the Dark. He was clever, old Hasdruban, you had to give him that, Dirk thought to himself.).

In one room, there was a display of little miniature soldiers, a diorama of the last battle between the army of the Commonwealth and the army of the

Darklands, fought in the foothills of Mount Dread. There was a little model of Hasdruban, holding a strange glowing crystal in one hand and his staff in the other, and also one of Dirk in his form of the Dark Lord, all horns, bony skull, skeletal talons and undead, goat-legged armour, standing in a black lacquered ornate chariot – the Midnight Chariot in fact. Chris stared at it in fascinated horror.

'Is that really you…?' he whispered. 'I mean, look at you, you're so…so evil!'

'Dark Lords are Dark Lords,' said Dirk. 'What did you expect? A fairy? A little bespectacled gnome? Maybe a bloke in a business suit like a banker back on Earth or something?' said Dirk with irritation.

Chris looked at Dirk, uncertainty in his eyes. Dirk folded his arms defensively. 'Well, I'm not like that now, am I?' he said.

Chris nodded. 'That's true, you've changed, haven't you?'

Dirk nodded…and then frowned in thought. He had changed. But he wasn't sure if that was a good thing or not. Was he ever going to be the same again? Could he ever be a true Dark Lord again?

The next display took Dirk's mind off things.

It was a great painting in three parts, what they called a triptych. The first part showed Hasdruban, dark eyes blazing, shattering some kind of crystal. The second part showed the Dark Lord falling and falling into a black, empty abyss. The third part showed people cheering wildly as Hasdruban trotted past on a great white horse, accepting the people's adulation graciously, waving a hand at them like the Queen of England.

Dirk stared at it in horrified fascination until his concentration was broken again, this time by the Fat Teacher.

'Now, children, for something very special indeed. You know that after the exile of the Dark Lord, his betrothed, the Dark Lady Sooz, returned to the Iron Tower to begin once again a campaign of nefarious evil in his name, don't you?' said the teacher.

'Yes, sir,' chorused the school children. Dirk and Christopher froze in shock at the mention of her name.

'Well,' continued the Fat Teacher, 'Hasdruban defeated her too, outwitting her with ease, and destroying that evil monster, the Black Slayer, in the process!'

Dirk's eyes narrowed. 'Hah, he doesn't mention that Hasdruban was allied with the Black Slayer at the time,' whispered Dirk angrily.

'And now, the White Wizard has the evil Dark Lady locked up, here in the Tower!' said the Fat Teacher.

Chris was staring open-mouthed at the Fat Teacher. 'What is it?' said Dirk. 'We knew she was locked up here. What's the problem, Chris?'

'He said "betrothed",' said Chris. 'That means like getting married, doesn't it?'

'Yes, it does, what's that got... Oh, I see!' said Dirk, equally surprised.

Chris turned on him angrily. 'She's gonna marry you when she grows up, is that it? You never said you'd asked her to marry you! I can't even believe she said yes! And worst of all, you didn't tell me! Neither of you. How could you?'

'Whoa, Chris, hold on there, it's the first I've heard of it believe me! I didn't ask her, of course I didn't!'

Chris's eyes narrowed. 'Really? REALLY? Only you're not exactly known for telling the truth now, are you Dirk?' said Chris bitterly.

'No, honestly, I swear it by the Nether Gods, Christopher, I never asked her to marry me. I mean, why would I? No, it's just some propaganda thing by the White Wizard to make out she is in league with "the Evil One" to justify them attacking her.'

Chris paused. That actually sounded quite convincing. But still…

Suddenly the Fat Teacher interrupted their conversation. 'Shut up, you two at the back!' he said, craning his neck to get a look. 'Who is it making all that noise – Picgreg, is that you? Be quiet or you'll get the cane again!'

'Not me, sir!' piped up a little voice near the front – Picgreg presumably.

Chris and Dirk ducked back out of sight. 'We'll talk about this later,' whispered Chris, glaring at Dirk.

Dirk shrugged. 'Whatever,' he muttered.

'Anyway, we've got a special treat today. Look, children, see the fate of those who oppose the great Wizard!' said the Fat Teacher. He pointed to a kind of telescope set into the wall.

'This device uses a clever arrangement of mirrors to show us the cell in which the Dark Lady is imprisoned, deep below the ground,' he said. 'Now, one at a time, look through the telescope.'

The kids took it in turns to look through it. Chris and Dirk did the same after the school party had finished. It showed a dirty stone-walled cell, where Sooz sat alone on a slab of rock, dressed in tattered black rags – shoeless, her face streaked with tears and with only black bread and water to keep her alive. The sight was heartbreaking. Tears welled up in Chris's eyes, but Dirk's face set hard into a mask of rage.

As the children trooped out of the room, Dirk hissed under his breath. 'Hasdruban will pay for this, oh yes, I will make him pay, I swear by the Power of the Nine Hells!'

'Yeah, but first we've got to save her,' said Chris.

'We will,' said Dirk, 'we will. For now, we must lose the Fat Teacher and his Goblin horde, see if we can get left behind, as it were.' He put his hand on Christopher's arm to hold him back as the last of the schoolchildren left the room. Dirk pointed to a nearby door. Quickly he opened it.

'Just as I thought,' he said. 'It's a broom cupboard.'

Dirk and Chris nipped inside, to find themselves

standing amidst a mess of pails, mops, brooms and other janitorial equipment. They shut the door. Total darkness wrapped around them like a blanket.

'What now?' whispered Chris.

'We wait,' said Dirk.

After a few minutes, someone spoke up nearby.

'All clear here, Pyter,' said a deep voice, a warrior's voice. 'All clear here, too,' came the reply.

'Right, let's lock the vault door then,' said the deep voice. 'The Lower Levels are clear!'

The footsteps began to recede. After a short while, Dirk said, 'I think it will be safe for us to venture out now, Christopher. All the visitors and tourists will be gone.'

Suddenly something moved at their feet! Chris shrieked in horror. 'Quiet, you fool,' hissed Dirk, although he was almost as terrified.

Something else rattled and moved. Then the door swung open, bright light hurt their eyes. They looked down squinting. A metal bucket was waddling out of the cupboard into the room beyond, waddling on four tiny little legs. A broom and a mop followed after, floating an inch or two off the ground.

Then came a rush of mops, brooms, buckets, dusters, cloths and pails from the back of the cupboard, taking Chris and Dirk with them, leaving them sprawled on the floor beyond. The various brooms, buckets, mops and pails started sweeping, cleaning, mopping and washing the floors. Damp cloths floated on the air to wipe down the tables and walls, light feather dusters gently brushed off the paintings and other delicate displays.

Dirk got up, helping a flabbergasted Chris to his feet. 'Magic janitor, basically,' said Dirk. 'A trivial enchantment, really. I could do better!'

The Chambers of Correction

Dirk and Christopher were walking down a long corridor, lit by torches set into the walls. It slanted downwards, and seemed to go on forever. Side doors were frequent. Most of these rooms were trophy or display rooms, showing off events, triumphs and famous battles from the histories of the Commonwealth of Good Folk, or strange curiosities and unusual things, or else they were storerooms full of weapons or food or whatever. A little placard on each door gave a brief outline of the contents. There were many off-shoots into different passages and areas, a veritable maze of tunnels, but fortunately the way to the Chambers of Corrections – 'Pah! Fancy name for a dungeon, basically,' commented Dirk – was regularly signposted.

Often they heard approaching footsteps of guards

Detention, Hasdruban style

or servants or workers, but it was an easy matter to hide in a storeroom.

They came to a room that was labelled, 'Gamulus vs Oksana'. This was too much for Dirk, he had to open the door and take a look. Inside was a circular room with a domed ceiling, in which burned another artificial sun, though this one was much smaller than the one in the main entrance hall of the Tower. Around the walls were many carved and painted panels, a kind of sculpted mural, depicting the story of the Wizard Gamulus the Good and his struggle versus an evil Vampire Queen called Oksana the Pale.

'Who are they?' said Christopher, awed by the sight.

'My father and mother,' said Dirk, as he followed the story around the walls.

'Your…' But that was all Christopher could get out, he was so flummoxed by the idea that Dirk had a real father and mother.

So Christopher examined the walls too – and was amazed by it – for Gamulus the Good was the third White Wizard, and Oksana was the Vampire Queen of Sunless Keep.

'But it doesn't say anything about you or Dark Lords, it just shows a great battle, and the forces of Good kicking the arses of the vampire hordes!' said Chris.

'I know, it is only half the story. Once they loved each other. Sort of. Until my father slew my mother, right before my eyes,' said Dirk.

'Wow! That's awful, Dirk, you poor thing!' he said sympathetically.

'Don't be ridiculous, Christopher! I have no need of your petty human empathy and least of all your wretched pity!'

'Sorree!' said Chris sarcastically.

'In any case, it made me what I am today, the Great Dirk, a mighty Dark Lord and everything!' continued Dirk.

'Yeah, well, I guess that explains a lot, doesn't it? Those psychologists – wotsit and thingy – I bet they had a field day with you!'

'Those fools Wings and Randle you mean? Hah, I ran rings round them! Though they did get a couple of books out of it. Anyway, enough of this, let us go on.'

They made their way deeper into the labyrinthine

depths of the White Tower.

Leaving the storerooms of the White Tower behind, they eventually came to an archway labelled 'The Chambers of Correction'. Beyond was a long, gloomy corridor lined with heavy steel doors, each door with a little plaque upon it. At the far end, they could see light streaming out from behind a half-open door, and muffled voices talking.

They examined one of the doors. 'Chamber 1: Empty Due to Recent Execution'. It was ajar. Inside, they could see a bare, stone-walled room with a dirt floor and a stone bench. Then the next. 'Chamber 2: Koff the Warlock – Awaiting Trial for Heresy.' And another. 'Chamber 3: Winny Probes – Awaiting Trial for Disrespecting the Office of the White Wizard.' 'Chamber 4: Dimdam Watertoes – Awaiting Trial for Publication of Inflammatory Pamphlets Contrary to the Truth.'

There were quite a few in this vein. Then finally they found the one they were looking for. It said, 'Chamber 13: Sooz the Black. Indefinite Incarceration by Executive Order of the White Wizard, for Being the Dark Mistress of the Tower of the Moon, and for Agreeing to Marry the Dark Lord.'

Dirk frowned. 'Tower of the Moon? What's that then?' he said in a low voice, almost to himself.

Christopher was also frowning. 'It says she agreed to marry you! Again!' he said, annoyed.

Dirk put a finger to his lips. 'Quietly, Chris, and I've told you once already, I didn't ask her, it's just the Wizard's propaganda. They do it all the time, always smearing the Dark.'

Chris glared at him suspiciously.

'Anyway, the important thing is we've found her,' said Dirk, examining the door carefully. There were three keyholes at the top, middle and bottom with three massive locks.

'Thrice-locked steel door. Enchanted too, by the smell of it. Hmm…' muttered Dirk.

'How are we going to open it?' whispered Chris.

'We can't, not without the key,' said Dirk.

Suddenly one of the voices at the end of the corridor grew louder. 'I'm off, then. I'll be back for the morning shift. Night, Imbolg,' said the voice.

'G'Night!' came the reply. Footsteps began to echo out of the far room.

'Quick,' hissed Dirk, 'in here!' They darted into an empty cell, and hid. Dirk knelt down and peeked out through a thin sliver of space between door and wall. A large man, dressed in a studded leather jerkin and heavy leather trousers ambled past. Various key rings and a big club hung from his heavy leather belt. Obviously he was one of the jailors.

After he'd gone, Dirk sat in thought for a moment or two. He turned to Chris. 'We must get the keys to Sooz's cell,' he said.

'Well, yeah, Sherlock, but how?' said Chris.

'A Sher Lock?' Dirk said, examining the door closely once more. 'No, no, they look like standard enchanted locks to me.'

'No, Sherlock is… Oh it doesn't matter, just forget I said it, OK?' said Chris.

'Alright. In that case, I will have to use the Sinister Hand, send it down to the guardroom. Try and steal the keys,' said Dirk.

'What, after the last time? You said it'd damaged you or something, that it wasn't safe to use any more,' said Chris.

'Quite so,' said Dirk. 'It is not safe any more, but we have no choice. What else can we do? But it is a grave risk, it could even…' His voice tailed off as if he didn't want to consider the possible outcome.

'But what else can we do?' he continued, as if to himself.

'I don't like it, Dirk. I mean, you were in real pain the last time, weren't you?' said Chris.

Dirk squared his shoulders, as if he'd made his mind up about something. 'Yes, yes, but what's a little pain between friends, eh?' he said with a reckless grin. With that he mumbled the words of the Sinister Hand spell, making an arcane pattern in the air with his other hand.

Dirk gasped. His left arm fell away just below the elbow to lie on the cell floor, twitching. His face was a mask of agony. Sweat broke out on his brow. It was all he could do to keep breathing through the pain, let alone control the Sinister Hand.

Chris stared at the hand in horrified fascination. The Sinister Hand... Yuk!

Dirk gritted his teeth. Slowly the disembodied hand began to drag itself along the floor by its fingers, inching its way out of the cell and down the corridor towards the guardroom. It was obvious that it was much harder for Dirk than it usually was and that the effort was causing him a lot of pain.

Chris shook his head. He couldn't bear to see

Dirk like this, he had to do something. Quickly he got to his feet, and picked up Dirk's arm.

'No, don't do it!' hissed Dirk.

Chris ignored him. He crept down the corridor up to the half-open door of the guard room. He lay down, and gingerly poked his head around the bottom of the door. At the far end of the stone-walled room, two men sat at a big oak table, playing cards. Beside them were a pile of empty plates and a big jug of water or ale. A roaring fire filled the room with heat. There were also some shelves stacked with documents and records, but mostly it was a pretty functional guardroom.

What interested Chris were the numbered hooks along one wall, upon which were hung various keys, one for each cell. Chris would have been spotted immediately if he'd gone for them, but Dirk's arm was a different matter. Chris put it down on the floor inside the room. Slowly it began to inch its way to the keys. It creeped him out how Dirk knew where to go – spirit sense or something he'd called it.

Suddenly, one of the jailors glanced over at the door. Chris whipped his head back out of sight, heart hammering like the loud drumbeat of a

A helping hand

hardcore dance track. He crouched outside as quiet as he could, praying that the jailor hadn't seen him.

But he hadn't been spotted, no one came out to haul him off to a cell or to beat him with a heavy jailor's club. After a few minutes, Chris heard a shallow scraping sound. Out from behind the door came Dirk's hand, grasping a bronze key with the number '13' inlaid on it in white.

Chris grinned in triumph, and picked up the Sinister Hand. He hurried back to the cell. Dirk was sitting by the door, slumped forward, his face pale and drenched in sweat.

'Here,' said Chris, handing his arm back.

'Thanks,' muttered Dirk as he took it with his other hand. Carefully he placed it back where it belonged, muttering a few more words of the spell. The flesh knitted together, but the join was livid, raw and red with dark, purple welts. It didn't look right at all. In fact, it looked like it was infected.

Dirk groaned as he got to his feet. 'Can you make it?' said Chris concerned.

Dirk looked up at him. 'Have to,' he said. 'No choice.' Dirk hobbled out, holding his arm, his face screwed up in pain. They headed straight to Cell 13. Dirk tried to put the key in the top lock, but he couldn't do it, his strength failed, and the key fell to the ground with a loud clatter. They both froze in fear…but no one came, no one heard them. Chris picked up the key. He reached up, unlocked the topmost lock. He reached down to do the middle lock, but Dirk shook his head. 'Bottom lock next, or you'll set off an alarm,' he said. Chris nodded, and reached down to open it. Then he unlocked the final lock…

Chris pushed the door gently – it opened slowly and silently on well-oiled hinges.

Dirk and Christopher stepped into the cell. And there was Sooz! She was huddled in a corner, trying to get as far from the door as she could, her eyes red from crying, her hair dishevelled, her clothes tattered and torn, and her bare feet covered in scratches and scabs.

Her jaw dropped at the sight of them and then her face lit up with joy. She leapt to her feet, jumping up and down on the spot excitedly. 'Dirk, Dirk, I can't believe it's you!' she said, and then she ran up and hugged him, so hard that Dirk gasped in pain. He paused for a moment, caught out by this unexpected welcome, but then he hugged her back.

'Oh, it's so good to see you,' she gushed.

'Good to see you too, my little vampire,' said Dirk affectionately. 'Are you alright?'

'Yeah, basically, yeah. They've been feeding me and that, but I've been so lonely!' Then Sooz gave him a little kiss on the cheek.

'Right, well, so, Mr and Mrs Lloyd is it?' said Chris waspishly, unable to help himself. She hadn't even noticed him!

'What!' said Sooz, embarrassed, stepping away from Dirk rather sharply. Even Dirk straightened up, and coughed. Sooz began to blush.

'Good to see you too, Sooz,' said Chris, rather sarcastically.

Sooz didn't notice his tone. 'And you, Chris,' she said, her eyes welling up with more tears, but this time tears of joy. She gave Chris a big hug but he stood there stiff and unmoving.

'What's the matter?' said Sooz, confused.

'What's all this stuff about getting married to Dirk then?' said Chris.

'Oh, give it a rest, Christopher,' said Dirk, holding his arm.

'No, it's OK. I should explain,' said Sooz. She stood

there for a moment, looking embarrassed, gathering her thoughts and then said, 'Well, it was the Ring you see. When Gargon saw me, he thought you'd given me the Ring, Dirk, because...you know, as... well, you know.'

'As an engagement ring,' said Chris.

'Yeah, and then Agrash and the Goblins and the Orcs, they all believed it too, and that's why they made me their queen, why they followed me and that, coz they thought I was the rightful queen, betrothed to their Dark Master and everything,' she said. 'So I thought I'd better go along with it.'

'So you're not really engaged then?' said Chris.

'No, of course not! I mean, why'd I marry him, even if I could? I mean, duh! Don't be a dork all your life, Christopher,' she said, looking at Dirk the whole time to see what his reaction would be. But Dirk was holding his arm in obvious pain. 'What's the matter, Dirk?' said Sooz.

Chris blinked. They were wasting time. He was wasting time, here they were in a cell in a dungeon, in a fantastical tower in another dimension and he was getting all jealous and angry!

'He used the Sinister Hand spell to get the key to

the door. But something's gone wrong – he's used it too many times and now it's really hurting him, and we've got to get out of here,' said Chris in a rush.

'That doesn't sound good,' said Sooz, concerned. 'How did you get here anyway?' she said.

'Well, first of all we… Actually, it's a long story. We'll tell you later,' said Chris, leading her by the arm towards the exit.

'Yeah, there's a lot of catching up to do,' said Sooz. 'I can't believe you came to rescue me. I'm so lucky to have friends like you! I'm so happy! Not to mention chuffed to be getting out of this horrible cell!'

'That's nice,' said Dirk hoarsely, shuffling his way to the door, 'but what happened to the Ring?'

'I'm sorry, Dirk. Hasdruban took it from me after he ambushed my army and captured me. Ripped it from my fingers in fact, the big bully. He did say he was unable to use it, as its power was "infected by the Dark" or something, so he hid it here in these very corridors. If it's any help, I heard him say "Put it in the Dark Reliquary" which isn't far actually! Oh, it's just so good to see you both!' Sooz said.

'Didn't we see a sign to the Dark Reliquary?' said Chris to Dirk.

Dirk nodded. He was hunched over, holding his arm. He looked up at Sooz and smiled. 'You have changed,' he said. 'You're not just a little girl any more, are you?'

Sooz smiled back and shook her head. No, she wasn't a little girl any more. She'd fought battles, governed a kingdom, been imprisoned. She had changed.

Dirk grimaced. The pain seemed to be getting worse. Chris and Sooz frowned.

'Come on,' said Sooz. 'We can't stay here, we've got to get moving.' Dirk could barely walk, they had to hold him up between them.

'Oh, by the way,' said Dirk, shrugging off the bag on his back. 'Here's your AngelBile backpack, with your make-up and phone and everything.'

'Wow, that's great. Thanks Dirk, how'd you get it?' said Sooz.

'The nanny,' said Dirk.

'The…the what?' said Sooz.

'Yeah, the nanny. It's a long story,' said Chris.

The Lair of the White Witch

Chris and Sooz staggered down the corridor, carrying an almost unconscious Dirk between them. His arm was swelling up and the discoloured purple welts were darkening and spreading towards his shoulder. It was also beginning to smell foul.

Up ahead was a kind of crossroads, where four corridors met. Each corridor was signposted. Straight ahead the sign read 'Display Rooms and Exit'. To the right it said 'To the Dormitories'. To the left it said 'The Lair of the White Witch'.

They were about to head off to the exit when suddenly, up ahead, they could hear many voices and the tramp of booted feet coming towards them.

'Guards,' hissed Chris. 'Right in front of us by the sound of things!'

'Well, we'd better head to the dormitories then!' said Sooz.

'No,' groaned Dirk. 'No, go left…'

'What?' said Sooz. 'To the Lair of the White Witch? That sounds far more dangerous than some dormitories!'

Dirk and Chris exchanged looks. 'She won't be there,' said Chris.

'Really? How do you know?' said Sooz.

'We know,' said Chris, 'trust me. She's the nanny.'

'The nanny – what in the Nine Hells are you talking about?' said Sooz.

Dirk looked up at her and smiled weakly. Nine Hells, eh? It was like she was becoming part of the Darklands, taking over from him, almost as if she belonged here.

'I'll tell you later – but the White Witch won't be there, honest,' said Chris.

The marching feet were drawing closer. They dragged Dirk down the corridor to the left as fast as they could. The soldiers or guards or whoever they were tramped on past, heading to the Chambers of Correction.

As they slowly made their way down the corridor,

Dirk suddenly gasped, 'Oh!' At his feet lay his arm, unmoving and rotten looking.

Sooz put her hand to her mouth.

Chris stared at the arm in horrified fascination. How could it just drop off like that? And it had gone almost completely black. Chris bent down, picked it up and handed it to Dirk. Weakly, Dirk tried to reattach it, mumbling the words of the spell, but it just fell to the floor again. Dirk stared at it in consternation.

'Black Rot,' he said. 'Bad. Very bad. Just as I feared.' His elbow and upper arm were veined with a livid dark purple colour. The Black Rot was spreading. 'If only I had returned to my original form on my return, got all my powers back, none of this would be happening!'

Chris picked up the arm again and handed it to Dirk. 'No good,' said Dirk, shaking his head. Chris frowned. He moved to put the stinking rotten arm in Sooz's bag but she made a face. Chris shrugged. 'Well, what do you suggest? We can't just leave it here can we?'

Sooz blinked and then nodded resignedly. Chris put the rotting arm into her AngelBile bag.

'What shall we do, Dirk?' he said. 'What happens? I mean, will the Black Rot fade now that the arm is gone?'

Dirk shook his head.

'Well,' said Sooz, 'what will happen?'

'Death,' said Dirk. 'Soon.'

Chris and Sooz said together, 'No!'

Dirk smiled at that. It was nice to know someone cared. But there was nothing that could be done. He felt light-headed, and so weak. Little figures appeared to be capering and dancing at the edge of his vision. He was getting delirious. Or were they tiny devils, waiting for him to die so they could drag him off to one of the Nine Hells? But which one? Hah, they'll have to create a special hell, just for him! The Tenth Hell. He laughed at that, a mad delirious laugh.

Chris and Sooz exchanged panicked looks. 'He's losing it,' said Chris.

'We can't let him die!' said Sooz. 'We can't.' Her eyes filled with tears and her lower lip began to tremble. 'It would be just awful to lose him again so soon!'

'Maybe there's something in the White Witch's

lair that can help,' said Chris.

'Yeah!' said Sooz, hopefully. 'You never know! A witch's brew or something.'

Quickly they dragged the dying Dirk down the corridor until they came to a bead curtain composed entirely of little white gems. They swept it aside, revealing a white oak door, with a black plaque with the words 'The White Witch of Holy Vengeance' picked out in white ink.

'Yeah, this is it,' said Chris.

'Really?' said Sooz, sarcastically. 'Are you sure?'

'Yeah, OK, very funny,' said Chris, as he pushed at the door. It wasn't even locked and it swung open easily. Dirk was slumped between them, barely able to stand. They took him into the chamber beyond.

It was a large circular room with a domed roof, painted entirely in white, except for pale blue or pink skirting boards and trim here and there. At the top of the dome burned another miniature sun.

Everything in the room was white and lacy. One area of the room, covered off by a white wooden screen painted with a mural of a twee woodland scene, had a sunken bath of white marble, fed by water from an underground spring that constantly bubbled up with cold, clear water. At the far end was another door.

They looked around in amazement.

'Wow,' said Sooz. 'This is weird! It's all so white and…well, namby pamby and girly! I hate it!'

'Actually, it explains a lot,' said Chris.

Dirk groaned. They led him over to the bed, and laid him on it. 'Ugh,' Dirk mumbled, 'so white. Hurts eyes…' Then he passed out, breathing shallowly and irregularly.

Dirk and Sooz rushed over to the Witch's workbench. There they found a cabinet of little drawers with various labels on them, like 'Dried Tan-tan Berries', 'Pickled Lipweed', 'Trollbile', 'Nuclear Beans', 'Pus-wort Mushrooms', 'Ghost Spit', 'Beetle Juice', 'Powdered Fairy Farts' and so on.

'Nuclear Beans! What the…?' said Chris.

Sooz shrugged. 'I wouldn't touch 'em if I were you.' Then she found one that said 'Goblin Snot'. 'Hah,' she said. 'I wonder how much she'd pay for Goblin Snot? I know where I can get a lot of that!'

'Forget the ingredients,' said Chris. 'We need the finished thing.'

They searched around some more, until they

found a glass-fronted cabinet. Inside were stacked many phials, vials and potion bottles, full of all sorts of different coloured liquids, each one carefully labelled in white ink on black card.

The potions were labelled with things like 'Skimskam: For the Relief of Skim and Skam', 'Nephritising Slimeguzzler: For the Removal of Zombie Warts', 'Wish Wash: For the Righting of Wayward Wishes', 'Pink Shandygaff: Just Nice in the Morning. Warning: Do not confuse with Blue Shandygaff!'. Next to it was a bottle of 'Blue Shandygaff: The Laxative of Doom'. There must have been a hundred different potions and brews in that cupboard.

'We might find what we need in this lot, I guess,' said Sooz.

'Yeah,' said Chris. 'Maybe Dumpsy will turn out to have been quite useful in the end!'

'Dumpsy?' said Sooz. 'Who is this White Witch dude?'

As they opened the cabinet and began to examine the potions inside, Christopher told her the whole story about Dumpsy Deary and how she'd come to Earth to kill Dirk and everything. Sooz listened

Fancy a brew?

avidly as they searched. She'd begun to tell Chris about her own adventures, when suddenly she gave a cry of joy. 'Here, Chris, look, we're in luck!' she said, holding up a small phial of green, glowing liquid, 'Chromatic Hydromel: For the Relief of Black Rot'.

'Fantastic!' said Chris.

'Wait,' said Sooz, 'there's some small print.' She read it out loud. '"Note: will not cure Black Rot, but will relieve symptoms for a short time". Oh dear. Quick, see if there's any more.'

They searched, but that seemed to be the only bottle.

'Ah, well,' said Chris. 'It's better than nothing!' They rushed over to where Dirk was lying and put the phial to his lips. He began to cough and gag as they poured the contents down his throat.

He then slumped back, asleep, though at least now his breathing was a little more regular.

'I guess that's all we can do for now. We'll have to let him rest for a bit,' said Chris.

'We should search her desk, see if she has a recipe book for potions. If we find a way of making Chromatic Hydromel ourselves, we can keep Dirk alive for ever!' said Sooz.

They rummaged through the White Witch's desk for quite a while but could find nothing. Behind them someone coughed. They turned – it was Dirk, up on his feet at last.

'So, the Lair of the White Witch,' he said, looking around, squinting against the bright white glare.

'Dirk, how are you?' said Christopher.

'My arm stump is sore, but other than that, I am well,' he said. 'For now. I'm guessing you found a Chromatic Hydromel potion, yes?'

'Yes, Dirk,' said Sooz, 'but there was only one and now we're trying to find a recipe so we can make another.'

'Very admirable of you, but unfortunately I doubt that she will keep a written record, at least not one that she doesn't keep with her at all times. A witch's recipes are her most precious secrets, she won't leave them lying around.'

'But if we can't make another… Well… You'll… I mean…' Sooz couldn't bear to finish the sentence.

'I'll die. Indeed,' said Dirk. 'It could happen at any time, there is no real way of knowing. I have a day at most, if I'm lucky.'

Tears welled up in Sooz's eyes. 'No,' she said. 'I couldn't bear to lose you, Dirk,' she said, 'Not after we just found each other again!'

'Me neither, I don't…' Dirk began to say, but then he paused, frowning in puzzlement. He reached up with his good hand, and brushed a tear from his own eye.

'What's this?' he said. 'A tear? How…'

'You're crying,' said Chris.

'What? Me?' said Dirk.

Sooz smiled through her tears. 'You're crying because you'll miss me and Chris,' she said. 'Because you don't want to say goodbye to your friends.'

Dirk raised an eyebrow. 'Pah, don't be absurd! I'm just feeling sorry for myself. And I cry for the world, because it will be losing me, my genius, my creativity, oh how the world will suffer when I die!' his voice rising maniacally at the end.

Sooz and Chris looked at each other and raised their eyes. 'He's certainly feeling a lot better, isn't he?' said Christopher.

'Yup, just like his old self,' said Sooz, shaking her head.

'Anyway,' said Chris, 'we need to save you Dirk,

I mean we've got to, after all, for the sake of the world, right?'

Dirk frowned. Was that sarcasm? Again?

'So, other than the Chromatic wotsit potion, how do you stop the Black Rot?' said Chris.

Dirk rubbed his jaw. 'Short of some kind of polymorph or shape changing spell – of which I am currently unaware – well…hmm…nothing comes to mind,' he said. He shook his head in despair.

'What about the Tower?' said Sooz. 'Could there be a Hydromel recipe in the Dark Library?'

'Yes, it's possible, there could be a copy of the recipe in there somewhere. Actually, it's got thousands of years of accumulated knowledge – we might even find a cure!'

'How long would it take us to get there?' said Chris.

'Maybe a week, maybe quicker if we could find a magical shortcut,' said Dirk. 'It'll have to be quicker, mind, I'll be dead way before a week's out.'

'There's a problem even if we can get there fast enough. The Tower of the Moon – I mean the Iron Tower – is under siege. In fact, they may have surrendered already,' said Sooz. 'Besieged by a small army. If we could get there, maybe rescue them, we could…'

'Rescue who?' said Dirk.

'My friends, Gargon, Agrash, Skabber and Rufino, and my people,' said Sooz.

'Your people? My people you mean!' said Dirk, irritated.

'Oh yes, of course, your people, that's what I meant,' said Sooz diplomatically. But Dirk didn't seem to be listening any more. He was coughing too much. After a moment or two the coughing subsided. 'What… What was I saying?' he muttered. He stared at the floor, swaying. He still wasn't well, not well at all.

'It doesn't matter. We have to get out of here, try and find a way to the Tower,' said Chris worriedly.

Dirk shook his head to clear it. 'Yes, indeed,' he said, a little more like his old self, 'but not before we make a few adjustments first! Sooz, find yourself some shoes and fresh clothes. Chris and I will sabotage the bed!'

'Sabotage the… What do you mean?' said Chris.

Dirk winked. 'You know, a few pointy hair brushes and that, in the bottom of her bed. A little welcoming present for Clumsy Dreary, should she ever return!'

'Hah,' laughed Chris.' Good idea!' Together they set about remaking her bed, whilst Sooz ransacked the White Witch's wardrobe.

A short while later, the three of them stepped out of the Witch's Lair into yet another corridor. Sooz was dressed in a lacy white dress, though she'd managed to rip up her old dress to make some half decent black lace bows and sashes to lessen the total white-out effect. She'd found some nice silver jewellery as well: a necklace, a bracelet, some rings for her fingers and some earrings. They weren't really her style but they weren't too bad. The only problem was footwear – the White Witch had nothing that would fit Sooz, so she was still barefoot. Though she'd added one or two silver toe rings and an ankle bracelet.

Still, a visit to the magical wardrobe in her room in the Tower would sort all that out... She glanced over at Dirk. In *his* room in the Tower, she thought to herself with a twinge of jealousy.

They walked on slowly – Dirk couldn't keep up much of a pace, as he was rather weak, and getting weaker. They came to a T-junction. As usual, the corridors were signposted. One read 'To the surface'. The other read, 'To the Dark Reliquary'.

'The Dark Reliquary!' said Sooz. 'That's where Hasdruban told them to put the Ring. I knew it was nearby.'

Dirk perked up at that. 'We must investigate it,' he said.

'Bound to be guarded or locked though,' said Sooz.

'Still, we must try. There could be something useful. And in any case, I can use the Ring to get us to the Tower,' said Dirk weakly.

Sooz nodded. 'I agree. Let's do it!' she said.

Dirk and Chris looked at her, surprised at her authoritative tone.

Crikey, Chris thought to himself, one bossy Dark Lord is bad enough, but a bossy Dark Lady as well? How am I going to cope?

The Dark Reliquary

After a short while, the corridor became shrouded in darkness. Chris took a burning torch off the wall. He returned – to reveal a big, craggy stone face set into the side of the corridor. Above it, a stone plaque read 'The Dark Reliquary'. The corridor continued beyond, to join up with the maze of corridors that led to and from the Chambers of Correction.

Suddenly, an eye opened on the stone face, and it glared at them. Chris started back with a cry of surprise. Sooz and Dirk glanced at each other and smiled. They were much more used to this sort of thing.

'Who's that waking me up with that light?' said the face stonily.

Dirk cocked his head. 'I know that voice... Tin Tallon, is that you?'

'What? That name! I haven't been called that in a hundred years! Yes, Tin Tallon – that's me, isn't it? I remember now!'

'Indeed. Tin Tallon, a spirit of the earth, of rock and stone. What are you doing here?' said Dirk.

'Well, you know, guarding things, as usual,' said Tin Tallon with a pebbly sigh. 'Hasdruban bound me here into this rock many years ago, to open only for those who know the password. Now, tell me, who are you, that knows my name of old?'

'Ah, I am the Dark... Err... I am Dirk. Dirk Lloyd, and I know many things, for I am a wise and mighty sorcerer!' said Dirk.

'Hmm, that's just as well,' said Tin Tallon. 'I thought for a moment there you were going to say the Dark Lord. That would have been no good, no good at all, for I've got a bone or two to pick with him, after what he did to me in the Caverns of...'

'Yes, yes, well, enough of that! I'm not the Dark Lord, obviously. It was a simple slip of the tongue on my part, that's all,' said Dirk hurriedly.

'Oh yes, Dirk does sound a little like Dark, doesn't it? Though I have to say, you don't look like a mighty sorcerer. Actually, you look more like a child. As

334

The Rock Face

do your friends, in fact.'

'Indeed,' said Dirk. 'Though it is…' Suddenly Dirk froze in pain. He gasped, and fell to his knees, clutching the stump of his arm.

Sooz and Chris knelt down to hold him, panic in their eyes. Thin tendrils, like swollen veins full of black blood, had appeared on his neck.

'Goodness me, are you all right, dear boy?' said Tin Tallon politely.

'He's got the Black Rot,' said Chris.

'The Black Rot! Some spell that went wrong, eh? Used it too often, no doubt. Tsk, tsk, you sorcerers just don't know when to stop, do you? Very serious, Black Rot is, oh yes, very serious. Well, for mortal folk of flesh and blood that is – wouldn't bother me, of course, not in the slightest!' scraped the stone face.

Dirk spoke through gritted teeth, 'We need to get into the Dark Reliquary. Will you let us pass?'

'Certainly!' said the door.

The three of them looked up, expectantly. Nothing happened.

'Well,' said Chris, 'are you going to let us in, then?'

'Of course,' rumbled Tin Tallon. 'But first of all

you have to tell me the password and then answer…'

'Diatonic Fizzbuzz!' spluttered Dirk.

'Hah! Very good. But no, that's an ancient password that one is, I'm afraid. It's been changed since then. Now it's Monochrome Mustard… Oh dear! Ah! Umm… Oh my!' said Tin Tallon.

'Monochrome Mustard!' yelled Chris, laughing as he did so.

Sooz grinned from ear to ear. 'Silly old door,' she said, giggling. Even Dirk managed a wan smile.

'Yes, well,' said the door, 'I guess I'm not quite as sharp as I used to be. Ho hum.'

Dirk sank down to the floor. 'Open up, then,' he said.

'What? Oh no. Not so easy, I'm afraid. The password just entitles you to hear the riddles. If you can get them right, then I'll open up for you,' said Tin Tallon.

'Riddles! Whose ridiculous idea was that?' said Dirk hoarsely.

'The White Witch. She got the idea from something called "Fairy Tales" from another dimension she's been visiting recently. Or so she claimed. They're quite hard, you know. Even Hasdruban himself was flummoxed!

That's why he thought they were such a good idea,' said Tin Tallon in a voice like grinding rocks.

Dirk sighed. He looked up at Sooz and Chris. 'Well, it's up to you. I've always hated riddles. But if they're from Earth, maybe you two will know them.'

'Maybe,' said Chris.

Sooz shrugged. 'Possibly. OK then Mr Tallon, let's hear these riddles!' she said.

'Yes, of course my dears. The first one goes like this: "I have cities, roads, forests and villages, but no people." What am I?'

'Oooh, oooh, I do actually know that one!' said Chris. 'That's easy – it's a map!'

'Ho, ho!' said Tin Tallon. 'You're right, it is indeed a map! Well done, little fellow. Now, how about this one: "My skin is mail, my legs are tail, sea is my jail; when men I hail, their souls will fail. What am I?"'

The three of them all frowned at once, puzzled looks on their faces.

'I read something about mail in a book about riddles for History at school. It was an old Anglo-Saxon riddle about fish, I think. You know, mail and scales and that. But fish don't "hail" men, do they? They don't talk to us. And what's with the legs…? Hmm…'

Dirk coughed and lay back. 'Oh I don't know…
Riddles, *bah!*' he said in frustration.

'Lobsters or prawns maybe?' said Chris, thinking
out loud. 'They live in the sea and have legs. But
they haven't got scales. More like plate armour
rather than mail, right?'

'Mermaids!' said Sooz. 'Mermaids! They sing and
the souls of men fail, and that. And they're half-fish,
half-human, with fishy tails for legs!'

'Correct, young lady,' said Tin Tallon. 'You are a
bright one, aren't you!'

Sooz smiled at the door and bowed graciously.

'You're doing well, and with such good manners
too! Now, the last one,' continued Tin Tallon. 'A
poor man has it. A rich man wants it. If I go wrong,
it is right. I am what I seem.'

The three of them stared at the door. And stared.
They shifted from foot to foot. They hummed and
they hawed. They scratched their heads and their
ears and their noses but nobody could come up
with the answer.

'By the Nine Hells, nothing comes to mind!' said
Dirk.

'Indeed, that's it! Well done, young man,' said the door.

Sooz and Chris looked bemused. Dirk's face lit up for a moment as the answer dawned on him. 'Yes, simple really,' he said, desperately trying to pretend he hadn't got the answer by a total fluke. 'You see, a poor man has nothing. A rich man wants for nothing. If nothing goes wrong it is right. And nothing is what it seems!'

'Brilliant. You are a genius, young man!' said Tin Tallon. 'Right, stand back then, I'm going to open up.' The stone door began to creak and crack. Seams appeared around the edges, and it rolled forward a little with a horrible grinding sound. Then it shifted off to the left, revealing a doorway into a brightly lit storeroom.

Everywhere artefacts and curiosities of a thousand years of the Dark were laid out and labelled. Most were fairly mundane things like examples of orcish armour, or Goblin weapons, or a stuffed Nightgaunt, but there were also a few special items in display cabinets like the Spear of the Ogre Lord, Gallons Blubberbelly ('I remember him!' said Dirk in-between coughs. 'He served me well until he died after eating some bad oysters – or was it humans? I forget.') or the Sword of Ven

– a sword so massive none of them could lift it ('So that's where it ended up,' gasped Dirk. 'I wondered what happened to it!') and a strange metal helmet shaped like a camel's two humps ('That belonged to the two-headed Troll King, MishnMash,' Dirk croaked. 'The White Wizard's axeman got double pay the day they executed him.'), and books, lots of books, mostly histories of battles and wars between the Darklands and the Commonwealth of Good Folk.

In one corner, near the door, they found some recent placements that hadn't even been labelled or properly laid out yet. They found Sooz's big black Goth boots and her Moonsilver tiara crown with the black onyx set in it. She was overjoyed to find them and put them on immediately. She also found a kind of egg box, with six many-sided blue crystals in it. The box was labelled 'Anathema Crystals'. Shrugging, she picked it up and put it in her AngelBile bag, making a face as she caught a whiff of Dirk's rotting arm as she did so.

There was also a beautiful black wooden box, inside of which was the Great Ring, resting on an elegant bed of black velvet. Next to the wooden ring box was a small bottle, filled with a black, shiny, viscous liquid.

Dirk, who was so weak he couldn't stand, was staring at the bottle. He reached for it, but couldn't get there. He signalled to Chris. 'Give me that bottle,' he said. Chris looked at him. And then at the bottle. He had a good idea what it might be, and he really wasn't sure it was a good idea for Dirk to have it. Especially as it was obviously interesting Dirk more than his Ring – and that was saying something.

'Now, Christopher, give it to me now!' said Dirk angrily.

'I don't think that's a good idea, Dirk,' said Chris.

Dirk glared at him, but he was too weak to do anything about it.

'What about the Ring?' said Sooz. 'Doesn't anybody want that?' She leaned forward, took it and put it on her finger. She looked at it and smiled. It felt so right on her finger, like it belonged there. It began to glow in welcome, bathing her in its glorious dark light.

Dirk's jaw dropped at the sight of that, the bottle of black oily stuff forgotten. Chris was awed. Sooz stood there looking at her finger, a crown on her head, radiating majesty and power and dark, dangerous beauty. Even her white dress seemed to shine with an aura of pale moonlight. Behind her, the shadow of what looked like a mighty Sorcerer-Queen flickered faintly on the wall.

'Wow,' said Chris.

Dirk smiled a wry smile. 'Indeed, you are a dark and terrible Queen.' He glanced down at the Ring on her finger. 'And the Ring knows it. The Ring gives itself to you. Hah! I would never have thought it in a thousand years! All hail Dread Queen Sooz, Dark Mistress of the Darklands!' said Dirk weakly as he lay back, barely able to move.

Sooz looked at them as if noticing them for the first time, her face full of imperial authority and regal splendour.

Chris stared at her. Susan Black. Thirteen years old. Lives in a council house. Serious Goth. Swimmer. Always in trouble. Good at English and History, bad at Maths and Geography (but only because she didn't like them). AngelBile fan...

And Queen of the Darklands, a fantastical world in another dimension! He could hardly believe it. Without thinking, still staring at Sooz, he reached over and grabbed the bottle of Essence of Evil (for that is what it was) and slipped it into his pocket.

'You are a fitting heir to my throne, my little Child of the Night, though you are a child no more!' coughed Dirk. 'For soon I shall die…' With that Dirk sagged back – he no longer had the strength to even sit, or speak. Thin black tendrils spread across his face.

'No!' said Sooz, coming out of her dark reverie. 'No!' She knelt down beside him. A tear rolled down her cheek. It was filled with a shadowy radiance, that tear. It glowed like liquid moonlight. Chris stared at it, fascinated by its dark beauty. And by her. Dirk closed his eyes.

'We've got to get him out of here,' said Sooz.

They picked Dirk up between them and dragged him out past the stone door.

'Oh dear, I hope he'll be all right,' said Tin Tallon.

'Thank you, Mr Tallon,' said Sooz. 'You may close up now.'

'As you wish. Goodbye then, little ones!' said the door as it rolled back over the entrance with a grinding shudder.

'See ya,' said Chris, wrestling with Dirk's unconscious body.

'Umm, before you go…' grated Tin Tallon.

'Yes?' said Sooz, hefting Dirk's good arm over her shoulder.

'You won't mention anything to Hasdruban will you? You know, about the password. Terribly embarrassing, you know!'

'Huh! No, don't you worry, we won't be saying anything to him, not if we can help it!' said Chris.

'Yeah, we're not planning on talking to him any time soon!' added Sooz.

'I'm so pleased, thank you so much,' gravelled the door politely.

They dragged Dirk down the corridor, his feet trailing along between them, following the signs that read 'To the Surface'.

Eventually they came to a simple wooden door at the end of the corridor. It opened easily into the back end of a cave up in the hills upon which the White Tower was built. A little path led down from the cave to some open farmlands, beyond which lay the town of Magus Falls. Chris and Sooz dragged Dirk to the cave entrance, and onto a nearby grassy hilltop where they collapsed, exhausted, with Dirk lying between them.

It was evening and the sun was setting in the west. 'He's going to die, isn't he?' said Chris, looking over at Sooz. They were sitting outside a cave on a grassy hilltop.

She nodded, her eyes welling up with silvery tears.

Dirk coughed and his eyes flickered open. He grabbed Chris by the arm. 'Give me the Essence. It's my only hope,' he croaked.

'What do you mean?' said Chris.

'If I drink it, it might restore me to my original form. And by doing so, restore my arm too. If it doesn't – well, I'll die anyway, but it's my only chance,' said Dirk hoarsely. He coughed and lay back, closing his eyes.

Chris stared at him, unsure. 'What's the Essence, Chris?' said Sooz. 'What's he on about?'

Chris felt in his pocket. He drew out the little bottle of black, oily liquid. 'Essence of Evil,' he said. 'Dirk's Evil.'

'You mean that stuff that the White Beast took? In the car park back on Earth?' said Sooz.

'Yeah,' said Chris. 'Looks like Hasdruban

extracted it and bottled it. Trouble is, if we give it to Dirk it might turn him back into… Well, you know, a proper Dark Lord and everything. Proper evil and that.'

Sooz thought of the suit of armour in the Sanctum Sanctorum in the Iron Tower. She shuddered.

'But if we don't give it to him, he'll die,' she said.

Chris and Sooz looked at each other, unsure of what to do.

'We've got no choice, have we?' said Sooz.

'I guess not,' said Chris, hand in his pocket.

'Well, go on then,' said Sooz.

Chris did nothing. If he did nothing, Dirk would die. And right now, that didn't seem such a bad thing. Sooz would take over, and he'd be with her, by her side. He frowned and shook his head.

'What's the matter, Chris?' said Sooz.

'It's the stuff in the bottle. It's affecting me, making me think… Making me think bad thoughts,' he said. 'It's dangerous.'

'Give it here, then,' said Sooz.

Impulsively, Chris jerked the bottle out of his pocket and tossed it to the ground in front of Sooz, obviously glad to be rid of it.

Sooz didn't hesitate. She picked it up, pulled the stopper out and poured the contents into Dirk's mouth. It seemed to trickle down his throat of its own accord, like a glittering black oily snake slithering home to its lair.

They stood back and waited...

Part Five:
Metamorphosis

A Dark Puberty

Dirk lay there unmoving. Sooz and Chris were staring at him expectantly, but nothing seemed to be happening. And then suddenly Dirk's eyes flew open and he cried out, 'Noooo! Not that!'

Dirk's limbs began to twitch uncontrollably. Then something really weird started to happen. He began to shake and hum, like some kind of living rattle. He was shivering so fast they could barely see him.

Sooz and Chris recoiled in horror. 'Dirk! Oh no, it's killing him. Oh Dirk, no!' cried Sooz.

'Aaaaiiieeee!' shrieked Dirk in agony. Suddenly a pair of huge hands burst out of him. Bony, leathery hands, ending in long, black talons. They reached to either side of Dirk's boyish body, and began to haul themselves out. Heavily muscled arms followed, covered in dark leathery skin, with bony ridges.

Sooz and Chris stared in open-mouthed terror.

A typical schoolboy from Surrey

Dirk's body was being torn to shreds, and from the gory wreckage a vast new form was emerging.

A head and shoulders came forth, a head with two huge horns and fierce yellow cat-eyes, and a great, fanged and tusked mouth. Its face was gnarled, leathery and bony. It rose up out of the tatters of Dirk the child to stand like a colossus as Dirk the Dark Lord. The body was mightily muscled and its legs were shaped like those of a goat, ending in heavy hooves. It was at least twelve feet tall.

Chris and Sooz cowered down before it. 'What have we done...?' said Sooz under her breath.

The creature raised its arms, put its head back and howled at the heavens in a voice deep and dark and resonant with power.

'Free! I am free at last! I have returned, I, the Dark Lord, the World Burner, Master of the Legions of Dread! All shall fear me! All shall bow down before me, the Evil One, the Nameless One, the Lord of...'

Then the vast creature paused, and frowned.

'Wait a minute,' it said, in its deep, vibrant voice. 'I'm not the Nameless One any more, am I?'

The creature raised its head to the heavens once more. 'All shall fear me, the Dark Lord Dirk! Dirk, the World Burner, Dirk the Master of the Nine Hells, Dirk the Magnificent!'

Dirk, for that is who this creature was, lowered his great horned head and chuckled, a rolling, rich laugh.

'Cool!' he said. He turned, and gazed down at the two human children. He put a taloned finger to his chin, and tapped. 'Hmm, now what have we here? Two little man-things by the look of it!' he said.

Chris said in a voice full of fear, 'Is that really you, Dirk?'

'Indeed it is, Christopher. Or should I say Brother Christopher!' said Dirk. He put his huge head back and laughed. Then he turned to Sooz, who was looking up at him, eyes wide with fear. The ring on her finger was pulsing with energy. The Dark Lord frowned, a huge, meaty, bony frown.

'Give me the Ring, Sooz,' he said commandingly.

Sooz just stared up at him, speechless. Dirk leant down and shouted into her face, 'GIVE ME THE RING, GIRL-CHILD! NOW!!!'

Sooz quailed back in terror. Quickly she removed the Ring with quaking fingers and handed it over. Dirk smiled. The Ring swelled in size in his hand,

and it slid onto his finger. Instantly, the runes began to glow with terrible energy.

Dirk put his head back and laughed, '*Mwah, hah, hah!*' but this time the sound was loud and mighty and full of evil intent. He admired the Ring on his finger for a moment. Then he leant down and chucked Sooz under the chin with a black taloned finger.

'Thank you, my little vampire!' he said, smiling fondly at her. Well, as much as a giant, twelve-foot tall Dark Lord could smile fondly.

Sooz blinked, regaining some of her composure. She smiled back. 'That's OK, Dirk,' she said nervously. 'I guess you've been cured of the Black Rot, then?'

The Dark Lord looked at his left arm, which was strong and whole. He smiled. And then frowned for a moment as if he didn't want to be reminded that it was they who had saved him. But then he made a face, just like Dirk used to, as if admitting something to himself.

'Yes, it worked. You will find that I am not ungrateful! I won't forget it, you have earned your reward,' said the Dark Lord forcefully. Actually, he pretty much said everything forcefully.

'Reward? But we did it because… Well, we're your friends,' said Chris, still not quite able to believe what had just happened.

'Friends!' said Dirk, laughing insanely once again. 'I do not have friends, you addle-pated boy-child!'

Then the Dark Lord stopped laughing. He put a great hand to his bony chin once more, just like the boy Dirk used to do.

'Well…on the other hand. Maybe a Dark Lord can have friends. I'm not sure,' he said thoughtfully. 'This is new territory for me.'

'Do you remember being Dirk?' said Sooz. 'All that stuff on Earth, with the school and the Pavilion, and the nanny, and rescuing me and everything?'

'Oh yes,' said the Dark Lord. 'Indeed I do, I can remember it all. *Bah*, I was weak! I should have killed that witch! I should have enslaved your parents, Christopher, and destroyed that petty villain, Grousammer! And as for Wings and Randle – oh, what punishments I could devise!'

The Dark Lord shook his head, and continued. 'I mean, what was I thinking? Infected with human mercy, I suppose. Hah, absurd!'

Sooz and Chris exchanged glances. They were scared, but on the other hand, Dirk was obviously still in there somewhere. Sort of. But not the Dirk they once knew.

'So, what's next, Dirk?' said Sooz, worried about what he might be planning.

'Do not call me Dirk,' said Dirk. 'You may address me as your Imperial Darkness, or Dark Lord.'

'But we've always called you Dirk,' said Chris.

'That will change. Though I suppose, as it's you two, the Great Dirk will be acceptable,' said the Dark Lord imperiously.

'And what if we don't?' said Sooz, a little angry at his arrogant tone.

'I will destroy you utterly, of course,' said the Dark One.

Sooz and Chris stared at him in astonishment. 'You wouldn't!' said Chris.

'Of course I would, you fool! Do I look like I'm joking, you puny human... No wait, you puny numpty! Hah, hah, yes, you puny numpty, Christopher. Do not make the mistake of thinking I wouldn't!' said the Lord of Darkness.

Sooz frowned. 'But we saved you. We're your

friends. We took you in when you needed us, when you were alone on Earth. We helped you!'

The Dark Lord Dirk grimaced, his huge face wrinkled up in annoyance. '*Bah*, I suppose so!' He folded his arms and stared at them. Then he said, 'Perhaps it would be best if we return to the Iron Tower. Once I've broken the siege, re-enslaved – ah, I mean rescued – my people, I'll find a way to send you back to Earth. With a reward or something. It is probably best that way – each to their own and all that.'

Chris nodded. 'Makes sense,' he said. Sooz nodded too, but less enthusiastically. She had friends here, good friends, and though she missed Earth terribly she didn't feel comfortable about leaving her new friends in the hands of this version of Dirk.

The Dark Lord Dirk continued. 'You don't really belong here, you see. It is too dangerous. I can't guarantee your safety, even from myself. It's just the way things are,' the Dark Lord said in his deep, powerful voice. 'Things have changed.'

Dirk and Chris looked at each other. That was certainly true. This Dirk was pretty scary, to put it mildly.

'So,' said Sooz, 'how do we get to the Tower?'

The Dark Lord's face lit up with unholy glee, just like Dirk's face used to.

'Aha, well, I shall show you! You're going to like this, my little morsels, oh yes, you will!' The Dark Lord raised his hands to the sky, and began to chant something in deep, sepulchral tones.

Chris looked at Sooz. 'Morsels? That doesn't sound good,' he said under his breath.

'No it doesn't,' said Sooz. 'I think we'll have to humour him, you know, flatter him. That sort of worked with the old Dirk, didn't it?'

'Yeah, I guess,' said Chris, not entirely convinced it would work with the Dark Lord Dirk – but what else could they do?

The Dark Lord's voice was getting deeper. It began to vibrate with ominous power. They could feel it in their chests, like the sound of really loud heavy metal music. Suddenly a column of dark energy burst from the Great Ring, and hurtled upward into the cloudy heavens where it exploded like a firework, scattering little motes of sparkly shadow all over the sky.

'To me, Abrakulax, to me!' howled the Dark Lord

at the top of his mighty voice. The motes of glowing darkness began to fade and fall, until nothing was left. Silence reigned. Nothing happened.

'That went well then,' said Chris.

The Dark Lord whirled and leant down towards Chris, a bony finger raised threateningly. 'Ah! Now that is sarcasm, I'm sure of it! Be careful, little man, or I'll…'

'What?' said Chris angrily, his jaw jutting. 'Kill me? Sacrifice me, maybe? Again! Without me, you wouldn't even be here, you'd be a prisoner of the Skirrits or dead from Black Rot, you…you big bully!'

The Dark Lord blinked at Chris for a moment – a blink like that of a lizard or a bird – a sideways blink.

'You have courage, I'll give you that, Christopher,' said the Dark Lord. 'And you have been useful. I will let you live. But be warned, there are limits to my patience! As for the success of my summoning, wait and see, faithless mortal!'

As if to underline his words, a small speck appeared far away in the sky. It grew larger and larger as it drew near.

The Dark Lord Dirk turned to face the black spot, taloned hands on his hips. Christopher made a rude face behind his back. Sooz stifled a giggle.

'Here comes Abrakulax, the Dragon King!' said the Dark Lord.

Swooping down through the clouds came a great dragon, its scales shining and black, its eyes huge, and of a bright, luminescent amber colour. Trails of red fire wisped from its nostrils. All along its back, from neck to tail ran spiky barbs of horn.

Abrakulax, the Dragon King.

Sooz and Christopher stared at it in open-mouthed astonishment.

'Wow,' said Sooz. 'A dragon, a real, actual dragon! How cool is that!'

'Assuming it doesn't eat us, that is,' said Chris, rather less enthusiastically.

'Look how beautiful it is!' said Sooz.

The Dark Lord turned, and smiled at her. 'Isn't he magnificent?' he said. He leant down and chucked her under the chin again with a taloned finger. As he turned to welcome the dragon, Sooz glared at his back. She really wished he wouldn't do that with his finger, it felt so…patronizing.

The dragon perched on a nearby heap of shattered rock, looking regal and quite magnificent.

'Welcome, Abrakulax, King of the Dragons,' said the Dark Lord Dirk imperiously. 'Bear me and my companions to the Iron Tower with all haste, and all your ancient obligations to me will be discharged!'

Abrakulax looked over at the two children as if to say, 'These two humans are your companions? Really?'

The Dark Lord gestured with a taloned hand. 'Strange times, strange company,' he said.

The dragon seemed to shrug. Then it came down and lay before them, offering up its great neck for them to climb up on. The Dark Lord leaped easily onto the dragon's back. Abrakulax looked at Chris and Sooz, its huge, amber eyes gazing at them curiously.

'We're going to ride this thing?' said an astonished Christopher. The Dragon shifted a little, snorting flames.

'Indeed we are, Christopher, and do not call him a thing! He can understand every word you say. Remember, he is the King of the Dragons and should be treated with all due respect. You do not wish to anger him, believe me!'

'I've always wanted to ride on a dragon!' said

Sooz, stepping forward and stroking the great beast on the nose. 'Thank you, Abrakulax!' she said. The dragon looked at her placidly out of one eye. It began to make a strange noise, as if it were purring.

Sooz climbed up behind the Dark One. 'Come on then, Chris, it'll be fun!' she said.

'Fun? Riiight… What's to stop us falling off, for a start?' he said.

'You must hold onto the spines as tightly as you can,' said the Dark Lord Dirk. 'Now come on, Christopher, we haven't got all day. We must get to the Tower before sunrise!'

Christopher shook his head. 'This is crazy,' he said under his breath, as he clambered up the glistening black scales of the enormous dragon.

When they were ready, the Dark Lord shouted, 'Up, Lord of the Dragons, up and away!' Abrakulax began to run, building up speed, before he leapt into the air, great wings beating like giant black sails, buffeting the air with unimaginable force. The mighty beast powered upward, climbing high into the sky.

Down below, Christopher and Sooz could see the land falling away beneath them. The little town of

Magus Falls looked like a model village, and just beyond it, the White Tower gleamed like a shaft of light. The Dark Lord shook his fist at it and bellowed exultantly. 'I have returned! And now I shall exact my vengeance! Prepare to suffer, Hasdruban, you crack-brained meddler! *Mwah, hah, hah!!!*'

Then they streaked away through the clouds. Howling winds battered them, threatening to pluck them from their fragile perches and send them hurtling to their doom. They shivered in the freezing wind and clung onto the spiny ridges of horn along the dragon's back. Down below they could see a great lake, and then farmlands and villages, which gave way to rolling moorland, with scattered woods and forests. And then, after some time freezing in the high winds of the upper skies, they came to a bare, blasted heath, the Plains of Desolation. Beyond that, in the distance, they could see a dark tower pointing up at them like a finger of gnarled black iron.

'Down, your Dragon Majesty, down!' screamed the Dark Lord exultantly. 'To the Iron Tower of Despair!'

Return of the Dark Lord

As they descended, they could make out more detail below – a small army had surrounded the Tower. Colourful banners and flags fluttered amidst the neatly ordered rows of tents and improvised buildings where the soldiers were camped.

'Hasdruban's army of Paladins and Spearmen,' said Sooz in the Dark Lord's ear as the wind whistled past them.

The Dark Lord nodded. 'Yes, I see them. Elves too, by the look of it. Not many though. We shall drive them off.'

Sooz frowned. 'How?' she said.

'Abrakulax can slay many with his fiery breath, and I shall use the ravening power of the Ring to kill many more. They'll be running for their lives in seconds!!' said the Dark One with obvious relish.

'No!' said Sooz.

The Dark Lord Dirk turned and stared at her. 'No? What do you mean, no?'

'We don't have to kill them,' said Sooz desperately. 'You could blast the ground near them, burn their tents with dragon breath, they'll soon get the message and flee anyway. After all, you're really tough and strong and that. They're scared of you already!'

'Hah, true, but where's the fun in that? What's the point?' said the Dark Lord.

'Please, Dirk. I mean the Great Dirk, my Lord, my Dark Lord, please, just for me? Will you spare them, please?' said Sooz imploringly.

The Dark Lord Dirk frowned. 'Spare them? Well...' He looked down, rubbing his chin. Then he turned to look at Sooz. For a moment his face took on a look of feral bloodlust, but then the madness in his eyes faded.

'Oh all right, just for you, my little vampire,' he said. With that, he turned and whispered into Abrakulax's ear. The dragon banked, swooping down over the besieging army's camp. Out from his mouth came a great roaring blast of flame, setting light to tents, wooden towers and carts and storage pens.

Hundreds of figures boiled out of the tents like little ants, running and screaming in terror. The Dark Lord unleashed powerful bolts of energy from his Ring, blowing holes in the earth, and knocking people to the ground. The dragon and its dark rider flew back and forth, dealing out destruction, plunging the encampment into chaos.

The Dark Lord began to laugh maniacally – he was having fun. Christopher and Sooz clung on behind, trying not to fall off as the dragon banked and wheeled. The army below began to break and run, streaming away westwards in a chaotic riot of terrified men. Sooz grinned happily – they'd been driven off and with hardly anyone at all getting hurt, as far as she could see – just like the last time she had liberated the Tower.

The Dark One whispered again in the dragon's ear, and it swooped down towards the Iron Tower. As they drew near, the gargoyle heads above the Gates of Doom looked up.

'Is that the Dark Lord himself?' said one of the heads.

'Yeah! On the back of the Dragon King,' rasped another.

'Now there's something you don't see every day,' said the first.

Abrakulax thudded into the ground in front of the gates, almost throwing Chris and Sooz off in the process. Gingerly they slid off its back, sore and tender from their rollercoaster ride through the sky.

'Thank you, beautiful dragon,' whispered Sooz. The dragon bowed its regal head to her.

'The Dark Lord has returned from exile! All hail the Dark Lord!' shrieked the gargoyle heads.

Lord Dirk stepped down from the back of the dragon. 'Hmm, I see you sorted the paint job out, Sooz. Well done,' he said. He leaned down to chuck her under the chin again, but she turned away, scowling.

The Dark Lord put his hands on his hips. 'Don't you get all huffy with me, little girl,' he said. But then the Dragon King gave a great roar. Dirk turned to the dragon. 'My thanks, Abrakulax, you have served me well. You are free!' he said regally. The Dragon King gave another roar and then took to the skies.

And then the Gates of Doom opened.

'All hail the Dark Lord,' screamed the gargoyles.

'Oh be quiet,' said the Dark Lord Dirk as he

He's just a big pussycat really. No, honest, he is.

strode towards the gate.

'Yes, my Lord,' said one of the heads.

'We'll be quiet,' said another. 'I promise.'

The Dark One stopped and put his horned head in his hands. 'By the Nether Gods, I'd forgotten how irritating you were!'

Then some figures emerged from the Tower.

'Gargon!' said the Dark Lord, smiling. Dirk the Dark Lord frowned, thinking to himself. Smiling? What's the matter with me? I'm smiling. At Gargon, of all people!

Gargon stepped forward. Behind him were Agrash, and Skabber. Agrash was half cowering behind Gargon's thick legs. Behind them, stood Rufino the Paladin. He looked over at Sooz, and waved. Sooz nodded and waved back. Then he looked up at the Dark Lord, concern written all over his face.

Gargon, too, looked at Sooz. He nodded, and smiled his sulphurous smile. Then he looked up at the Dark Lord, somewhat fearfully, and dropped to one knee. Sooz had never seen Gargon scared before. Ever. That worried her.

'Welcome, Master, to your realm! We have

guarded it as best we could during your exile!'

The Dark Lord nodded. 'And who is this?' he said, pointing at Rufino.

Gargon looked around shiftily for a moment. 'Ah…that is Rufino. An ally.'

'A friend,' said Skabber Stormfart.

'An ally? A friend? Orcs don't have friends, you deluded simpleton!'

Skabber blinked, totally tongue-tied in the face of the Dark Lord's anger.

Then the Dark Lord spoke silkily, like the calm before a storm. 'And we ally with Paladins now, do we?'

Gargon could read these signs. Trouble was coming.

'It was your betrothed, Master!' said Gargon, quickly. 'Queen Sooz, she make peace, Lord! We only do what the Dark Mistress tell us, my Lord!'

'She spoke with your voice, had your Ring, your Imperial Darkness,' piped up Agrash from behind Gargon's legs. 'She made us ally with the Paladin!'

Sooz frowned. Talk about dropping her in it – straight off too, without even thinking about it! Some friends.

'It was the right thing to do,' said Sooz. 'We needed time to regroup.'

'That is correct, your Mightiness,' said Agrash, finding a bit of backbone at last. 'In fact, the Dark Lady took the Tower with only a handful of Goblins! We were terribly weak. We had to buy time. She did well!'

That made Sooz feel a little better. But then Rufino stepped forward. 'They are right, Dark One! I am the Paladin Rufino of the Order of the Unicorn. I have sworn to serve Queen Sooz, for she has taught us a new way to live, a way of peace and harmony. You should continue with this policy, for…'

'Silence!' said the Dark Lord, raising a taloned hand. 'Take him to the Dungeons of Doom. I will interrogate him later.'

Rufino blinked in shock. Gargon shuffled his feet. Skabber Stormfart looked around uncomfortably.

'TAKE HIM TO THE DUNGEONS, NOW!!!' shrieked the Dark Lord at the top of his voice. 'OR BY THE NINE HELLS I WILL EVISCERATE HIM WITH THE CLAW OF RIPPING DEATH! AND ANYONE ELSE WHO DOESN'T JUMP TO IT RIGHT NOW!'

Gargon blinked. He gestured with a hand. 'Take him to the Dungeons, Skabber.'

Rufino frowned and reached for his sword.

The Dark Lord Dirk smiled at that. 'Go on,' he said. 'Try it, you puny human! I'd love to peel the flesh from your bones, I really would!' he said.

'Noo!' said Sooz. 'Just go Rufino. Go, or he'll kill you!'

Rufino's eyes flicked over to look at Sooz, and then back to the Dark Lord. His hand fell away from his weapon. Skabber took him by the arm. 'Sorry 'bout this, old son,' he said.

Rufino looked around angrily. Then he sighed resignedly. 'So be it. For your sake, my Queen,' he said, nodding at Sooz. Skabber led him away to the Dungeons.

'Oooo, my Queeeen,' said the Dark Lord putting on a mocking Dirk-the-kid-like voice. 'Pah! I am the ruler here!'

With Rufino gone, the Dark Lord relaxed a little. 'Good, right, that's that out of the way,' he said. 'And now, one more thing. This ridiculous girl-child is not my betrothed or any such nonsense, right? Got that through your bonehead skulls? I mean really, when was the last time I had a girlfriend even? It's absurd! If I did, it wouldn't be some sappy human anyway, it'd be... Ah... I don't know... Well, anyway, just forget it, guys, OK?'

Gargon and Agrash stared up at the Dark Lord. Guys? Did he just say 'guys'?

Sooz, though, looked crestfallen. Ridiculous girl-child? she thought to herself. Is that what he really thought of her? That hurt, it really did, even though the whole marriage thing was obviously absurd – especially now.

Then she frowned, and a determined look came over her face. 'Promise me you won't mistreat him or torture him!' said Sooz.

Agrash put his hand over his mouth in shock. Nobody spoke to the Dark Lord like that! Gargon stared at Sooz, making a face to attract her attention. She glanced over at him.

'No,' he mouthed, shaking his head from side to side theatrically and gesturing with his arms.

'What? What did you say?' said the Dark Lord with rising anger.

'Don't hurt him. Don't hurt Rufino. He's my friend. If you do, I won't speak to you ever again!' said Sooz.

The Dark One gaped at her for a moment, as if he couldn't believe what he was hearing. But then, instead of blasting her with some kind of spell like he would have in the old days, he crossed his powerful arms, and looked her up and down. 'You won't talk to me! Is that it? Hah! Do I look bothered, little girl, do I?' he said.

'I mean it! You won't be my friend any more and I won't talk to you ever again, not EVER!' said Sooz, stamping her foot.

Chris watched this exchange with fascination. Sure, Dirk was twelve feet tall and a Dark Lord, but it could just as easily have been in the school playground back home on Earth, and that gave them some hope.

The Dark Lord blinked his sideways blink. He was thinking about what life would be like if Sooz never spoke to him again. 'Well… Well… OK then, as it's you, my little vampire. I promise not to hurt him. There – are you satisfied?'

Sooz nodded. 'Yeah, OK, that's cool.'

'I'm not letting him out though! He stays locked up! Got it?' said the Dark Lord Dirk.

Sooz shrugged a 'whatever' shrug.

Agrash and Gargon exchanged looks that said 'What's going on?' The Dark Lord was back, that was for sure and he was mostly behaving like himself i.e. like a terrifying dictatorial bullying monster – but something was different. He had changed somehow. He may not be betrothed to the Moon Queen, but there was clearly some bond between them. It was all very odd.

Gargon stood up. 'Your Imperial Darkness?' he said.

'Yes, Gargon,' said the Dark Lord Dirk.

'We have several hundred Orcs, Goblins and Humans... Err several hundred of our people inside who have not eaten properly for days. Can you open the storerooms for them?'

'Oh right, yes, of course!' said the Dark Lord. 'In we go! I can't wait to sit once more on the Throne of Skulls anyway!'

In the Court of the Dark Lord

Dirk the Dark Lord sat on his Throne of Skulls, arms resting on either side, hooves firmly planted on the platform. Dark light shone up at him, haloing him in majestic shadows. Where Sooz had looked beautiful, mysterious and queenly, Dirk looked terrifying, powerful, and dangerous.

The skulls on the Throne were constantly moaning – a low, barely audible moan as if the weight of the Dark Lord itself somehow pained them.

At his feet, sitting on the throne's dais, were Sooz and Chris. Before them, stood Gargon, Skabber and Agrash.

Chris was dressed in the uniform of an elite Goblin Guard, black leather armour with the Seal of the Dark Lord emblazoned on his chest and a

Goblin chopper at his side – basically a kind of long bladed meat cleaver. It didn't look right on him, the weapon and the armour, but he had been given the titles The Mouth of the Great Dirk and Commander of the Goblin Guard, and that was his uniform.

Sooz, though, had been allowed a whole new outfit from the magic wardrobe and she was wearing a new dress with lots of lovely black lace, inlaid with threads of Moonsilver. Dirk had 'officially' confirmed her title as the Moon Queen, and Our Lady of the Dark. Her own Seal was wrought in Moonsilver on her dress, and she had a long white scarf patterned with little versions of her Seal too. She looked majestic. She still had her Goth boots on though, and her AngelBile bag. Dirk's human arm had been taken out of the bag, and pickled. Then they'd hung it in a glass cabinet on the wall in the Dark Lord's trophy room as a reminder of the time he had been cursed to wear the body of a human boy-child. It all added to the mythology and legend of his never-ending struggle with the White Wizard.

Dirk the Dark Lord gestured at Agrash. The Goblin stepped forward and spoke loudly. 'All

Hail the Great Dirk, the Dark Lord, Master of the Legions of Dread, the World Burner, the Dark One, Master of the Nine Hells and…'

'Yes, yes, just get on with it, Agrash,' said the Dark Lord. Normally he liked to listen to his titles but today he was eager to get on with things.

Agrash continued. 'His Imperial Darkness will issue an edict! Listen, all ye gathered here, and obey or be forever consigned to the Dungeons of Doom!' he said portentously.

The Dark Lord Dirk leant forward. 'Right,' he said. 'I'm going to create a unit of Goblin Battle Balloons, just like we discussed at that absurdly twee church fête, Christopher. You remember, don't you?'

'Right…' said Chris, unsure as to where this was going.

Agrash raised a snotty eyebrow. 'Balloons? What are balloons?' he muttered under his breath.

'To this end,' continued the Dark Lord, 'I have drawn up some blueprints for the making of a Dirigible Battle Balloon, to be crewed by a team of ten Goblin Bombardiers, powered by magically enhanced gas! Here, Agrash, I'm putting you in charge of construction.'

He handed to Chris, Agrash and Sooz several sheets of paper upon which were carefully drawn various cutaways and plans for the building of a Goblin Battle Balloon.

'Wow, cool!' said Chris.

'I know!' said the Dark Lord. 'Agrash, I want fifty of them ready in two weeks' time for an assault on Gam, the City of Men. We'll be using exploding rock grenades – or Cakes of Doom, as I call them. Hah, hah, hah! Geddit, Christopher?'

Christopher smiled up at the Dark Lord, trying to laugh, but inside he found the whole idea rather disturbing. He glanced over at Sooz. She looked just as worried. After all, Dirk was basically talking about bombing a city. And that meant people – humans – getting killed. And all because of his neighbour's rock cakes and a hot air balloon.

Agrash frowned too, though his concerns were of a different order. 'Two weeks? It's not possible, Sire, we don't have the workers… I mean, it would take…' he said.

'I know, I know. That's why we're going to re-open the Slave Pits. All those annoying humans wandering about having fun in that absurdly named town you built – Soozville, was it? Well, it's over. Round 'em up and put 'em in the Pits. They'll be working round the clock on my Balloons, and don't spare the lash!' said the Dark One.

'What?' said Sooz. 'You can't do that! I promised them there would be no more slaves, no more overseers and whips and that. It's cruel! It's wrong! No, worse than that, it's…it's evil!'

The Dark Lord raised his eyes. 'Duhhh! Hello! Am I not the Lord of Darkness? Anyway, what do you think we should do, send Hasdruban some flowers?'

'Well, yes actually, in a way. We should be making peace! Living together in harmony and…' said Sooz, but the Dark Lord Dirk wasn't listening. He was looking away, distracted.

'Hmm, actually, sending him some flowers might not be such a bad idea,' he said, thinking out loud. 'Exploding flowers, of course…'

'Don't do this, Dirk, please don't!' said Sooz, raising her voice.

The Dark Lord frowned and glared at Sooz. 'I've told you, you can't call me Dirk. Either the Great

Hanging out with the gang

Dirk or one of my other titles. The boy Dirk is gone.'

Sooz put her hands on her hips. 'I don't care! You shouldn't have slaves, it's wrong, and that's that!'

'Oh, give it a rest, Sooz,' said the Dark Lord, waving a taloned hand dismissively. 'I've issued the edict, and that's that.'

He turned to Agrash. 'What are you doing, standing there, you snivelling greenie! Get on with it! And take Skabber with you, you'll need his Orcs to round up the humans.'

'Yes, your Imperial Darkness, right away!' a frightened Agrash said. He glanced at Sooz, as if to say 'Sorry, there's nothing I can do' before he and Skabber left to carry out the Dark Lord's orders.

Sooz folded her arms and screwed her face up. 'I'm not going to let you get away with this,' she said, stamping her foot.

'Oh really, and what are you going to do, little girl, put me in detention?' said the Dark Lord. Then he leaned back in his throne and laughed out loud at the thought of it. 'Detention! Hah, hah!'

Sooz shook her head in disgust. 'Come on, Chris, I've had enough of this,' she said, and began walking away. Chris turned to follow her.

The Dark Lord made a face. 'Eeeuuuw, grumpy Sooz!' he said, just as if he were back in the playground on Earth. Sooz ignored him, nose in the air, stomping her way out of the Hall of Gloom.

The Dark Lord shrugged. '*Bah*, go! I don't care!' he said. 'As for you Christopher…'

The Dark Lord Dirk signalled and several Goblin Guards stepped forward to block Christopher's exit. He turned to the Dark Lord. 'What? What is it?' said a worried Chris. Behind him, a determined looking Sooz hurried on, throwing a resentful glance behind her.

The Dark Lord grinned at Chris. 'I want to show you something, something fun!'

'Fun? What do you mean, fun?' said Chris.

'Come with me! You're going to love it my old friend, really you are!' said the Dark Lord, as he got down from his Throne. He walked over to Chris, laid a massive hand on his shoulder and led him away, like two friends leaving school to go home and hang out together. Except that one of them was tall, dark – really dark – and very, very dangerous.

Darklands: The Game

Chris stood in astonished wonder at what he saw before him. Dirk the Dark Lord had led him out of the Tower and down to a large open space behind it. He had covered this field in hexagon shaped tiles that seemed to be carved from wood and then enchanted in some way. Each tile had various pieces of terrain modelled upon it, lifelike but smaller than real life. There was a little range of mountains, a river, forests, marshes and so on. And also model towns, cities and forts. Each model had been magically enhanced in some way. Leaves on trees rustled, towns were inhabited with tiny mannequin people, rivers flowed, small ships sailed upon their waters, little clouds passed over tiles and rained on them, and suchlike.

The Dark Lord waved his hand. 'Remember that game we used to play on your computer back on

Earth,' he said. '*Fantasy Wars* it was called, wasn't it?'

'Oh yeah, the one you always used to win,' said an awed Chris.

'Yes, indeed. Well, I have recreated it, but instead of computers we can play it in the real world. I've sort of modelled it on the Darklands. See there – my Iron Tower. And at the other end, the White Tower. See?' He pointed to the far end of the field where Chris could see a model of the White Tower, but where the great telescope observatory rested on the top of the real Tower, on this little model there was a comfortable looking chair.

'That's where you sit,' said Dirk the Dark Lord. 'You'll be playing white of course, and I'll be black.'

Chris shook his head. 'Wow, Dirk, this is great! And these tiles can be moved around, so we can play on different boards over and over again, right?'

'Of course,' said a pleased looking Dark Lord. He hadn't even noticed that Chris had called him Dirk.

'What about the playing pieces, what do we use for those?' asked Christopher.

'Aha, you'll love this even more,' said the Dark Lord and he clapped his hands together, creating a loud booming sound.

Several figures marched out of the tower, and began to approach the board to take up various positions. Some were Orcs, representing orcish brigades, others were Goblins with bows and javelins. Other Orcs and Goblins were dressed as human Paladins or archers, or knights or light cavalry. The horsemen straddled fake wooden hobby horses, or for the orcish cavalry, fake looking wooden wolves. Except for the heads. These were enchanted so that the horses neighed and tossed their heads, whilst the wolves growled and bared their teeth.

Chris was amazed. 'Real live playing pieces, how cool is that!' But then he frowned. 'But why use Orcs dressed as humans? Why not real humans?'

The Dark Lord hesitated. 'Well, you know. The humans are…otherwise engaged as it were,' he said.

Chris looked up at him. 'You shouldn't have done that, Dirk, putting them in the Slave Pits like that. It's wrong.'

'Well, whatever, let's just play for now, OK?' said Dirk the Dark Lord, striding over to the model of the Iron Tower. 'The rules are exactly the same as for *Fantasy Wars*, so you shouldn't have any trouble learning the ropes. All you have to do is give orders to your units, and they'll go where you want 'em to.'

Chris couldn't help himself – it did look fantastic and so, so cool! A real-life game with real life Goblins and Orcs and everything. He strode over to his position. Maybe this time he could beat Dirk for once, though that was unlikely. Still, it was going to be fun trying. He reached the model of the White Tower and sat upon it. Next to him he found a kind of wooden megaphone – he was going to need it for shouting orders. Dirk the Dark Lord didn't though, his voice was booming and commanding anyway.

'So, you get the first move, Christopher! Off you go!'

Chris grinned as he ordered a burly Orc dressed as a Paladin of the Order of the Whiteshields forwards. The Orc grinned a feral grin and set off – his wooden horse floating over the terrain a bit like a witch's broom. He tried to pass over a small river, but the Dark Lord shouted, 'Hey, you can't do that! You're a Paladin, right? All that armour weighs you down, you can't move that far!'

The Orc paused in mid-travel. 'Oh, sorry, my

Dark Master, sorry,' he said, a worried look on his face.

The Dark Lord raised his eyes. 'You're supposed to be a Paladin, you don't call me Master, you have to say things like "Die, you hell-spawned fiend!" or "I have sworn an oath to hunt down evil wherever I find it – and I have found it right here, you black hearted villain – prepare to be annihilated!" and suchlike.'

The Orc blinked in confusion – there was no way he was going to risk talking to the Dark Lord like that! Gingerly he backed his floating horse up a tile. Then he dismounted, planting his feet on what looked like a bush. There was a yelp of pain. The Orc stepped back in surprise. He had trodden on a little Goblin hidden beneath some foliage on a tile representing a small wood.

'*Bah*, you lucky dog,' said the Dark Lord. 'You uncovered one of my Goblin Light Infantry Units hiding in ambush. They'll have no chance against Paladins! A thousand curses!'

'Great! Destroy them, my Paladins,' said Chris, getting into the spirit of the game. The Paladin Orc raised his sword in the air – a real sword! The little

Goblin cowered down, and whimpered, one arm raised feebly in the air.

'Whoa!' said Chris. 'Hold on there a mo. It's just a game, right, we can't really kill people, surely?'

'What, why not?' said the Dark Lord. 'That's half the fun!'

Chris got up, outraged. 'No way, I'm not playing like that. It's sick,' he shouted.

The Dark Lord made a face. 'Yeah, yeah, I know, dude, I was just joking, really. Don't worry, no one's going to actually die, all right?'

Chris frowned at him suspiciously.

'No, really, I'm serious,' said the Dark Lord. 'No one's going to die – it'd be a waste of good soldiers, for a start! Better they die on the real field of battle than on this gaming table.'

'All right then,' said Chris mollified, as he sat back down.

'I knew you'd make a fuss if we tried to do it properly,' said the Dark Lord, mischievously, a Dirk-like grin on his massive face.

Chris sensed the Dirkness in that smile, and he laughed too, realizing the Dark Lord really was joking. He got back into his role, and said, 'You are the Evil One, and I shall destroy you and all your works. Proceed my Paladin!'

Dirk put his head back and laughed loudly. 'That's it, Christopher, that's it!'

The Orc Paladin looked back and forth between the two, a confused expression on his rough features. The Dark Lord nodded at him. 'Get on with it, you fool,' he said.

'Oh yes, my Dark Master, of course,' muttered the Orc.

'No, no, you're supposed to be… Oh, never mind,' said the Dark One.

The Orc brought down his sword lightly on the Goblin's head, who then pretended to die most horribly, which made Christopher and the Dark Lord laugh even more. It was as if they were in Christopher's room back home, playing together on his computer. And so it went for a while until a little Goblin messenger rushed up to the model of the Iron Tower.

'Well, what is it?' said the Dark Lord, annoyed at the interruption. He was just planning an assault on the model of Gam, the City of Men, with an elite unit of orcish Storm Troopers.

The little Goblin blinked up at the Dark Lord, terrified. The Dark Lord raised his eyes. 'Oh, for evil's sake, I'm not going to eat you, what is it?'

The Goblin handed the Dark One a piece of paper. 'A message, your Imperial Majesty. From Og the Torturer,' squeaked the Goblin.

'Og, Overseer of the Slave Pits? What does he want?' muttered the Dark Lord, snatching the note from the Goblin's hand.

He quickly read it – and scowled. Then he stood up, raised his face to the darkening sky and howled a howl of rage. Without another word, he strode off towards the Iron Tower.

Chris leapt to his feet and ran after him. 'What, what is it, Dirk?' he said, breathlessly. He'd had to run pretty fast to catch up with the Dark Lord.

'It's your annoying little girlfriend, Sooz – and don't call me Dirk!' said the Dark Lord.

'Oh come on, she's not my girlfriend and you know it. Anyway, what's she done?' retorted Christopher.

The Dark Lord narrowed his eyes. 'She has interfered. Meddled! There's nothing I hate more than do-gooding meddlers! I'm going to...to...' As

Chill, Dark Lord, chill!

he said this he balled his taloned hands into fists and began to growl incoherently.

'Hold on,' said Christopher, putting a hand on the Dark Lord's arm. 'You need to calm down before you do anything rash!'

The Dark Lord stopped, and glared down at Christopher. His yellow eyes gleamed with rage. He leant his head down and hissed threateningly into Chris's face. 'You dare lay your hand on…'

Chris flinched, but then the Dark Lord blinked his weird reptilian blink.

'Just pause for a moment, think it through, take a deep breath or two,' said Chris, and he took the Dark Lord's great hands in his, and looked up into his face.

A calmness seemed to wash over Dirk.

'No, you're right, Christopher, quite right. Sooz must be handled…delicately,' he said.

In for a Penny,
In for a Pound

The Dark Lord gritted his teeth, trying to contain his anger. 'So, you just let them go, eh, just like that?'

'Yes, I did. I sent them home, and closed down the Slave Pits. I did it. It was me,' said Sooz, chin raised defiantly, hands on her hips.

'And what, the guards just let you? Are they mutinous dogs too?' said the Dark Lord.

'Oh no, no,' said Sooz. 'I ordered them to do it, and so they did.'

The Dark Lord frowned in puzzlement. 'You… ordered them?'

'Yes,' said Sooz. 'Have you forgotten that I was in charge here, before you returned? I saved most of them. They loved me, they chanted my name and called me their Moon Queen and everything!'

The Dark Lord glared at her. '*Bah*, love!' he said contemptuously.

'You agreed to it too, you told them all that I was the Moon Queen. It's not their fault, leave them out of it!'

The Dark Lord folded his arms. 'Well, I suppose so. Which means it's all your fault.'

The Dark Lord towered over Sooz. A moment of silence followed as they stared at each other, each uncertain about what to do or say next. Christopher stood to the side, trying to think of a way to mediate between them.

They were in Sooz's personal chambers. The Dark Lord had reclaimed his Inner Sanctum for himself, but he'd given Sooz an extensive suite of rooms of her own which they had renamed the Moon Wing. She'd had a lot of fun gothing it up. (She'd had her bedroom made up as an almost exact replica of her room back home.)

The Dark Lord narrowed his eyes. 'I'm going to put them back to work in the Pits. I need those slaves to make my Battle Balloons, and those rock grenades, the Cakes of Doom!'

'You can't make them work like that. You can't

have slaves, it's wrong!' said Sooz.

'Don't tell me what I can and can't do, little girl!' said the Dark Lord, his features contorting with anger.

'Why not? What are you going to do, lock me up? Kill me?' she said.

The Dark Lord angrily raised a taloned fist.

'I've got an idea,' piped up Chris.

'What?!' said the Dark Lord and Sooz angrily at the same time. They turned to Chris.

'Umm...the problem's really slavery, isn't it, Sooz? That's what you object to?'

'Well, yes, mostly that – plus I promised there'd be no more of it. But also there's the war stuff, and...'

'Yeah, but slavery – that's why you started paying people with fair wages and that.'

'Yes,' said Sooz. 'What about it?'

'Well, what if you did the same, Dirk – started to pay them to build your stuff? And with decent hours, and if you want 'em to work harder, you could pay overtime, like they do on Earth. It really works – people work better if they're paid!'

The Dark Lord shook his head. 'Don't be ridiculous, Christopher. Why should I hire humans when I can enslave them? And overtime, hah! You must be joking!'

'But what if you minted your own coins to pay them with?' said Christopher.

'What do you mean?' said the Dark Lord.

'You know, with your face on them. You could put your Seal on one side, and then your face on the other.'

The Dark Lord looked thoughtful for a moment. 'My face…' he said. 'Like the Queen of England back on Earth…'

'Yeah,' said Chris, encouraged to see he was having some effect. 'And it could say stuff, like "Year of Our Dark Lord blah", or "All Hail the Great Dirk the Marvellous", or "In the Name of his Imperial Darkness", and so on!'

'Yeah, yeah,' nodded the Dark Lord. 'I like it!'

'And you can have pennies and shillings and pounds or whatever you want – like gold pieces, or groats, or something more Darklandsy!' continued Chris.

'Or "Dirks", you could call the currency "Dirks",' added Sooz. She turned to Chris, grinning. 'Brilliant, Chris,' she mouthed silently.

Chris beamed from ear to ear.

The Dark Lord went on. 'Dirks! Yes, perfect. I could have Copper Dirks, Silver Dirks and Gold Dirks – I love it!'

'And there could be ten Copper Dirks to a Silver Dirk, ten Silvers to a…' said Chris.

'No wait,' said the Dark Lord. 'We can't have Copper Dirks, and Silver Dirks, there can only be Gold Dirks!'

'OK, so what do we call the others?' said Chris, egging him on.

The Dark Lord paused. 'Hmm, Copper Christophers, and Silver Soozes. How does that sound?'

Chris frowned. 'Why do I have to be copper?' he said.

'Hah, hah! 'Cause you're Christopher, why else?' said the Dark Lord.

'Well, OK, if I get my head on the coin,' said Chris.

'What? No, of course not! Every coin will have my head, they'll just be called Christophers and Soozes, that's all,' said the Dark Lord.

'So,' said Sooz. 'Does that mean no more slaves?'

The Dark Lord raised his eyes. 'Yes, yes, all right

then, no more slaves.'

'You'll pay them properly, with decent working conditions and overtime and everything?' she said.

The Dark Lord narrowed his eyes. 'You're pushing it Sooz…'

'It's the fastest way to get your coins into circulation, so everyone is using them!' interrupted Chris quickly. 'You could design them yourself, of course, get the right profile of your head and that, so you look your best!'

The Dark Lord paused. And then nodded grudgingly. 'True, true, gets them into circulation… They'll be all over the place, won't they? Hmm… Oh, all right, you can have this one Sooz, we'll do it your way!' With that he turned on a hoofed heel and strode out the door, calling out as he did so: 'Agrash! Agrash, where are you? We've got work… You've got work to do!'

Chris turned to Sooz and let out a sigh of relief. 'Wow, that was close!' he said.

'I guess,' said Sooz, 'but we still have a problem.'

'What?' said Chris.

'The Battle Balloons,' said Sooz.

'What about them?' said Chris.

'He's still going to build them, and then he'll use them to kill lots of people. I can't allow that,' she said forcefully.

'You can't allow… Come on, Sooz, we've been lucky so far. There's still some Dirk in there but if we keep pushing this, he's going to flip. And then there's no telling what he'll do.'

'I don't care! He can't start a war like this, it's crazy! And we're not just talking about the people of Gam or whatever. Hasdruban will hit back, and there'll be battles and lots of our people will die too. My people, that is,' said Sooz passionately.

'Your people? But Sooz, you're a girl from…'

'Yes, Christopher. My people,' said Sooz, interrupting. 'I have to stop him, and you're going to help me.'

Christopher stared at her for a moment as if she were mad. Then he put his face in his hands and said, 'Oh no, we're going to get into so much trouble!'

Bad Judgement Day

All was quiet. The Dark Lord was sitting on the Throne of Skulls, chin in one hand, and he was gazing at Sooz, thinking. Sooz, aware he was staring at her, stood there uncomfortably, looking at the floor. The atmosphere generally was not good. Agrash was getting stressed and his nose began to dribble. As it dripped, snot splashed to the floor where it vaporised with a hiss. Desperately, he tried to stop the flow, terrified he might anger the Dark One.

The Dark Lord was calm now, but earlier he had been striding up and down the Great Hall shouting and screaming like a two-year-old.

It was Christopher and Sooz, you see. After weeks of work, the Dark One had amassed a force of Battle Balloons, along with an arsenal of the Cakes of Doom, but Christopher and Sooz… Well, they'd let them go. Untethered them. Let them float off into the skies on their own to be lost forever, crewless and unmanned, but full of all the bombs he'd had made. Now he had no balloons and no bombs. He'd have to start all over again. And that made him angry – very angry.

So he'd got most of the anger out of his system before bringing Sooz and Chris before him. But now they were here.

'What to do with you,' said the Dark Lord. 'I mean, really it's mutiny, isn't it, what you did? I mean, letting all the balloons go up into the air like that… What a waste. You deliberately did it to mess up my plans! How could you?' He shook his horned head ruefully. 'I really ought to punish you both. Harshly.'

'We saved lives and stopped a pointless war, that's all,' said Sooz, gazing at the floor.

'*Bah*, you have delayed the war, that is all,' said Dirk the Dark Lord.

Sooz looked up at him. 'There's no need for war, you can make peace. Everyone can live together!'

The Dark One made a face. 'Don't be ridiculous! There will be war, and with Earth technology I will be victorious. The only thing stopping me is you and Chris. And I have to do something about that. I don't want to hurt you, really I don't, but something has to change. So…'

Sooz gave him a sideways glance.

He stared at her, blinking strangely, stroking his chin in thought. 'I could arrange for you to become a real vampire if you like, Sooz. I have friends, Vampire Lords, in fact. Relatives, actually. They could bite you, transform you. What do you say?'

Sooz's jaw dropped. Become a real vampire? Wow! She had to admit, back home on Earth, she'd dreamed of that sometimes. She was a Goth, after all.

'You could be immortal. Be by my side forever. You'd be truly part of the dark. I could trust you utterly then,' said the Dark Lord.

Sooz frowned. To dream about vampires was one thing. To actually be one was another. And she didn't want to live forever anyway, and certainly not with a twelve foot Lord of Evil.

'But then… Well, I'd have to drink blood. You know, kill people to live, right?' she said.

'Well, yeah! Duhh!' said the Dark Lord. 'You'd

be a vampire, dude, of course you'd drink blood! Anyway, that's half the fun.'

Sooz shook her head. 'I can't do that. Sorry.'

The Dark Lord leaned forward. 'What do you mean? Why not?' he said, annoyed.

'I can't kill people so that I can live, Dirk, I can't. It's wrong!' she said.

The Dark Lord's face creased up in anger. 'Foolish child, the path of mercy leads only to weakness and death! And I've told you, do not address me as "Dirk"!' he said, his voice rising at the end. But then he paused, the anger fading as another thought came to him. He sank back into his throne.

'Well, what if we arranged for you to use donors? You can feed without actually killing anyone you know, if you're that squeamish,' said the Dark Lord.

'No, my Dark Lord, no. I don't want to be a vampire. It's just too…well, not for me,' said Sooz as diplomatically as she could.

'But why not? I don't understand,' said the Dark One.

'Look,' said Christopher, 'she doesn't want to be a vampire, all right? Leave it!'

'What did you say?' said the Dark Lord.

Christopher couldn't take it any more. He jumped to his feet and shouted, 'She doesn't want to be a vampire because she doesn't want to be with you for ever and ever, you crazy tyrant!'

Gargon visibly flinched. Agrash began to back away. The Dark Lord sat there unmoving for a moment, gazing at Christopher. Christopher blinked. Uh oh, that temper of his... He gulped.

Suddenly, the Dark Lord's face became a mask of insensate anger. He grabbed Christopher around the throat and pulled him up to his face, so that Christopher's legs were several feet off the ground. Christopher's eyes bulged and he couldn't breathe. He dangled like a rag doll. Feebly he batted at the Dark Lord's taloned hands but he was only a child, a puny human child. The Dark One reached up with his other hand, as if to crush Christopher's head like a melon.

'Nooo!' shouted Sooz. 'Don't do it, Dirk!'

The Dark Lord looked down at Sooz. Then back at Chris, who was starting to turn blue. His fierce yellow eyes narrowed. He pointed a taloned finger at Chris. And then stabbed it into the side of his face. He ran the razor-sharp talon down the side

Sometimes Dirk could be a real pain in the neck

of Chris's cheek. Blood flowed freely. Christopher squirmed in pain. Then the Dark Lord Dirk blinked.

'It's me, Chris,' gasped Christopher. 'Your friend.'

The Dark Lord frowned.

'*Bah*!' he shouted, tossing Christopher to the ground. 'You are not worth killing!' Chris lay there gasping for breath, trying to staunch the blood running from his cheek.

'How could you, you monster!' said Sooz. She stood there stamping her foot. 'He was your friend. He saved your life, you big, horrible bully!'

The Dark Lord looked away, unable to look her in the eyes. He actually felt... What was it? Ah yes, guilt. How absurd!

Behind Sooz, Christopher began to cry. Agrash ran forward to offer his handkerchief. Christopher looked at it in disgust and waved the Goblin away.

'You should say you're sorry,' shouted Sooz, 'and start behaving yourself!'

Agrash, Gargon and Skabber shifted their feet uncomfortably. It wasn't wise to tell a Dark Lord to behave himself, especially as Christopher had actually got off quite lightly, all things considered.

'Behave myself?' said the Dark Lord, all feelings

of guilt gone. 'BEHAVE MYSELF? I am not some schoolchild, some brainless human boy to be put in detention when they have become inconvenient! I AM THE DARK LORD! I AM THE INCARNATION OF EVIL! I AM THE BURNER OF WORLDS AND IT IS YOU WHO HAS MISBEHAVED, DEFYING ME LIKE THIS!'

As he said this, he rose to his feet, his yellow eyes blazing, his Ring burning with energy, his face livid with a kind of angry madness.

Sooz stepped back, terrified, her arm raised in futile protection. Chris desperately tried to shuffle away, his blood hissing as it dripped on the self-cleaning floor. Gargon, Agrash and Skabber had already moved well back. The Dark Lord raised his arms, and began to mutter the words of an awful spell. Terrible energy began to crackle and flow between his hands. But then he stopped. A kind of sanity washed over his face, a kind of calm.

He put his hands on his hips. 'Gah, perhaps you don't deserve death. But you do deserve detention for what you have done, Darklands style! No more weak-minded mercy and friendship and all that nonsense! Take them away, Gargon, and put them with that idiot Paladin in the Dungeons of Doom.'

Gargon frowned. 'Are you sure, Master?' he said.

Anger flickered across the Dark Lord's face. 'Don't push it, Gargon! Take them to the Dungeons or there will be blood, and it won't be mine, I can assure you!'

Sooz looked up at Gargon. 'Just do it,' she said. 'It's best for everyone.'

Gargon stepped forward. Tenderly, he held Sooz and Chris by the arm. 'Sorry about this, my Lady,' he whispered.

'What are you doing, Gargon, by the Nine Hells?!' said the Dark Lord. 'What is the matter with you people? You've all turned into milksops and weaklings since I've been gone! Skabber, put 'em in irons first. We're doing this properly, just like the old days, got it?'

So it was that Sooz and Chris were led away in manacles to the Dungeons of Doom beneath the Iron Tower of Despair. Behind them, they could hear the Dark Lord Dirk declaiming from the Throne.

'Right, with those millstones around my neck out of the way, we're going to get on with things!

I want the Slave Pits reopened. I want round the clock work shifts – get all those humans back into the Pits, and no more cursed treasury-draining wages! Old skool slavery is back! And get RakRak here, I want messengers sent to the Ash Mountains and the Plains of Blood. Summon the Orcs! All of them! And reopen the Breeding Silos. We need to put together a big army as soon as we can, for we're going to war!'

The Daily Massacre

18th of the Month of the
Dark Moon of Sorrows
Year of our Dark Lord 5321

THE DARK LORD RETURNS

Our great master, his Imperial Majesty, the Dark Lord Dirk the Magnificent, has returned at last to save us!

Our mighty Lord drove off the besieging army of the White Wizard and once again has imposed his wise and benevolent rule upon us all!

Even now, Hasdruban the Meddler will be shaking in his boots! All hail the Dark Lord.

In further news* - the Dark Lord has sentenced those troublemakers and traitors, Sooz the so-called Moon Queen, that milksop hugger-of-skirts, Christopher Purejoie, and the preposterously absurd Paladin, Rufino, to indefinite detention in the Dungeons of Doom.

The Dark Lord is merciful however, and they won't be given over to the Racks of Pain, the Iron Maiden of a Thousand Needles or the Gibbet of Grue. Well, not yet anyway.

As dictated by the Dark Lord Himself to Agrash Snotripper, Editor-in-Chief, The Daily Massacre...

The Dungeons of Doom

Sooz, Christopher and Rufino were sitting on rough stone benches inside a stone prison cell. Quite a large prison cell, but still… A bloody scab marked Chris's cheek. It was going to leave a permanent scar, running from cheekbone to chin. No one was going to believe how he'd got it either! Assuming he ever got to show it to anyone, that is.

The walls of their cell were of rough stone, and the floor of compacted dirt. Beside them was an old wooden tray with a water jug, and a hunk of black bread. At least it wasn't mouldy, and that's about all you could say that was good about it.

The door was of black iron, with three locks. The jailor, an Orc called Grimgrunge, had said they were enchanted locks and that there was no way anyone could get 'em open without the key. Grimgrunge had been quite polite, in fact. He knew Sooz had been ruler here quite recently, and you never know with Dark Lords – she was out of favour now, but could be back in favour tomorrow. It was best to hedge your bets.

On the door of their cell a plaque had been hung. The Dark Lord had written on it himself. It read 'Dungeon Cell Number 13: The Dark Lady Sooz and her toadying lickspittle playmate, Christopher – for Insubordination, Mutiny and Talking Back to the Dark Lord. And the Paladin Rufino for… Well, for being a Paladin'. Christopher had been particularly annoyed that he'd been relegated to 'Sooz's mate' and little else.

The three were talking amongst themselves in low tones. 'Well, I haven't been tortured, which was a surprise, I must say!' Rufino said.

'Yes,' said Chris absently. He was examining one of the crystals that Sooz had in her bag, the Anathema Crystals that she'd found in the Dark Reliquary. 'Sooz insisted.'

'What do you mean?' said Rufino.

'Oh, nothing, it was nothing,' said Sooz, embarrassed.

Chris looked up. 'It wasn't nothing! She made

Dirk promise not to torture you or harm you in any way. He nearly blasted her for it. But then he gave in – it was something to see, a huge Dark Lord giving in to little Sooz! Hah!' said Chris.

Rufino looked over at Sooz. 'Thank you, my Lady. Thank you,' he said. 'You risked much for me. I shall never forget it, never!'

Sooz made a fluttery gesture with her hands, and went red with embarrassment.

Rufino, seized with a feeling of chivalrous gratitude, as was the way with Paladins, dropped to one knee and bowed his head before her. 'I swear to serve you, my Lady, to die for you if needs be!' he said theatrically.

Sooz looked even more embarrassed. Chris raised an eyebrow. 'Cool,' he said under his breath. It wasn't every day a knightly Paladin swore to serve you, after all! He nodded at Sooz encouragingly. Sooz stared back. 'Go on, Sooz, be queenly and that,' he whispered, gesturing towards Rufino.

Rufino glanced over at Chris, and then lowered his eyes once again. Sooz blinked.

'Umm...' She stood up and laid a hand on Rufino's head.

'I… Um, I Sooz…'

'Queen Sooz!' interjected Chris.

'Er, yes, Queen Sooz… I, Queen Sooz of Whiteshields Comprehensive, do…errr, recognize the Paladin Rufino as my…errr…right hand dude! Arise, Sir Rufino!'

Rufino got to his feet. 'Thank you, my lady,' he said. 'I will not fail you!'

'No, I'm sure you won't,' said Chris, a wry smile on his face.

'What's with the crystals anyway, Christopher?' said Sooz, kind of wanting to change the subject.

'Well, when me and Dirk – good Dirk, that is, not bad Dirk, that is not-so-bad-Dirk, I suppose really, as opposed to really-bad-Dirk – were skulking around in the White Tower we found this room with a kind of diorama of the Dark Lord getting banished and turned into a boy by Hasdruban. He used some kind of crystal to do it – looked a bit like one of these. Very much like one of these in fact.'

'Anathema Crystals? Hmm,' said Rufino. 'Interesting. Do we know how to use them?'

'No, we don't,' said Chris. 'But if we did… Well…'

'We could turn him back into a little boy!'

said Sooz excitedly.

'Yup,' said Chris. 'Maybe we could. Get our old Dirk back.'

'That would be better!' said Rufino. 'But how can we find out how to cast the spell?'

'I don't know – short of asking Hasdruban himself, but he's as likely to bang us up as talk to us,' said Chris. 'Or maybe he's got it written down somewhere in his book of spells or his White Library or whatever he'd call it.'

'The Library!' said Sooz, excitedly. 'I don't know about a White Library but I do know the Dark Library is full of stuff, thousands of years of stuff,' said Sooz.

'Perhaps,' said Rufino. 'But how do we get in there?'

'There must be a way. Somehow…' said Sooz. The conversation tailed off as they realized there was no easy way of doing so. They were trapped here in the Dungeons of Doom. Each sank into their own thoughts.

Some time later, Grimgrunge slid open a small panel on their cell door. 'Got a visitor for ya,' he growled. 'Stand back in the corner, away from the doors.'

The trio stood back, as each lock was laboriously opened by the great Iron Keys Grimgrunge kept at his belt. In came Agrash Snotripper.

'Hello, my Queen. And Christopher, Rufino,' said Agrash. In his hands he held a big plate of fine food from the storerooms – a spiced stir-fry, and a bowl of one of Sooz's favourites, Syndalon Lamb Curry, plus some honeyed oatcakes and some chocolate brownies.

Once the chocolate brownies had been made with real chopped up Brownies (a kind of Gnome) but nowadays, it was just regular stuff, the recipe having been brought to the Darklands from Earth by a famous Skirrit chef.

The faces of the imprisoned trio, who'd had little more than black bread and water so far, lit up with delight at the sight and smell of the food.

'Hello Agrash, it's good to see you,' said Sooz.

Agrash grinned and stepped forward. Unfortunately, as he did so, a large droplet of snot was dislodged from his improbably long nose to fall with a splash into the curry.

'Just put it down on the table. We'll eat it later,' said Sooz. Agrash put the plates down.

To change the subject, she said, 'So, what's happening up top?'

'Not good, my Lady. The Dark Lord is amassing another big army. He's started casting the Black Vapours of Gloom to cover the sky in darkness, though that one takes a few weeks. He's going to invade the Commonwealth, but instead of Goblin Battle Balloons, this time he's got some plan for getting inside the White Tower to plant a magical bomb or something so he can take out Hasdruban from the start.'

'How's he going to do that?' said Chris. 'He'll never get in there, not as the Dark Lord! Nor will any of his minions – it's protected against evil and that.'

'I know, that's why I've come to tell you. He wants you to do it, Christopher.'

'Me? Why would I do that? Especially after what he's done to us!'

'Well,' said Agrash. He glanced over at Sooz. 'That's why I came… He's… He says…'

'Yes, yes, spit it out, Agrash, we can take it,' said Sooz.

'Well…he says he's going to make Chris do it.

If you don't, he'll take it out on Sooz. Torture her or something. He's ordered up a special rack to be made for her and everything.'

Sooz's jaw dropped.

'That evil swine!' said Rufino.

'Wow,' said Chris. 'That's really twisted.'

'He wouldn't really do it though, would he?' said Sooz, visibly upset.

Agrash shrugged. 'Maybe, yes. He's falling back into his old ways more and more,' he said. 'It wouldn't surprise me. Though he did say he'd get someone else to do the actual torturing, if that's any consolation. One of the Orcs probably. Some of them are quite nasty, you know.'

Sooz was ashen-faced.

'It's a hollow threat,' said Chris. 'Anyway, I'm not going to blow up a bunch of innocent people for him, even if one of them is that nutter Hasdruban!' said Chris.

'I shall tell him,' said Agrash. 'But…he really is gettiing more Dark Lordish. He might…well…he might actually…' But he couldn't bring himself to say what he might do, and his voice tailed off.

'Right, well, we've got to do something,' said

Chris. 'Agrash, can you get us out of here?'

Agrash turned a paler shade of green. 'Ah... That'd be... That'd be really dangerous. I'm sorry, I'm not the heroic type, I mean, they'd kill me...'

'All right, Agrash, don't worry,' said Sooz. 'But if you can't rescue us, can you get into the library, find something out for us?'

'Oh, I can do that, my Lady,' said Agrash. 'He lets me in there quite often to work on the newspaper, the Daily Massacre.'

'Great, this is what I want you to do...'

The Fall. Again.

Sooz, Christopher and Rufino were staring at the door expectantly. The locks were clicking open one by one. At last the great iron door swung towards them with a creak. Gargon, ducking his head, stepped into the room. He stared at Sooz for a moment, his face sick with worry. Then he stood to one side and held the door open.

In walked the Dark Lord, along with a particularly burly looking Orc wearing a hood and carrying some kind of large leather bag.

Christopher and Sooz backed away. Rufino stepped forward fists raised defiantly. The Dark Lord muttered a few arcane words and waved his hand. The Great Ring glowed and Rufino found his arms encased in dark, shadowy chains. Around his feet, heavy black clamps held him motionless. Dirk grinned.

'A new spell I have been working on,' he said. 'Shadow Shackles. Actually an idea I got from those car clamps back on Earth.'

Rufino struggled against his bonds, but he could neither move nor speak.

'So much for the Paladin. Now, Christopher, you have refused my command, even though you know you are the only one of my servants who could enter the White Tower.'

'I'm not your servant, and I'm not going to murder people for you, either,' said Chris.

The Dark Lord leaned forward, his horned face a few inches from Chris's.

'Oh yes you are,' he hissed.

'Oh no I'm not!' said Chris.

The Dark Lord's hand formed a fist – dark energy flickered and flowed around it.

'You going to cut my face again or something?' said Chris.

The Dark Lord just smiled a sinister smile. 'No, no, Chris, I'm not going to hurt you. Instead…' Rather than finish the sentence, he turned and gestured at the big hooded Orc.

'This is Og. Og the Torturer, a real old skool Orc,

oh yes, and a long-standing favourite of mine.'

Og the Torturer grunted, and bowed. He let the leather bag he was holding fall open to reveal a row of rusty torture tools – blades, hooks, thumbscrews, branding irons and the like.

Sooz gasped. Chris shuddered. Rufino strove to free himself but to no avail. Gargon frowned. Og laughed. It was an evil sound.

The Dark Lord turned towards Chris and Sooz. He grinned at them.

'So, it's do as you're told, Christopher, or Sooz will be spending some time with Og and his bag of hideous horrors!'

'You wouldn't!' said Sooz, aghast.

'Wouldn't I?' said the Dark One.

'No, you wouldn't, I know you wouldn't,' said Chris but his voice shook with doubt.

'Hah, oh yes I would!' said the Dark Lord. With that, he waved Og forward. 'Do your best – or do I mean your worst, eh, Og? *Mwah, hah, hah!*'

Chris and Sooz stood there, frozen. They simply couldn't believe this was happening. Chris was about to give in and say he'd do whatever Dirk wanted when Gargon bellowed at the top of his voice.

'Noooo!' he screamed. And then Gargon gave Og such a buffet with his mighty hand that the burly Orc flew through the air to crash into the corner of the cell, where he lay, unmoving.

The Dark Lord blinked. His great jaw dropped.

'Gargon… What have you done?'

Gargon paused, staring up at the Dark Lord with an expression of confused anger and guilt on his face.

'Has it come to this, after all these years, Gargon? Betrayal? Mutiny? You too? I can hardly believe it!'

There was a moment of silence, as the two gigantic creatures stared at each other. Then the Dark Lord shook his great horned head. 'You have left me no choice, old friend!' He raised his hands, readying a spell.

Meanwhile, Sooz reached into her bag and took out a tattered scroll, a scroll that Agrash had smuggled into her cell, wrapped up in a copy of the Daily Massacre. Then she took out one of the Anathema Crystals and began to read the scroll muttering the words under her breath as fast as she could.

'No, Lord,' said Gargon, recoiling. 'I did it for you – because I love you!'

The Dark Lord paused, astonished. 'Did you just say… Did you just say "love"? What are you blathering about, you crazy demon! I mean, really, Gargon, that's ridiculous…'

The crystal in Sooz's hand began to glow with power. The Dark Lord Dirk noticed it for the first time…

'Wait, what are you doing, Sooz? That's not… No, not that! No, it can't be… Noooooooo!!!'

Sooz threw the crystal to the floor and shouted a word of magic from the scroll. The crystal shattered. Time seemed to slow to a crawl.

A great white light blossomed up from the pieces of crystal, engulfing all of them in its cloudy glow. The floor began to dissolve beneath them, yawning open to reveal a great black abyss of nothingness.

They began to fall slowly, like they were falling through treacle. The Dark Lord's cry of 'Nooooo!' deepened and slowed to a rumbling roar of unintelligible sound.

And then suddenly everything returned to normal

Falling. Again.

speed, and they found themselves plummeting down through a dark gulf of total nothingness, each of them screaming with terror.

The Dark Lord howled in pain as he began to change.

Back to School

Dirk and Christopher stood outside the Purejoie's house. Christopher was wearing black leather armour covered in red glyphs. Dirk was wearing his Dark Lord's robe, a big black cloak, marked with his Seal and far too big for a teenage boy. On his shoulder sat Dave the Storm Crow. It cawed into the night sky, happy to have its dark master back.

Dirk and Chris looked at each other.

'Here we go then,' said Chris.

'OK then,' nodded Dirk.

Christopher rang the doorbell. It chimed pleasantly. Dirk made a face. One of these days he was going to change that doorbell chime – maybe to a kind of alarm siren, like they used in Second World War films. Or maybe a '*Mwah, hah, hah!*'. Yeah, that'd be cool.

The door opened. Mrs Purejoie stood there, looking down at them, her face a mask of astonishment.

'Christopher! Oh my goodness, Christopher! Thank heavens you're alive!' she said before gathering him up in her arms so tightly she nearly squashed him.

Chris hugged her back, tears coming to his eyes. Dirk looked on, an expression of mild distaste on his face. *Bah*, soppy nonsense, he thought to himself. Then Mrs Purejoie glanced over at him. Dirk began to panic.

'And Dirk! We were so worried. Come here my darling,' she said as she gathered him in for a family hug.

He fell into her embrace, face screwed up in horror. Dave the Storm Crow flapped up with a caw of annoyance, feathers flying. Not hugs, thought Dirk, anything but hugs! It wasn't long ago that he'd been a twelve foot tall Dark Lord, terrorizing thousands, and now here he was in a group hug with his 'mother' and his 'brother'.

Still, it wasn't so bad.

Then he noticed someone standing behind Mrs

Purejoie. It was the White Witch, Dumpsy Deary. She was staring at him, her mouth open.

Dirk just grinned at her. She shook her head in horror, as if coming to her senses and then, without warning, she just ran out of the door and down the street as fast as she could.

'Miss Deary… What, where are you going…?' stammered Mrs Purejoie.

'She's off to report what she's seen to the White Wizard Hasdruban,' said Dirk matter-of-factly.

Mrs Purejoie frowned. 'Who… Now hold on a moment. Where have you been? What's happened to you? I mean, really, we've had the police, social workers, neighbours, practically the whole town out looking for you all! Are you all right?'

'We're fine, Mum, don't worry,' said Chris.

'Don't worry! What do you think we've been doing all this time, young man? Nothing but worrying, I can tell you. Now get in the house, you've got some explaining to do, both of you! And what are you wearing? Is that… I mean… What is that? And…your face! Goodness me, Christopher, what happened to your face?'

And so the questions began…

Dirk and Christopher were eating a big hearty breakfast. They were dressed in their school uniforms – they'd got back to Earth just in time to start a new term at school, much to Dirk's annoyance. Although from their point of view they had been gone for weeks, time ran differently on Earth than it did in the Darklands and only a few days had passed here. Still, as far as the people of Whiteshields were concerned, Sooz had been missing for several weeks, and Dirk and Chris for several days.

At first, they had been overjoyed to see them, but soon their joy turned to anger and they had been thoroughly grilled, not just by Mr and Mrs Purejoie but also by the police and the social services too. Dirk had invented a complex story involving 'a live action role-playing game' – hence their strange clothes – in the local woods and then Sooz got lost and later Dirk and Chris set off to find her, which they did, but then they got lost too, and they had to live rough in the woods for a while. Dirk said that Chris had tripped over and gashed his cheek on a fallen branch. Chris hadn't been too happy about that, but what else could he do – say that Dirk the schoolboy had turned into an evil Dark Lord and had cut his face with a taloned claw for sabotaging his army of Orcs and Goblins?

No one really believed their story anyway but there was little more the authorities could do about it. The children seemed safe enough, and unhurt. Indeed, they had a strange new air of confidence about them, and stuck to their stories in a most un-child-like way. Something about them was different... More grown up. Nevertheless, Dirk was deemed the ringleader, and he had been electronically tagged, which he really hated.

But for now, Mrs Purejoie, so happy to see her son safe and sound, was spoiling them with a big breakfast of bacon, pancakes and maple syrup. Or as Dirk called it: 'The crispy flesh of his slain enemies with pancakes made from the Dough of Doom, and covered in the sweet succulent syrupy blood of Angels.'

'Yes, dear,' said Mrs Purejoie. She was so glad to have them back that she didn't mind Dirk's weirdness. Though that probably wouldn't last.

There was a knock on the door. It was Sooz. She'd come by to join them on the walk to school. Mrs Purejoie pressed packed lunches into their hands and kissed them all far too much and generally made a fuss.

Eventually they got out and on the road, taking the short walk to school. 'So, how was it for you, my Child of the Night – or should I say, My Lady of the Dark?' said Dirk.

'Not too bad, Dark Lord,' she said. 'It was great to see Mum again, it really was, but she got angry pretty quick and gave me a real bad time. Nothing compared to Hasdruban and his armies though, or you for that matter… Umm… Anyway, so… Well, I stuck to my story and that was that.'

'Just like us, then,' said Chris.

Sooz nodded.

'So,' said Dirk, as they ambled down the street towards the school gates. 'We've got Rufino and Gargon camped out in the woods, but they can't stay there forever. What are we going to do with them?'

'We've got to send them back to the Darklands, it's the only way,' said Chris, running a thumb along the scar on his cheek.

'True enough, but how? We can't do that ceremony again and we've lost the Voyager Boots,' said Dirk.

'Maybe we don't need to send them back

433

straightaway,' said Sooz. 'I've been thinking of starting a band, actually.'

'What? What do you mean, a band? Like a warrior band? But there are no Agrashes or Skabbers here, Sooz. Who's going to fight for you? Year 8?' said Dirk.

'No, no, a music band. You know, like AngelBile.'

'Oh yeah, of course, a music band, I keep forgetting,' said Dirk. 'Well OK, but what's that got to do with anything?'

'Well, it's gotta be a heavy Goth band, right? So Gargon could be in it. You know, like Morti, they've got a lead singer who dresses in a monster suit, looks like Gargon.'

'Gargon in a band. Really?' said Chris, as they turned into the school gates. All around them, children were streaming through the gates jostling, shouting, bickering, laughing, texting, and generally behaving like school kids.

'No, it'd work! Everyone would think he was in a monster suit. Then he could walk around a bit with us, like he was promoting the band or something!' said Sooz.

Dirk laughed. 'Gargon in a band indeed, hah, hah!' he said, as he pushed open the doors to the school assembly hall. They walked in to line themselves up in the Year 8 section, along with everyone else. 'He'd probably eat the other band members or chop their heads off and put them on his belt!!!'

'No, he wouldn't. He's actually rather gentle, you know,' said Sooz.

Dirk looked at her as if she were mad. Then he frowned. 'Well, actually…maybe. He does seem different now – with you anyway. Hmm, maybe it'd work.'

At the far end of the assembly hall, several teachers were standing on a raised stage. One of them reached for a microphone. It was time for the start of term lecture.

'What about Rufino?' said Chris.

'Well, that's a bit easier, once we've taught him…' Dirk was interrupted by a teacher.

'Welcome back to school, children,' said the teacher, her voice echoing loudly around the hall. Dirk scowled. He hated to be interrupted by anyone, let alone do-gooding, interfering school teachers, may the Nether Gods eat their souls!

'Anyway, as I was saying,' continued Dirk, 'we could show him how things work on Earth and then maybe we could kind of employ him or something. I was thinking as my bodyguard maybe…'

'Your bodyguard?' said Sooz. 'He swore one of those oath things to me. He'd have to be my bodyguard!'

'SILENCE AT THE BACK THERE!' said the teacher.

Dirk frowned. 'We'll talk about this later,' he said in a whisper.

'Now, children, I am delighted to announce that Whiteshields School has a new headmaster!' she gestured and a figure stepped up to the microphone. He was tall, with white hair, a long white beard and improbably bushy white eyebrows. He was dressed in a white suit, and he held a white cane in one hand, and wore a white hat with a blue headband. The pupils of his eyes seemed oddly dark. He grinned a sinister grin, and said:

'Hello everyone. I am Dr Hasdruban, your new headmaster…'

The End

Acknowledgements

I, the great Dirk, take credit for everything. *Mwah, hah, hah!*

Sigh. Chris and Sooz are insisting that I 'Do the right thing' and actually acknowledge those who have aided me in the crafting of this magnificent tome. *Pah!* When will I ever be free from meddling do-gooders?

So, I must… Well, I was going to say 'thank', but I don't need to thank my ghost-writer-slave Jamie Thomson, for he is a slave. Same goes for Thomson's friend, Dave Morris, who helps Thomson out from time to time in the writing of my life story. They do it for the love of me, (or is it fear?) and that should be enough. In fact, they should be thanking *me*!

Oh, and I must thank Darren Cheal, the Fish Lord, once more. He was genuinely useful, though I may still have him assassinated anyway. Though probably not.

And also Megan Larkin, publishing director at

Orchard Books. Not just for her editorial help, but out of respect. You see, I freely admit that I am not good at taking criticism. And, well, that's really her job – to hand it out. So I keep losing my temper and then hatching evil plots and setting traps to destroy her. But she has survived them all! You have to respect that, you really do. And her perseverance. Most of the witless, spineless humans I know would have given up long ago.

And finally, I must not forget my agent, Piers Blofeld. Whilst it is obvious he is actually Ernst Blofeld, the head of SPECTRE, hiding undercover as a literary agent, he has been useful. Also, I can see what he was trying to do with SPECTRE (look it up, if you've never heard of it), although I think his methods were bordering on the insane. Unlike mine. Which are quite rational.

No, really, they are.

The Author

Originally from a world beyond our own, Dirk Lloyd lives in the town of Whiteshields, in England, where he spends most of his time trying to get out of school and back home to his Iron Tower in the Darklands.

He has been a Dark Lord for more than a thousand years. Some of his achievements include: building the Iron Tower of Despair; raising vast armies of Orcs and Goblins; the waging of great wars; the destruction of many cities; the casting of mighty spells and enchantments; and exceling in English, Science and Maths classes at school.

Now he is a writer. Reviewers who adversely criticize his work may end up joining the others who have not been totally effusive with their praise. Join them in death, that is.

Well, all right, not actual death, but a long time being tortured in the author's Dungeon of Doom.

Oh, all right, not actually tortured. By the Nine Hells, not even incarceration in my Dungeon of Doom either, OK?

They will be in trouble though. Oh yes, most definitely! They might get cursed, or suffer the Charm of Sudden Baldness or the Cantrip of Uncontrollable Flatulence. Possibly.

So there.

The Seal of Dirk

Look out for the final book in the Dark Lord series!

GREETINGS PITIFUL HUMAN!
I, the Great Dirk do command you to set forth at once and buy a copy of my new book, Dark Lord: Eternal Detention

If you already own a copy, well done! But go and buy another one anyway.

Yours insincerely,

The Great Dirk

978 1 40833 025 8   £6.99 Pbk
978 1 40833 028 9   £6.99 eBook

ORCHARD

www.orchardbooks.co.uk

Read on for an extract of

Dark Lord: Eternal Detention

'AAAAaaaarghhhh!' howled Dirk. 'That hurts!'

The bathroom door swept open, and Dirk's foster brother, Christopher, poked his head round the corner, a look of panic on his face. He was blue-eyed and yellow-haired, and would have been rather angelic-looking but for the livid scar that ran down one cheek.

'Are you OK, Dirk?' he asked. Dirk turned to Christopher, a plaintive look on his face.

'Why does it suck so to be a human child?' he said. 'I mean, squeezing spots is such agony!'

'Ohhh!' said Chris. 'Yeah, that hurts, doesn't it? Still, not as bad as having your cheek gouged open by a twelve foot high, horned and hoofed evil Dark Lord, though, eh?'

Dirk turned away, unable to meet Chris's eye. He looked for a moment as if he were going to...well, *apologise*. But Dark Lords never say they are sorry. Instead he scowled at himself in the mirror and said, 'Are you going to upbraid me with this every time we talk, Christopher? I'm not that...thing any more. I'm not like that, it wasn't me!'

'It wasn't me! It wasn't me!' mocked Christopher, fingering his scar. 'That's your excuse for everything, isn't it, true or not!'

Dirk turned and glared at Christopher. 'Do not address me in such tones! I am no petty-minded boy child who must justify himself or face detention. I am the Great Dirk, and you will address me with the proper respect I deserve!'

Christopher raised his eyes. 'Oh, pleeease,' he said, before ducking out of sight and slamming the door.

Dirk turned back and examined the angry face that was looking out at him. Suddenly, instead of a slightly podgy, dark-eyed boy-face in the mirror, Dirk saw a massive, skeletal skull, fanged and horned, like the face of evil itself. But it was fleeting, so fleeting Dirk wasn't sure if it had really happened. Maybe it was all in his mind. He shrugged.

'What's a Dark Lord to do...?' he muttered under his breath as he leaned forward into the mirror and put his hands up to the offending black-headed spot, and began to squeeze once more.

His face knotted up in pain. 'Might be worth considering spot squeezing as a new form of torture in the Dungeons of Doom,' he said to himself.

Suddenly, there was a disgusting plopping sound and the spot burst, spraying pus all over the mirror. Dirk's face wrinkled up in disgust. How vile human children were. But then...

'Wait a minute, that's not pus!' said Dirk. And indeed it wasn't. It was black, and oily and shiny. Astonishingly, it began to move...drawing together...forming itself into a glistening blob of ebony mercury, hanging on the mirror like a parasitical egg.

'Essence of Evil!' whispered Dirk. He stared at it in fascination. He stared and stared. He reached out a hand to the glittering blob of blackness.

Essence of Evil. There must still be some left inside me from the time I was a Dark Lord, thought Dirk. A magnificent, mighty, all-powerful, spell-slinging Dark Lord, commander of armies of Orcs and Goblins and ruler of the Darklands! Dirk paused, hand held out stiffly.

But also selfish, cruel, and heartless. Thoroughly unpleasant, in fact.

Dirk blinked, coming out of his reverie. He didn't want to be that person ever again. The Dark Lord had imprisoned his friends and then almost destroyed them utterly. His friends – or minions, as he preferred to call them, though in his heart of hearts he knew they were really his friends – were all he had in this strange world. And all he had in the Darklands for that matter. He couldn't bear to lose them, not now that he was Dirk Lloyd the human kid. Well, sort of human. His friends had used a special magical crystal – an Anathema Crystal – to bring them all back here to earth, turning Dirk back into a boy and ripping out all the Essence of Evil inside of him. Chris had taken it, and hidden the Essence somewhere so that Dirk could never get his hands on it again. And that's just the way Dirk wanted it; he didn't want to know where it was, in case he got tempted once more. He had made his choice – he would be the boy, Dirk, who had friends, and went to school and lived in modern-day Earth, like everyone else. Well, probably. Maybe he'd go back to the Darklands and live there – he wasn't sure. The important thing was that he'd decided to stay as Dirk. Not any old Dirk, mind you, though.

Oh no! He would be the *Great* Dirk. Naturally.

Dirk put a hand to his chin. That was all very well, but what to do with the Essence of Evil? Not much of it, true, not enough to turn anyone totally Evil, but still, it was dangerous stuff. He'd have to store it somewhere, until he could work out what to do with it.

His hand reached for his foster mother's – Mrs Purejoie's – contact lenses case. He emptied the case, throwing the lenses into the bin without a second thought. Gingerly, making sure the Essence of Evil didn't come into contact with his skin, he used the lid to scoop the gelatinous blob into the small contact lens case. He screwed the cap on tightly, slipped it into the pocket of the black, skull-patterned dressing gown that he wore over his Grim Reaper pyjamas and left the bathroom.

My incredible story starts here in:

Dark Lord:
The Teenage Years

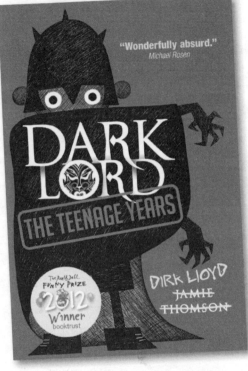

978 1 40831 511 8   £6.99 Pbk

978 1 40831 655 9   £6.99 eBook

OUT NOW!

Buy this book or endure my eternal wrath!
Yours sincerely, Dirk Lloyd